THE RIGHT
MISTAKE

THE RIGHT MISTAKE

THE FURTHER PHILOSOPHICAL INVESTIGATIONS
OF SOCRATES FORTLOW

WALTER MOSLEY

BASIC
CIVITAS
BOOKS

A Member of the Perseus Books Group
New York

Hardcover edition first published in 2008 by Basic*Civitas*
A Member of the Perseus Books Group
Paperback edition first published in 2009 by Basic*Civitas*

Books published by Basic*Civitas* are available at special discounts
for bulk purchases in the United States by corporations, institutions,
and other organizations. For more information, please contact the
Special Markets Department at the Perseus Books Group, 2300 Chestnut Street,
Suite 200, Philadelphia, PA 19103, or call (800) 810-4145, ext. 5000,
or e-mail special.markets@perseusbooks.com.

Design by Jane Raese
Text set in 10-point Utopia

Library of Congress Cataloging-in-Publication Data
is available for this book.
Hardcover ISBN 978-0-465-00525-3
Paperback ISBN 978-0-465-01852-9

2 4 6 8 10 9 7 5 3 1

For Harry Belafonte and his virtual Big Nickel:
www.thegatheringforjustice.org

CONTENTS

THE RIGHT
MISTAKE

THE RIGHT MISTAKE

1.

"Yeah, brothah," Billy Psalms said before he downed half a paper cup of Blue Angel red wine, "Freddy Bumpus made a *big* mistake when he married Vanessa Tremont."

"Vanessa Tremont." Martin Orr repeated the words lustfully, licking his lips and moving his head to silent music.

The other men sitting around Socrates' card table nodded and raised their paper cups in a toast. Then they went back to their game of dominoes. Psalms was ahead, as usual. He slapped down a four/three tile, closing off the play so that all the men had to give up their bones, affording him a two hundred and sixteen point advantage.

After they paid up (a penny a point) the group returned to the topic of Vanessa Tremont, and her husband Fred Bumpus—a house painter who was born and raised in Watts.

"What kinda mistake could it be to marry somebody like that?" Winston Twiner asked. "Van got a backside derail a train."

The men laughed. Even Socrates had to smile.

"Ain't you heard, man?" Billy said. "Vanessa done served Freddy wit' papers, kicked him outta his own damn house."

"What?" three of the five men cried.

Darryl, a boy of seventeen, sat in the corner watching his elders and adoptive guardian—Socrates Fortlow.

"Damn straight," Billy said. "Bumpus moved in the room upstairs from mines Thursday last. Said that Vanessa filed for divorce, got her a lawyer, an' moved his sorry ass out in the street."

"Took his house?" Martin was astounded. He had a perfectly round head and a face that would have been called pretty if not for the gray hairs that sprouted on his jaw line.

"That's a goddamned shame," Winston said.

"It ain't like they cut off his dick," Comrade Jeremiah said. "Somebody got to get the house."

"Excuse me . . . but you'ont know what you talkin' 'bout, Brother Jeremiah," Billy declared. "Freddy was born in that house. His father was born there. His grandfather built it with his own two hands back in the forties. That house more important to the Bumpus family than half the male chirren in they clan."

Billy Psalms and Darryl noticed Socrates leaning forward.

Psalms was a small man who made his living as a gambler mainly. He played cards and pitched pennies, went to the races when he was flush and to Victory Rooming House when the money was gone. He prided himself as a streetwise odds maker and so he watched Socrates closely whenever he got the chance.

Fortlow's an explosion ready to blow, he would say. *An' you know you cain't nevah get a even bet on a bomb blast.*

Billy reached for his Dixie Cup.

"What about the boy?" Socrates asked the gambler.

"What boy?"

"Fred an' Van had a son," Socrates said. "Peanut they called him, but his name is Bradford. I think he's three or maybe four years old."

"Yeah," Martin said. "They got a boy. I think he's been livin' wit' Vanessa's mama. She live over on Adams. She come an' took the boy when Vanessa an' Fred started fightin' all the time."

"What they fightin' about?" Socrates wanted to know.

"Beats me," Martin said.

"I think Van's backside derailed Too-Tight Floyd Grimm," Comrade Jeremiah announced. He had olive brown skin and generous lips. He was covered by an extra layer of fat that made him seem open and friendly. "Floyd been seein' Van an' Freddy didn't have what it take to break it."

"What you mean—what it take?" Socrates asked, the question sounding almost like a threat.

"Nuthin'," Comrade said defensively. "It's just that if a man gonna be fuckin' my woman he gonna have to answer t'me."

"So you kill him?" Socrates asked the middle-aged baker. "Thatta make you a bettah man than Fred?"

"Yes sir," Comrade replied. "Niggah gotta be a man in this world. He cain't have his woman givin' that pussy away like that. Shit—kill the man an' the bitch too."

Martin and Winston nodded while Billy and Darryl watched.

"What about Peanut?" Socrates, the big ex-con, asked.

"What about him?" Comrade replied.

Socrates didn't answer right away. He looked at Darryl and then at Winston. He didn't waste time with Psalms.

"Well," Winston said. "I guess Peanut's with his grandmother anyway. I mean they done give up on him already."

"An' you think that's right?" Socrates asked Winston, the eldest among them.

"No. No it ain't right but that's the way it is."

"But it ain't got to be," Socrates said. "An' you know it would hurt that boy if his mother dies an' his father ends up in jail. It hurt for a man to lose his blood like that."

"You right about that," Martin Orr said with a nod. "I mean a man get mad an' all, you could understand that, but afterwards a little boy like Bradford just be lost. They got chirren like that all up and down these streets."

The men were quiet then, nodding, agreeing with the logic that Socrates teased out of Martin's mouth.

"So I'm s'posed t'sit down an' let my woman walk on me?" Comrade said. "What kinda father could I be if I cain't show my son how t'be a man?"

"An' how do you be a man?" Socrates asked. "By callin' his mother a bitch?"

"Kill the mothahfuckah fuck yo' woman. Kill him an' her too."

A grin formed on Billy Psalms' handsome mouth. He liked danger. That's why he hung around Socrates so much of the time. The convicted rapist and murderer was the most danger-ous solitary man Billy had ever met.

Socrates was nearly bald with dark skin and a visage that was stern—even frightening. And though he was nearing sixty he was still a powerful man with bulging shoulders and vise-like hands that were nicknamed the rock breakers while he was do-ing hard time.

"So let's say that it was me with your woman," he said.

"What?" Comrade didn't like the turn in the conversation. He moved his right shoulder as if he were going to rise and flee.

"I'm fuckin' yo' woman," Socrates said slowly, deliberately. "She come ovah ev'ry day an' suck my dick."

The room went from quiet to silent.

"Stop fuckin' around, man," Comrade said.

"Ev'ry day she tell you she goin' out," Socrates continued, "an' when you ask her where she goin' she say, 'None'a yo' mothah-fuckin' business.'"

Socrates' eyes were on Comrade's. His left nostril lifted in contempt.

"I get that pussy whenever I want it. Ain't a damn thing you can do to make us stop. So what you gonna do now?" Socrates raised his hands, gesturing for a reply, daring Comrade to come toward him.

"Why you doin' this, Socco?" Comrade complained.

Suddenly Socrates' stern face broke into an almost friendly grin.

"Just messin' wit' ya," he said.

The rest of the men and Darryl exhaled in relief.

Comrade let a smile flit across his mouth.

"But it's a good question, right?" Socrates asked.

"What?"

"I'm a bad man, CJ. I spent twenty-seven years in the penitentiary. All I evah done is study how to survive when anothah man want me dead. You couldn't stop me from killin' you if you had ev'ry othah man in this room on yo' side. I'd kill ya even if it meant losin' my own life. That's what you learn in prison."

"I don't wanna mess wit' you, Socco."

"I know you don't but what would you do if I was fuckin' yo' woman ev'ry day?"

Comrade knew that he couldn't dodge the question. He had blustered and now he had to back it up.

"I'd kill you," he whispered.

"Oh shit," Billy Psalms murmured.

Darryl's eyes opened wide.

"How?" Socrates asked. "How would you kill me?"

"I dunno. I don't know how but you know I wouldn't let you walk on me like that."

"Stand up," Socrates commanded as he rose from his chair.

Fortlow was wide in the shoulder and thick in his chest. He stood six feet at least but his dimensions belonged on an even taller man. There was violence shot all through his bearing and he moved with the seamless grace of a man twenty years younger.

He took a step toward Comrade and the frightened baker leaped to his feet. The other men got out of their chairs too. The wooden legs moving behind them cried across the pine floor.

"If you were Fred Bumpus and I was Too-Tight what would you do right now?" Socrates asked.

"I, I, I would . . ."

"What if you had a knife?" said Socrates. "Darryl."

"Yeah?"

"Get Comrade a knife out the draw. That sharp butcher's knife."

Darryl moved to the kitchen side of the one room house. The boy pulled a whining drawer open.

"Don't do this, Socco," Comrade begged.

"Why not?"

"I ain't, ain't got no quarrel with you."

"It's not you'n me, Comrade. You are Fred Bumpus. I'm not Socco—I'm Too-Tight Floyd Grimm."

"No you not."

"But what would you do if I was?"

"I'd kill you," Comrade cried.

"You want the knife?"

"No."

"I'll turn my back," Socrates offered and then he turned around.

Darryl handed Comrade the knife.

The frightened baker took the haft of the blade.

Socrates could see the fear in Martin Orr's eyes. He could see

Comrade's shadow on the floor to his left. He didn't know if Comrade would take the bait or not but it didn't matter. He'd walked among men who wanted him dead day and night for years, decades; desperate men with violent hearts whose only pleasure was the destruction of their enemies. Socrates had been slashed, stabbed, battered, and garroted in the Indiana state penitentiary. Men had plotted his demise countless times. But he was still alive, living in his rent-free one room cottage behind a benefactor's house, surrounded by evergreens and a lush lawn.

He wasn't afraid of Comrade Jeremiah or any other man.

"What would you do," Socrates asked the man behind him, "if I was Too-Tight and you was Freddy B?"

"Why you doin' this, Socco?" Comrade whined. "I ain't done a damn thing to you. I said that I'd kill Too-Tight, not you."

"But what if it was me?" Socrates said as he turned to face the trembling man named for friendship. "What if it was me and your woman? Would you stab me in the back then? Or even if you couldn't, even if you just tried but I caught your hand and turned your knife, then would you lay in wait with a pistol and shoot me like some coward from behind a door or a corner?"

Comrade dropped the knife on the floor.

"Whatever it take," he said affecting the hollow semblance of courage.

"So if you shoot me in the back how's that gonna make you into a man?" Socrates asked then. "How yo' son gonna learn yo' last lesson if you sneak around and bushwhack me?"

Socrates sat down heavily. Slowly the other men got their chairs and returned them to the domino table. Darryl picked the knife up from the floor, put it in the sink and returned to his stool on the sidelines watching Socrates with hungry, proud eyes.

Comrade Jeremiah filled his paper cup with red wine.

Martin and Winston began turning over dominoes and shuffling them.

"So what you sayin', Socco?" Billy asked. "Man just s'posed to let his woman walk on him an' shame him in the street?"

The gambler was smiling because he knew that Socrates wasn't a true bully. Fortlow wouldn't threaten Billy for challenging his logic. The ex-con's actions with Comrade were just his way of showing that bluster doesn't mean a thing.

Still, Socrates glowered at the smaller Psalms.

"A woman treat a man like shit," Socrates said, "or the other way round—the only thing a smart person can do is to walk away. If he think he better for the boy then he should go to that grandmother and take him back."

"It's hard to swallow that much pain," Martin speculated. "Woman do you like that and you bound to get mad."

"Yeah," the elder Twiner added. "Woman do sumpin' like that to ya an' it just eat at ya—mornin' an' night."

Socrates was looking out the window into the idyllic green yard. Under a bush of yellow Sweetheart roses he spied the snow-white cat from the neighbor's yard. The hairy feline liked to slip through the fence now and then. For hours he'd sit in the foliage and watch the ex-con. But whenever Socrates went to pet it the cat darted away, back into his owner's yard.

"That's bein' a man," Socco said. "Pain in your heart and your dreams—that's the test of a man. If you can live life day after day with men treatin' you like a dog but you never bark or howl, cower or beg—if you can be a human being even when they want you to be a animal—that's got man all ovah it."

"So you think Bumpus done right," Billy said. "Movin' out, givin' up the house his granddaddy built . . . ."

"Naw, Billy," Socrates said—he even smiled. "I think *you* right, at least halfway."

"Me? What I say?"

"That Fred made a big mistake when he married Vanessa." Socrates chortled and shook his head.

When Billy's face had a serious caste to it he looked all of his forty-five years. At any other time he could have passed as a man of thirty.

"Shit," Billy said. "That don't take no deep thought. Woman do a man the way she did Freddy, that got to be a mistake."

"But," Socrates said, holding up an educating finger.

"But what?" Winston Twiner asked.

"What if it's the right mistake?"

"Right mistake? How gettin' with a lyin', cheatin', stealin' woman gonna be right?" Comrade asked.

Martin Orr cocked his round head as if he had just heard a strange sound somewhere in the room.

"That's you, CJ," the unemployed glazer said.

"Me? You bettah believe that a woman'a mine ain't gonna do me like Vanessa done Freddy."

"But you scared about it," Martin said. "I mean what you care about Fred? An' why you mad at Van fo' leavin' him? It ain't none'a yo' nevermind but there you are with the veins standin' out on your neck you so mad."

Comrade was tall and thin. His neck was longer than the norm. Everyone in the room could see the pulse in his throat from a swollen artery.

"Who the fuck you think you is, Marty," Comrade asked, "my mama?"

"Just sayin'," Marty replied with a shrug.

"But what about this right mistake Socco's talkin' 'bout?"

Winston asked. He was bald on top and thinner than Comrade. Even though he was midway past his seventieth year he had few wrinkles. The only traits that marked his age were his soft voice and fragile gait.

"Yeah," Billy added.

All eyes turned to the host.

Socrates glanced out the window. The cat was gone.

"What you think, Darryl?" he asked.

"Me?"

"Yeah."

"I'on't even know them peoples."

"But you heard what happened didn't you?"

"Yeah."

"So why would a man be makin' the right mistake to be with a woman like that?"

Socrates smiled.

Darryl sat hunched over on his stool. He was lanky and tall, dark-skinned with a perpetual frown on his face. He'd been party to the murder of a retarded boy when he was younger. Socrates divined the crime by just talking to Darryl and had, single-handedly, offered the lost youth absolution. From that day forward Darryl had been faithful to the severe minded ex-con.

"I'ont know," Darryl said. "I mean maybe if he was with her and she hurt him then maybe he could learn sumpin'."

"Learn what?" Billy Psalms said.

"I'on't know," Darryl said.

That was when Socrates decided that the boy needed another kind of education.

"Then maybe you wrong," Billy said.

"How could he be wrong," Socrates said, "when we all know that pain is the only way most men learn anything? A dog that bites, a match that burn. You learn right away from sumpin' like that."

"Some men never learn," the elder Twiner proclaimed.

"That's right," Martin agreed.

"Don't mean he didn't make the right mistake," Socrates said. "Just that he too stupid to get somethin' out of it. But there still something there he *could'a* known."

Even as Socrates spoke his mind was far beyond the conversation in that room. He was thinking about Darryl and all the things that the boy had yet to learn. All these years he'd sat at Socrates' feet trying to feel better about himself.

Socrates had murdered a man, raped the man's girlfriend, and then murdered her. He'd been drunk but that was no excuse. He'd spent twenty-seven years in prison but that was not justice. No, he lived by the good graces of his benefactor, who let him stay in this small garden cottage in the middle of SouthCentral L.A. But that wasn't right either.

Socrates realized that he'd been acting a fool with his friends; even worse, he was wasting time.

"Ain't nuthin' Fred Bumpus could learn worth the house his granddaddy built," Comrade said from someplace far away.

"What you say, CJ?" Socrates asked.

"That bitch done stole his family house," Comrade spat. "The lesson is too late."

"It ain't nevah too late," Socrates said slowly, softly—like a memory. "Not till the last man that knew your name is dead."

Socrates looked down at the wood beneath his well-worn shoes.

Martin Orr said, "Well, I better be gettin' outta here. I'ma be lookin' for pickup work in the mornin' down near Exposition. Sometimes they need a glass man."

The other men left soon after that. Socrates nodded when they said good-bye to him but he wasn't listening. Somehow he knew that this part of his life was over. There would be no more games of dominoes or bull sessions in his home.

"Socrates . . . Socrates . . ."

He looked up to see the boy.

"What?"

"You okay?"

"Where is everybody?" the big man asked.

"They all gone. I'm goin' over Myrtle Brown's house," the boy said. "I'll see ya later on this week all right?"

"Myrtle Brown?"

"Uh-huh." Darryl ducked his head and turned his chin toward his shoulder.

"She's at least forty."

The boy had no response.

Socrates wanted to talk about it, to advise the boy, but he couldn't find the words. Everything had been sucked out of him. He considered grabbing Darryl by the shoulder but his hands were like heavy weights on his knees.

"What?" Darryl asked after two minutes of this silence.

"I was wrong to bully CJ like I did," Socrates confessed.

"He a fool," Darryl said.

"And the next time you act a fool would I be right to shame you?"

"If I deserve it."

"No, boy." Socrates sat up and touched Darryl's elbow. "It's you and me out there in the world and in here too."

"You want me to stay?"

"Naw. You go on if you want. Go on."

2.

From the time Darryl left, about four in the afternoon, until sunset Socrates sat in his chair looking at his shoes. He wore size fourteens that were extra wide. Those same black shoes had carried him for years. They walked him out of Indiana and into Watts. They strode with him down block after block when he collected bottles and they brought him home every night when he lived in a gap between the outer walls of two abandoned stores. They'd taken him to the supermarket where he'd worked as a box boy until they had to fire him.

He'd worn them the day that he killed a powerful young thug in a lonely alley near his old makeshift home. They marched with him in the evil boy's funeral procession where his mother cried from grief and his grandmother shed tears of joy.

He'd shined those shoes every week and seven times he had the soles replaced. There were a thousand cracks in the shapeless black leather and fitted and sewn cowhide patches where his baby toes had burst through.

Socrates stared at his shoes hoping that they would give up some secret. They'd been with him all the years since prison, had been silent accomplices to blood that he'd shed. His shoes were closer to him than any woman, even closer than Darryl. He'd kept them because there was rarely enough money for a new pair and even when he had a few extra dollars there were no shoes made well enough to carry him half as far.

Socrates sat in his chair until the light failed and his feet merged with the darkness gathering on the floor. The night crowded in around him and the windows took on the weak glow of far away streetlights and a wan quarter moon.

In the darkness Socrates forgot his shoes. Now his attention fastened onto his breathing. In and out, his lungs working like a bellows, his heart a pounding blacksmith's hammer. He could feel his broad nostrils flaring and the darkness of his skin.

Somewhere along the way he'd gone wrong. Before the murders, before his wild youth. By the time Socrates was incarcerated he was already a bad man. He'd earned his imprisonment, paid for it with a score of robberies, beatings, and lies.

"Some people bad since the day they open their eyes," his hard-minded Aunt Bellandra used to say. "Some people study evil. They cain't he'p it."

"Mama says I'm bad to the bone," young Socrates had told his aunt in her kitchen while she cooked and he sat on the high stool.

"That don't make you bad," Bellandra said. She was making corn cakes for her nephew.

"But what if I am?" the boy asked. "I hit Cindy Rogers 'cause she wouldn't gimme some'a her candy."

"You know what to do about that."

"What?"

"You know," the powerful ghost spoke in the darkness of the room.

"Don't do it again," the man said.

"That's just right," Bellandra replied over the decades that separated them. "You got the will to do right. Ain't nobody could stop you if you set your mind to it. Don't strike that girl again. Don't let the other boys get to ya. Make up your mind that you would rather die than be a tyrant."

"But I don't wanna die," the nine-year-old had answered.

"We all gonna die, child. Ain't no relief from that. Men an' women, boys an' girls, even babies die. They die all the time. An' poor peoples die most of all. That's 'cause they's more of us. We got more than our share of sickness and bullies like you been to that girl."

"So I am bad?"

"You don't have to be."

"But I am today."

He could see that even now, when he was so far away from the lives he'd shared and shattered, he was still bullying, still using his fists and his hardened will to break down those he disdained.

"It's all been wrong," he said aloud in the empty room that was haunted by a woman who never gave up on him and never gave him a break. "But wrong is all right if you know it."

"All you got to do is turn around," the ghost whispered. "Turn around and you will be the man I know you can be."

"And then will the people I hurt forgive me?" the man asked.

"No."

"Will mama love me?"

"Never."

SOCRATES DIDN'T SLEEP THAT NIGHT. He sat in his chair, got up to urinate now and again, drank half a bottle of red wine, and wondered at the strong alchemy it would take to make something right out of something wrong.

"I thought I wanted forgiveness," the man whispered in the dark.

"Man don't have time for somebody else to say he okay," Bellandra's spirit replied just as if she was still alive. "An' God don't care. All a man can do is make a stand."

"But I'm just a boy," the child had said all those years ago.

"But you can be a man," Bellandra told him.

"How?"

"By knowin' what's right, by livin' by that even though it takes you away from your dreams," she said. "By puttin' away your bullyin' an' hate. Man can on'y do right. It's the scared boy do wrong."

"But what's right?"

Bellandra's hard face turned to a smile. She held a warm corn cake to the child's lips. The man bit into the darkness.

WHEN THE SUN CAME UP Socrates found himself walking down toward Florence. Three blocks past the wide boulevard he turned right. There he came to First Victory Rooming House—a place where poor men and women could still buy a room for fourteen dollars a night.

Baths cost sixty cents and there was only a single pay phone.

Scott Bontille was the daytime manager.

Socrates approached his office at the far end of the first floor hallway.

"Mr. Fortlow," Bontille said. "No rooms to let this mornin'. Maybe you could come back in the afternoon."

Bontille was a squat specimen with a face shaped like a chisel and an advancing hairline that made him resemble pictures of certain rattlesnakes that Socrates had seen.

The house manager got pleasure out of lording his power over those that were less fortunate than himself. On the street Socrates ignored him but now he felt anger rising in his chest.

Between his anger and his mission Socrates was momentarily frozen, trapped by his desire to strike Scott.

"You know I already got a house, Mr. Bontille."

"You don't have no regular job," the light-skinned manager replied, his natural smirk opening into a leer. He was missing one upper and two lower teeth. The rest had been stained brown from cigarettes and too much coffee. "And the last I heard people still had to pay rent fo' a place to sleep."

"I'm lookin' for Freddy Bumpus," Socrates said then. "I hear he's taken up residence with you."

As the words came from his lips Socrates blessed his shoes. They'd taken him to a new place on that long road. His muscles relaxed and he no longer wished to throw Scott Bontille down the hall. He smiled.

"What's funny?" Bontille asked.

"Us."

"What us?"

"You'n me, Mr. Bontille. Here we are doin' our dead masters' work an' here they been in the ground so long their bones have turned to dust."

"What kinda mess you talkin', Socrates?" the snake-faced man asked.

"Just mess," the ex-con agreed. He felt good saying these words. "Just mess."

"Who is it?" a man's voice answered when Socrates knocked on door D3 on the second floor of the Victory.

"Socrates Fortlow."

"What you want?"

"Open the door, Freddy. I wanna talk to ya."

"About what?"

There was a time, an eon and a day before, when Socrates would have been tempted to knock hard enough to shake the door off its hinges. But now he just said, "About your grand-father's house."

There was a moment of quiet then. It was a Saturday and the sun was muted through a small window at the end of the shabby and narrow hallway. Birds were singing their hearts out in a fruitless apple tree that stood just outside the glass.

Socrates flexed his toes against the tip of his shoes and smiled.

The door came open.

Fred Bumpus was a chocolate colored man built for the long haul but not for strength. He'd been forty-three for six months, though he looked older. Bony but not thin, Bumpus was tall and lean. His pupils were brown and the whites of his eyes were a lighter brown. His face was mature and haggard. He held his head hangdog style telling anyone who bothered to look that he'd been defeated by life.

"What about my house?" he asked.

"I wanted to use part of it for this idea I got last night."

"Ain't mine no mo'," Fred said. He moved as if to close the door on the big man.

"Yo' granddaddy built that house," Socrates said. "His name was Mr. Bumpus too."

Bumpus lifted his head to regard his visitor.

"What you sayin'?"

"That that's a nice house," Socrates replied. "You got them two lots an' that addition on the side is almost a full home on its own."

"Is," Fred said with wan enthusiasm. "Got its own kitchen and bedrooms an' a toilet too. Its own doors, front and back. If that ain't a house I don't know what is."

"I'd like to use that add on," Socrates said.

"For what?"

"Meetins'."

"What kinda meetins'?"

Socrates felt the smile but doubted that it made itself evident. He hunched his shoulders slightly and showed Fred Bumpus his palms.

"House ain't mine no mo'," Fred said again.

"You signed it ovah to her?"

"No."

"You been to court?"

"No. Her lawyer just send me the papers. I'm s'posed to sign 'em. Too-Tight tole me he was gonna kick my ass I didn't sign 'em."

"Let me in, Freddy. Let's sit down an' talk."

3.

The hardwood that Albert Bumpus used to build his house was stained to make it look like a mountain retreat and treated to resist the elements. This main house, which was on the north side of the property, was three stories high with a slanted green tile roof and windows bordered in red. A white garage was attached to the main house and then there was the add-on house on the other side of the garage, in the lot that Albert bought when he *couldn't get the buildin' bug outta his hands and shoulders.*

The second home was slender and only two stories. Socrates had no idea what wood the shorter abode was made from because Albert had completely encased it with hammered and treated tin siding. It was like a small castle gleaming on that street of shabby homes and plaster apartment buildings.

The street was filled with black people and Chicanos but Socrates only had eyes for the Bumpus compound.

It was one of the few structures that a solitary man had built for himself and his family in the whole community; certainly the only one that had passed down two generations.

Socrates walked up to the front door of the big house and knocked even though there was a doorbell.

He would have liked to have been there with Darryl but he hadn't seen the boy for a few days.

He was wondering if he should go see Myrtle Brown and ask after the boy when the door came open. Too-Tight Floyd Grimm stood there bleary eyed, wearing blue boxer shorts and a gray sweater.

"What?" he asked, none too friendly.

"Mornin', Floyd," Socrates said. "I've come to see Van."

"What the fuck about?" Floyd leaned forward, holding onto the doorknob. Socrates figured that this pose was supposed to be threatening.

"I have a message . . . from her husband."

"I'm her husband now," Floyd said, leaning even further.

"Not unless you wanna get her put away for bigamy you ain't," Socrates said. "I knew a few men got put in the joint ovah bigamy."

"He s'posed t'sign them papers," Floyd said in a tone meant to frighten Fred—wherever he was.

"He left outta here so quick he didn't have time to pick up a pencil," Socrates said.

"That s'posed to be funny?"

"Lemme talk to Van," Socrates said again.

There was no threat in his tone but Floyd let up on the doorknob and swung back into the house.

"Vanessa!" he shouted. "Socrates Fortlow down here."

"What he want?"

"I'on't know."

Floyd turned away from the door and moved out of sight.

Socrates stood in the doorway looking at the messy sitting room it opened upon. There were clothes and papers, dirty dishes and brown paper bags everywhere. The former box boy wondered what Albert Bumpus's grandfather would have thought of the mess.

Socrates noticed a pair of pink slippers at the foot of a yellow padded chair. They looked like tropical fish sleeping under the shadow of a gaudy stone.

While Socrates stared at the shoes a pair of bare feet appeared and stepped into them.

Vanessa Tremont was tall and wrapped in a purple gown that had a satin finish. The robe accented her voluptuous figure. She had a lazy eye which made her look both distracted and sexy. Her hair was a mane of brown ringlets but it was too early for her to have put on makeup.

"What you want?" she asked, firing up a cigarette with a bullet-shaped lighter.

"Can I come in?"

"I ain't dressed."

"I don't mind."

"What you want?" Vanessa asked again.

That's when Socrates' heart picked up its pace. Up until now it had all been a game. He was just taking steps one after the other with nothing standing in his way. The Legal Assistance Office, the lease Fred Bumpus had signed. All of that was just a list of hollow details like listening to men sit around street corners and barber shops talking about what they would do if only. . . .

But the next step wasn't just an empty motion. Socrates was about to do something. The anticipation immobilized him.

"Well?" Vanessa asked.

For a moment more Socrates hesitated. He remembered the day that he was released from prison. He wasn't ready to be out among civilians. He'd gone to prison for murder. He'd killed again in the joint. He'd lived by brutality and violence; that was all he had ever known. And then they opened the door and let him free on the world.

"Are you slow?" Vanessa Tremont asked.

Socrates reached into the left pocket of his jeans jacket and came out with a copy of the lease. He handed the paper to her.

"What's this?"

"The lease to this property."

"What the fuck you talkin' about? This is my house."

"No," Socrates said. "This house belongs to your husband. He owned it before you were married and your name doesn't show up anywhere on its papers."

"Floyd! Floyd!"

The heavy footsteps hurried from somewhere beyond the untidy living room. Too-Tight Floyd Grimm ran from a doorway and up to his make-believe wife.

"What's wrong?"

"Fred done rented the house to this niggah here."

"Say what?"

"Fred done signed ovah our house to this bum."

"Lemme see that."

Floyd took the lease and stared at it with unseeing eyes. He looked up at Socrates and grinned—then he ripped the papers into shreds.

Socrates reached into his right pocket and came out with another lease.

"That was a copy," he said. "This one is too. I got a dozen copies. You can tear 'em up all day long if you want."

"Niggah, is you crazy?" Too-Tight Floyd Grimm asked.

"I got a lawyer and this here lease," Socrates said. "I paid rent for five years on this property. All I got to do is call the marshal and you will be evicted."

"You try that and I will shoot you in the ass," Floyd said with emphasis.

"You might," Socrates replied. "If you miss you'll be lucky and if you don't it's yo' be-hind will be in stir. That don't have nuthin' to do with me. All I know is that this my house now and you got to go."

Too-Tight threw the screen door open and swung at Socrates. The ex-con leaned back and grabbed the fat man by the wrist.

Before that day he would have hit Floyd until he broke bones and loosened teeth. But now Socrates satisfied himself by holding on hard to his attacker's wrist.

Floyd felt it. The pain went all the way down into his elbow. He pulled but couldn't get away. He swung his other hand but Socrates grabbed that wrist too.

"Let me go, niggah!" Floyd cried. "Let me aloose!"

"This is my house," Socrates said.

"Let me go!"

"Take your hands off him," Vanessa Tremont shouted, moving as if she were coming to the aid of her man. But she didn't actually try to help. Socrates' power was nearly a legend in that neighborhood, even now.

"Are you gonna try an' hit me again?" Socrates asked Floyd.

". . . no."

"You gonna move out my house?"

"Alright, okay. Just let me go."

Socrates released his grip and put his hands up in a gesture of false surrender.

Floyd Grimm went down on one knee and Vanessa put her hands on his shoulders.

"I'm sorry about that," Socrates said. "I'm really sorry, Floyd. I came here intendin' not to fight. I got a legal paper and a righteous claim. I don't wanna fight you . . ."

"Fuck you, niggah!" Vanessa shouted. "Fuck you!"

Floyd rose to his feet with each hand holding the other's wrist. Hearing Socrates' apology seemed to scare him more than the Rock Breakers' rough embrace.

There was a wan, apologetic smile on the killer's lips, an entreaty in his eye.

While Vanessa was yelling curses Floyd began to tremble inside. He knew that the older man standing in front of him could have broken his bones but held back.

"Shut up, Van," he said.

"Bastid!"

"I said shut up, woman. Let's just go."

"What? What you say?"

"I'm sorry, Mr. Fortlow. We'll be out by tonight."

"I'll come back tomorrow noon," Socrates said. He smiled again and nodded. He walked away from the sputtering woman and the man holding his wrists.

THE NEXT DAY FRED BUMPUS and Socrates approached the family estate.

"Look at this shit here," Freddy complained. "She done lef' the do' unlocked and open too."

They walked into the sitting room, which wasn't as messy as it had been the day before.

"She took damn near everything," Freddy said. He was moving faster than his friend, taking inventory with his eyes. "The TV's gone and the stereo and all my records an' tapes an' CDs."

There was a doorway to the left of the room that led to dark stained stairs. Socrates was listening for something.

"My mother's silverware is gone," Freddy called from another room. "She even took the pots and pans."

The house reminded Socrates of Bellandra though it in no

way resembled her small Midwestern bungalow. Socrates inhaled through dilated nostrils hoping for a whiff of those corncakes he loved.

Freddy went through the door and up the dark stairs.

Socrates put his hands to his own cheeks, feeling the happy grin that eluded him even in childhood.

"She took the sheets," Fred Bumpus called from upstairs. "She even took my goddamned sheets."

He was standing at the head of the stairs looking down on the grinning felon.

Socrates looked up at the pained face of Fred Bumpus and laughed.

"What you laughin' at, man?" Freddy whined. "She done robbed me blind."

"I'm laughin' at us, Mr. Bumpus," Socrates said.

"What's funny?" Freddy asked. He was so upset that he shimmied his shoulders to punctuate his words.

"Here we are," Socrates replied, "two black men lookin' at the same thing but seein' somethin' altogether different."

"All I see is that that woman and that mothahfuckah done took ev'rything I got," Fred said.

"An' here they give me ev'rything I evah wanted an' didn't even know it."

Freddy didn't understand what Socrates was saying but the look on the ex-convict's face arrested him. Freddy knew that Socco had somehow scared Vanessa and Too-Tight away. He'd given the unemployed criminal a five-year lease on his second home for the favor. But the joy in Socrates' visage was something more than Freddy could comprehend. It scared him. Scared him more than Floyd Grimm had when he told him that he'd have him killed and inherit his property if he didn't give Vanessa a divorce and the house.

"You wanna see yo' new place, Socco?" Freddy asked, no longer thinking about his silverware and sheets.

"School," Socrates said.

"Say what?"

"It's not a house. From now on that big nickel next do' is a school."

THE BIG NICKEL

1.

Billy Psalms was in the kitchen making gumbo from a recipe his grandmother, Rita Psalms, had passed down to him. He fried the slime out of his okra and made a dark brown roux from white flour sprinkled into blistering hot Crisco oil. It was a real gumbo made with blue crabs, Andouille sausages, dried shrimp, and even a few oysters thrown in. The base was a chicken stock, made from a whole fryer, and it was finished off with powdered thyme and sassafras leaves for extra thickness and spice.

Socrates had worked an entire month doing pickup work down on Exposition to raise the money for the meal.

"Smell damn good in here," the ex-con said as he entered the room.

"Men's yo' best cooks, Socco," the gambler said. "You know all the big chefs is men."

"That's only because they got so many helpers," said the woman who was standing at Socrates' side. "If a chef had to do his own prep work and clean-up half the time dinner would never make it to the table."

"I'ont know, Cassie. Some men might surprise ya."

"Forty-one years and I haven't been surprised yet. Every man I ever met has made his way by standing on a woman's back—a woman or a slave."

Cassie Wheaton was tall and willowy. She possessed a slender figure and primal eyes. Her hair was matte orange in color, piled up on her head like a windswept mound of autumnal colored hay; her skin was the same hue and just a shade darker. She would have been beautiful if she wasn't so striking. Many men, who had seen that face and figure in profile, had come up to her looking for a little play. But most of them, once they looked into her feral eyes, walked away softly, their pickup lines dying on their tongues.

"You spend too much time in court, Miss Wheaton," Billy said. He was so much shorter than the lawyer that he had to look up to address her. "Bad element all up in there. I mean between yo' gangbangers and police, crooked lawyers and crooks you get a cockeyed view of our gender. I mean look at Socco here. He more like a rock than a man. Shit. You could have a whole woman's basketball team stand on them shoulders."

Cassie glanced at her host. He did seem like the immoveable object she'd read about in college. There might have been a barb in her throat but she swallowed it; swallowed it and smiled.

"You want Darryl to come out here an' make the rice, Billy?" Socrates asked. "He cain't do much in the kitchen but I taught him how to make a pot'a rice."

"Naw, baby. My mama told me that if I want to be proud'a what I cook then I got to do the whole thang. An' you know I learnt almost everything from my mama."

"Did she tell you to become a gambler?" Cassie asked.

"White man taught me that, Miss Wheaton," Billy said as he wiped his hands on a damp towel hanging from a hook over the sink.

"So you blame the white man for your own failings," the lady lawyer said.

"Who said anything about blame . . . or failins for that mattah? I'm proud to be called a gambler. My mama had a boyfriend took us to Vegas when I was fourteen or so. The minute I saw that roulette table it all come clear."

"What's that, Billy?" Socrates Fortlow, the convicted murderer and rapist, asked.

"Roulette," Psalms stated, his eyes wide with a teenager's amazement. "All them folks gathered 'round that wheel with so many slots you cain't even count 'em before it come to rest. But there they were layin' down their hard earned cash on the slender hope that their numbah comes up." Billy shook his head and grunted. "I knew right then that that was my church. The gravity hurlin' that wheel was my God. Oh yeah."

"What's that got to do with the white man?" Leanne Northford asked.

Billy hadn't seen her because she was so small standing behind Socrates and Cassie.

"White men owned that casino, girl," he told the seventy-one-year-old social worker. "Maybe he didn't invent the game but he distilled it just like he done with gunpowder and alcohol, white sugar and timepieces. White man take what's good and makes it pure."

"Which means it's better?" Socrates asked.

"No, sir," Billy replied, shaking his head. "Pure'll kill ya. Ain't no lie to that. Pure is yo neighbor's eighteen-year-old wife all of a sudden see you one day and set her sights. You know bettah. You know that the wife at home the one love you and who'll take care of you when you old and sick. But it's that lust, that pure lust will break you down every time."

"That's a man for you," Cassie said.

Leanne hummed a two-note agreement.

"You ladies can say that," Billy said as he sprinkled the last pinch of gumbo filet into the twenty-quart pot. "You know there's a man out there messin' 'round for every second spot there is on the clock."

"You got that right," Leanne said.

"But you know for every man messin' there got to be a woman whisperin' in his ear."

Socrates barked out a laugh.

"Women get fooled by you men," Cassie countered, maybe not as certain as she had been before.

"But it's men that's the biggest fools," Socrates told her. "You not gonna deny that are you, Miss Wheaton?"

"Women want to bring things together," Cassie argued. "Men take that goodness and drag it in the dirt."

"Baby, please," Billy said, holding his hands as if in prayer. "You know women out there right now fluffin' up their nest with their girlfriends' feathers. You know it's true."

"I got to go with the gambler on that one," Leanne said. Her voice was high and sharp. She wore a mid-calf checkered skirt and a navy sweater for a blouse. You could see the outline of her ribs in the dark fabric.

"You see that, Socco?" Billy said. "We ain't even had our meetin' and you done already solved the problem of men and women."

Upon hearing this Cassie sucked on her tooth and walked off toward the big sitting room.

"Who else is comin', Mr. Fortlow?" Leanne asked.

"Mustafa Ali from the soup kitchen. Marianne Lodz . . ."

"The singer?"

"Yes, ma'am."

"How you get her to come here?"

"I met her once and she gimme her numbah."

Leanne knew that there was probably more to the story. But she also knew that Socrates would never tell. She'd met the big ex-con in her office. He was always bringing dope addicts and winos to avail themselves of the private and government services she represented. He was in her place just about every week until she retired the year before. Socrates never divulged a secret, bragged, or gossiped in her presence.

"You already met Antonio and there's a young man named Zeal . . ."

"Ronald Zeal?"

Socrates nodded.

"Why you wanna have somebody like that in your house? He's a killer."

"I'm a killer, Miss Northford," Socrates said. "If I was to tell a man he couldn't come in my presence because he was a criminal I'd have to put my own self out."

"He shot two innocent boys right down the block from me," Leanne said, dismissing Socrates' claim with her intensity. "Shot 'em down in the street. You know I watched them boys grow inta young men."

"I'll understand if you don't wanna stay, Lee," Socrates said. "Billy?"

"Yeah?"

"How long?"

"It's just sittin' now. I'll put the cornbread in the oven twenty minutes before we eat."

Socrates nodded and walked past Leanne, leaving her standing in the middle of the kitchen while Billy chopped raw onion on the butcher's block cutting board.

2.

Antonio Peron was a carpenter. He had a limp and fifty-five years in Southern California. He was standing next to the dining table when Socrates came in.

The Mexican-American was short and well proportioned, for his age. He had dark amber skin and salt and pepper stubble on his jaw. He wore white carpenter's pants and a dark blue, long sleeved work shirt. As Socrates approached he smiled.

"This is some table you got here," Peron said. "One solid piece of wood. That tree must have been a mother. Thirteen and a half feet?"

"Fourteen seven," Socrates said proudly. "I got it from the basement of House of God Church when they knocked it down. Had to trim some'a the rot and damage."

"I like that it's irregular. Like it was a man who had some living behind him."

"Or a woman," Cassie Wheaton put in.

"Or a woman," Peron parroted. When he smiled the gold rims of his teeth glittered.

Cassie was sitting close to the head of the long and asymmetrical table. She smiled at the carpenter and he ducked his head.

There was a knock at the front door. Before Socrates could make it Darryl, the lanky teenager, ran from the den, where he'd been playing Grand Theft Auto on a portable screen.

He flung open the front door on Marianne Lodz and another woman. Even from the back Socrates could make out how excited the boy was to usher in the young soul singer. Lodz wore a form-fitting dark green dress. Her face was wide and beautiful, the color of café con leche. She had a generous figure that was matched by a friendly smile. The woman beside her caught Socrates' attention.

This woman was slender and very dark. She wasn't smiling and she wore black pants and a white blouse. Her hair was the only expression to her; it was wild, sticking out all over the place as if she had just run through the woods escaping the dogs.

"This is my, uh . . . Socrates, Miss Barnet," Darryl was saying as Socrates came up to join them. "Miss Lodz say that you know her cousin Leroy."

"He took Leroy to the hospital when no one else would," Marianne said. "And when I tried to pay him he said that he didn't need to be paid for doin' what's right."

Marianne shook Socrates' hand and then got up on her toes to kiss his cheek.

"Hi," she said. "This is my friend Luna Barnet. I hope you don't mind that I brought her with me."

Socrates had to concentrate to avert his gaze from young Luna's passive stare. There was something sensual in the woman's flat eyes. She seemed to be appraising the big man; he felt that she had put him up on the block as if he were being judged for his strength and stamina, his ability to take orders and lurking willfulness.

"Hi," she said in a slow urban patois that had once languished in the southern states.

Socrates winced, stung by her mild salutation.

"Why don't you ladies come on in?" he said, turning quickly, headed for the Big Table (as it came to be known).

Darryl hurried up next to him excitedly.

"Ms. Lodz said she'd sing for us if you wanted, Socco," he said.

"Did you say hello before you asked her to sing?"

"Yeah," he said defensively.

"This ain't no concert, D-boy. It's a meetin'."

"But after the meetin'..."

"It's not that kind of meetin'," Socrates said, pushing on ahead of his ward.

When he came toward the table, followed by the panting young man and the women, Socrates said, "Ev'rybody, this is Marianne Lodz and Luna Barnet. Say hello."

When he moved to the side for the people to come together Socrates noticed Luna still looking at him with the dispassionate interest of someone who had just roused from a deep sleep.

BILLY PSALMS BROUGHT IN a bottle of Blue Angel and a stack of Dixie Cups. The gambler and the lawyer, social worker and carpenter came around Lodz. She had a song on the radio at that time called "Bring it on over." It played around the city and she was getting a name for herself. Darryl hung on her every word. She was kind and gracious but a little distant, *like a friendly prison guard,* Socrates thought. Then he saw Luna watching him while pretending to be looking around the room.

Another knock at the door and Socrates was happy to turn away.

Mustafa Ali and Wan Tai had arrived together. Socrates thought that Mustafa had been at the Chinese man's dojo before coming to the inauguration of the Big Nickel School.

"Socco," the white bearded and brown skinned Ali hailed.

"Mr. Fortlow," Wan Tai whispered, making the slightest nod as he spoke. The karate master always looked directly into Socrates' eyes when addressing him.

The host put out a hand to each man.

"Welcome to the Big Nickel, brothers. They're almost all here by now. Go on in and introduce yourselves."

"Socco," a man called before the front door closed.

It was Ronald Zeal. Even hearing the voice Socrates felt a thrill of excitement; not fear, not exactly—but the inner clenching he always felt just before a serious fight. It was a kill or be killed moment that he had to climb over before saying, "Hey, Zeal. What's happenin', man?"

"Nuttin' to it," the young man replied in his studiedly casual approach toward the big felon.

Socrates turned his head into the house and called out, "Billy, put on the cornbread."

"Okay, Socco."

Ronald Zeal was at the door by then. He was tall and meant to be naturally thin but his upper body was over-developed by exercise and weight lifting, maybe even some bulk enhancing drugs. His skin was dark, as dark as Fortlow's. His face had been pretty, would still have been if it weren't for the scars and a hardness in his eye. He didn't smile, only took Socrates' hand in welcome.

He was six three at least, no more than mid-twenties. He wore a clean white T-shirt despite the cool evening temperature and black pants with matching sneakers.

Behind Ron a car passed slowly. From the car's passenger window a white man peered into the house.

Socrates grinned and gestured for his guest to enter.

"Come on in, brother," the host said warmly. "We almost all here now."

He led Ronald Zeal into the room dominated by the big irregular table.

Every chair at the table was of a different make. Straight-back maple, cane and wicker, a black stool and a dark stained piano bench. There were eleven seats in all with the capacity to hold a dozen people.

"This Ronald Zeal, everybody. We only got one more and he told me he was gonna be late because of his job."

"Hey, Ron," Cassie Wheaton said. She was looking at the stern-faced young man.

"Ms. Wheaton," he said in an oddly subdued tone.

"Have you been down to the courthouse yet?" the lawyer asked.

"No, not yet."

"They will put you away if you don't show up with those papers."

"Mustafa Ali," Mustafa said introducing himself. "Mission of Heaven services."

"Hey."

Socrates noticed that Leanne Northford had moved to the black stool at the other side of the Big Table. She'd stay, he thought, but she wouldn't welcome the killer or shake his hand.

From Leanne Socrates' attention went around the room. Most were aware of the famous killer. Darryl was trying to put on a gangster-calm while Marianne Lodz seemed flustered. Antonio, though he might not have known Zeal's story, could read the threat in the young man's bearing. Billy Psalms was in the kitchen but Socrates knew that the gambler would watch Ron the way he'd concentrate on a roulette table—wondering at what number would come up, and then the one after that.

Only Luna seemed unaffected by the notorious gangbanger's presence. She satisfied herself by observing Socrates watching his guests.

3.

"Help me with this, Socco," Billy Psalms called as he entered the meeting room laboring under the weight of the two-handled copper cauldron that Socrates had borrowed from Leanne.

Antonio and Mustafa rushed over to grab hold of the big pot. As soon as they had taken the weight the gambler announced, "Louisiana blue crab gumbo is in the house."

The guests began taking their seats.

"Darryl," Socrates said.

"Yeah?"

"Go help Billy with the rest of what he got to bring in."

Darryl's eyes were on the singer. He wanted to get to a seat by her side.

"Okay," he said.

Luna followed the boy out of the room. Socrates watched her leave, wondering why she made him feel so uneasy.

When he looked back at the table he saw that Ronald Zeal was also troubled. The hard-faced street-fighter was thrumming his fingers on the table. There between Mustafa and an empty seat Zeal was sitting lightly like a man about to take flight.

Socrates smiled and forgot Luna for a moment. He went to stand at the center of three spaces, at what might have seemed like the head of the table.

The Big Table resembled a dark rose petal that had been gnawed on by insect pests and then trampled underfoot. Longer than it was wide there was something vaguely oval about its form. There were light, almost blond highlights along the sides and at two places in top. It was a sturdy board of wood four and a half inches thick and hard.

Darryl and Luna came in: him carrying a big bowl filled with white rice and her with a pewter platter bearing two huge squares of cornbread.

The seat next to Marianne Lodz was the piano bench. After setting down the food Luna pulled Darryl to sit between her and the budding star.

Billy went to stand at the head of the table to Socrates' left.

There was an arc shaped indentation there, one of the gnawed-out spaces that had survived the giant footstep.

Next to the gumbo pot stood stacked a pile of a dozen porcelain bowls, also borrowed from Miss Northford. Billy used a teacup to put a dome of rice in the bottom of a bowl and then ladled the dark green stew on top of that—making sure that each serving received at least one of the small crabs.

Leanne carved the cornbread. People took the large squares as the platter was passed down the center of the table toward the front.

Socrates set his eyes on Darryl. When the boy looked up the host moved his head, indicating the empty seat next to Zeal.

To his credit Darryl took up his paper napkin and moved to keep the uncomfortable killer company.

When Billy finished serving he sat in his. Socrates remained on his feet.

"I thought you called these blue crabs," Wan Tai said across the broad plank to Billy. "But these are red."

"They turn red when you cook 'em," Billy said. "But you know them li'l suckers got the best tastin' crab meat anywhere."

Those were the last words before the table went silent, waiting for Socrates to address them.

"There's ten of us now," he said. "And later on there will be one more. We got all kinds 'a people at this big table. Mustafa, who belongs to Islam, Wan Tai is a Buddhist and prays the way those people do, Darryl an' me ain't seen the inside of a church, temple or mosque in many, many years. We got Baptists and Catholics and other Christians—some practicing, some not—at the table. The last man to come is something different yet again."

The guests were looking around at each other while Socrates, who seemed uncharacteristically nervous, took a deep breath.

"We got a gambler, a singer, a teenager, at least two killers, a carpenter, social workers, and even a lawyer sittin' right here in this big tin-plated house."

A few people, including Cassie Wheaton, snickered at the lawyer line.

"Not all of us were born in America," Socrates continued, "but we'll probably all die here."

These last words sobered many an eye gazing upon Socrates.

"Death is our moment of reckoning," he said. "It's what calls up our hardest prayers. And so death has to have a place in the words at the beginning of the meal. Also words of hope and truth. But not Christian or Muslim or Buddhist words. No. We are here to come up with a new kinda faith. Maybe not even a faith but somethin' true, somethin' that will give us some kind of, I don't know . . . wisdom.

"And so I will say some words today and then, the next time we get together for a talk, somebody else will say somethin'."

With that Socrates bowed his head and everyone else, even Luna, followed suit.

"I have eyes to see and a mind to think; I have feet to take me and lungs full of breath; I have arms and legs, a sex and a nose to smell trouble. I have everything I need . . . everything but a sign."

"Amen," Mustafa intoned.

Socrates sat and the people began gabbing and eating.

The seat to Socrates' left was empty. He turned right to Billy and said, "Damn good, gambler. Why don't you get a job as a cook?"

"Why don't you be a preacher?" Psalms asked back and both men laughed.

4.

The dinner had been going on for half an hour or more. Billy was telling jokes about gambling schemes he had come across that had nearly everyone laughing; all except for Luna, Ronald Zeal, and Leanne Northford. The gumbo was good, the whole table agreed on that. The small house was perfect for their get together.

"So why you got us here, Socrates?" Mustafa asked. He was half the way down on the left side of the Big Table.

"Wait a bit longer, brother. We have one more coming."

"No matter to me," Antonio said. "This food is good."

The assembly hummed their agreement and the volume of the conversation rose. They were so loud after a while that only Socrates heard the soft knocking at the door.

THE SMALL WHITE MAN LOOKED UP at the mountain of darkness before him and smiled.

"Mr. Fortlow," Chaim Zetel said in greeting. "Your house is so shiny I could see it all the way from Cheviot Hills."

"Maybe to you, Mr. Zetel," Socrates replied. "Some people couldn't see it if they had their nose pressed up against the door."

When the two men walked back to the Big Table the loud talk quickly dwindled to a murmur.

"This is my friend Chaim Zetel," Socrates said, using the correct guttural sound for the *ch*. "He's our last membah, at least for tonight."

"So now you can tell us what we're here for?" Cassie Wheaton said.

"I know you don't eat shellfish so I got some fried chicken for you in the kitchen, Mr. Zetel," Billy whispered behind Socrates' back. "I'll go get it."

"Thank you, Mr. Psalms."

"We are here because the world . . . the whole damn world is messed up," Socrates said simply and to the point. "An' all we do every day is shut our eyes hopin' that it'll get bettah while we ain't lookin'."

"Amen to that," Leanne chimed. "Amen to that."

"Grown men an' women sittin' on their ass like slaves chained in the quarters," Socrates continued, "markin' time and waitin' to die. A chance to do sumpin' good comes an' goes ev'ry minute but we just sit there."

"What difference can we make to the world?" lean, white-bearded Mustafa asked.

"Nothin'," Socrates admitted. "Not a damn thing."

"Then why try?" Antonio proffered.

"I got here by the back door, Tony," Socrates replied; still standing, still quivering from nerves. "I heard that Fred Bumpus had lost this place to his wife and her boyfriend. I took it as a fact and humiliated a man who connected so closely with Fred's pain that he hated him for his weakness. Then it came to me that I was passin' a chance by, that I could help Fred and make this a place where people could come an' take themselves seriously. A place where there was good food an' good company an' where the only question is what can I do?"

At that moment the tension released in Socrates' shoulders and neck. He looked around the table seeing that the struggle had passed from him to most of his guests.

"I know what you feelin'," the ex-convict said. "I might as well ask you to fly. But you know people dyin' ten thousand miles an' one block away from here. We go to bed knowin' it. And when we wake up it's still true. We bring chirren into this world. We make love here. At least we could take one evenin' every week or two and ask—just ask, what is it we could do about this shit?"

The small audience fell under a hush. Their eyes were those of people engaged in a serious conversation but their tongues were still, their lips closed.

"You see?" Socrates said. "I could ask you what the weather was and you might tell me I need an umbrella. I could ask you if you knew a joke and you'd have me rollin' on the floor."

"Especially Billy there," Leanne said.

A few people laughed.

"But if I ask you," Socrates said, "how can we save some child bound for prison or the graveyard you just sit there like some voodoo witch done sewed your lips shut."

Again Socrates paused. Again he appreciated the struggle in the bearings of his friends.

"Your mother or sister or child could come runnin' to you," the host added, "screamin' that there was somebody after them, somebody that was gonna do them terrible harm. And you would grab a knife or a baseball bat and run out to protect them—to kill if you had to. But when I tell you that there's millions runnin' and screamin' right now all you do is look like you got gas.

"I'm not tryin' say that it's just us here. It's like this all ovah Los Angeles and California, the United States—all ovah the world. In Israel and South Africa and Europe too. Ev'rybody sittin' there with a sour look on their face while the killers and their prey run in the night."

From Darryl to Cassie, from Leanne to Antonio there was profound, intense silence—even Billy Psalms kept his peace. The extraordinary hush didn't bother Socrates. He was ready for this deathlike response. If someone didn't speak up soon he'd make a toast and promise the assembly that he would have a dinner every Thursday until the day that they could speak out loud about what they felt.

He was reaching for his paper cup when Ronald Zeal said, "I got sumpin' t'say."

"Yes, Brother Zeal."

The dark-skinned young man sat back in his chair, balancing it on the two hind legs.

"You told me that we was gonna come in here an' talk about somethin' important," Zeal said, "sumpin' for the people."

"I sure did."

"I expected to see a room fulla black men ready t'stand up and tell the cops and the whites what we won't take no mo'. But instead I come into a house fulla bitches, beaners, an' chinks. And then you got this Jew. What the fuck am I s'posed to do with that?"

The faces of the dinner guests registered shock and dismay. Everyone was disturbed except Luna and Socrates, neither of whom were bothered by the killer's concerns.

Socrates laughed; not because he found the words funny but because he was surprised. It was rare that anyone could sneak up on the ex-con like that.

This laughter further disturbed his friends.

"Ron," he said. "You see Wan Tai over there? He teaches black chirren the discipline of the martial arts. Antonio here repairs the houses of poor people no mattah what color they are. Cassie Wheaton kept you outta prison when you know they coulda had your ass, and as far as Chaim goes . . . Mr. Zetel?"

"Yes, Mr. Fortlow?"

"Tell this boy sumpin' will ya?"

The little man, who was not an inch over five feet, stood up as Socrates sat down. He was maybe seventy wearing a gray suit cut from coarse cloth. His shirt was yellow and he wore no tie.

The hands he placed on the table were small, liver-spotted, with thick, blunt-tipped fingers. His hair was still full, a thatch of dull silver that needed a trim. His white skin had lost its luster to age but his eyes, equally gray and brown, seemed to be smiling.

"My grandfather was a ragman, my young friend," Chaim said gently. "Do you know what that is?"

Every eye was on Zeal. He resisted the pressure and then gave in to it.

"A homeless," he said.

"Almost," Chaim said with a grin. "He was poor, very poor. He had a horse so skinny that it looked like the one ridden by Death when the plague raced through our cities and towns. This horse pulled a wagon and my grandfather, Moses Zetel, would go around collecting things that people had thrown out. He'd trade those things with the poorest people who might have had some need for them. His father had done that and his father had too. There have been ragmen so far back in our family that I wonder why Ragman was not our name."

Out of the corner of his eye Socrates noticed Luna smiling for the first time.

"My grandfather wanted his son to go into the business," Chaim continued, "but my father was very lazy." The sad look on Chaim's face elicited a few smiles. "He would stay at home playing with the broken doll houses, dishware, and machines. One day Moses realized that my father, Aaron, was fixing the things he found, making them almost like new. All of a sudden my grandfather was a wealthy man. He took in broken things only good for the poorest people and made products that everyone wanted to buy.

"Moses died and my father married and came to America. He wanted me to be a doctor but I was too lazy. So I went into his business finding things that no one wants and making them

into something useful." With that the tiny man sat down in front
of a plate of fried chicken and macaroni and cheese that Billy
Psalms had provided.

"What the fuck . . ." Ron Zeal said, a spasm of rage going
through him. He moved too quickly and the legs slid out from
under the chair. But the young man was agile as well as strong.
He maintained his balance with both feet and caught the chair
before it could fall to the floor. "What the fuck that shit s'posed
to mean to me?"

Zeal looked as if he were about to attack the little tinkerer.

Billy leaned forward.

Wan Tai placed his hands on the table before him.

"It means," Socrates said, "that Mr. Zetel has twenty-five black
and brown chirren workin' for him. They drive around the city
lookin' for things thrown away that can be fixed. They work in a
little workshop he got up in Silverlake. They make a livin' and
learn a trade all under this man here."

"Prob'ly gettin' rich off 'em too," Zeal said.

"So what if he make a dollah?" Socrates said, coming to his feet.
"They gonna do bettah wit' you? Carryin' guns? Dealin' drugs?"

Ronald Zeal clutched his hands on imaginary weapons and
cut his eyes to laser points on Socrates. The fight brewing between them sent waves through the room.

"What about a niggah?" Leanne Northford said, obviously addressing Zeal.

Ron's eyes were still on Socrates but his hands loosened a bit.
He glanced briefly at the small social worker.

"What about a niggah," Leanne said again, "who kills his
brothers? Lays 'em out in a coffin for their mothers and fathers
to cry ovah."

"What you talkin' 'bout, woman?" Zeal said, turning his head
fully to regard her.

"What about you, niggah?" the previously sedate lady said. "You walkin' down the street laughin' an' drinkin' while Thomas King and Terry Lingham laid up there in the cemetery."

Zeal seemed stunned by Leanne's declaration. He looked at her as if he had not understood the words.

"Killer," she said. "Just a damned killer. Talk about that little white man like he was our enemy. You the enemy, niggah. I been alive seventy-one years an' I seen it all—but you are the first black man that I have evah called a niggah. The first one—niggah."

"I don't have to listen to this shit," Zeal said. He set the chair upright and turned.

"Sit down, Ron," Socrates commanded.

"You think you can make me?"

"I know I could," Socrates said simply. "But it's not an order. I want you to stay here. This woman not insultin' you. She hates you right now. She really do. But she got reason. You know it's true. I'm not askin' you to confess or apologize or nuthin' like that. I'm just sayin' sit down an' finish your gumbo an' tell us somethin'."

"Tell you what?"

"Tell me why it's okay for one black man to shoot down another one but it's wrong for Chaim here to make a buck while teachin' our youngsters a trade."

Something in Socrates' tone persuaded the angry young man. He banged the chair into position and sat. Leanne was staring across the table at him.

Luna was watching Socrates.

"You old people don't understand what it's like out here," Zeal said to the dark tabletop. "It's a fuckin' war out here."

"Did Thomas King and Terry Lingham attack you?" Leanne asked.

"I'm not sayin' nuthin' about them," Ron said. "That's for the court. Right, Miss Wheaton?"

"Yes," the lawyer said. "Mr. Zeal would be well advised not to address any crime still under investigation by the police and the district attorney."

"Yeah," Ron averred. "But if a niggah disrespects me you know we got to go. If one man walk on you out here then you ev'rybody's bitch. You got to stand up. You got to take care'a business."

"And is that right?" Mustafa Ali asked.

"Ain't got nuthin' to do with right. Niggah don't have no rights. All he got is his respect, his pride."

"But what about the question?" Wan Tai asked. "What about Mr. Zetel? Is what he's doing better than you, Mr. Zeal?"

"I ain't talkin' to no Chinaman," Ron said, his eyes glued to the white bowl between his fists.

"Then let me ask you," Socrates said. "Who's doin' better for our people—you or Chaim?"

"That don't count, man. He a rich Jew. I'm a poor man been pushed down by him and his kind from the gitgo."

"I'm a po' niggah too, brothah," Socrates said. "Me an' Billy an' Darryl an' Tony here. Po' don't mean helpless. Po' don't mean stupid. You could be down in Mustafa's soup kitchen tomorrow helpin' feed people got even less than you. Naw, man, Chaim's money ain't what makes his work good."

"Niggah," Leanne Northford said again.

"Bitch, you bettah shet yo' mouth," Ron told her. "You could get hurt."

"She just sayin' what she sees, Ron," Billy Psalms said. "You call yo'self a niggah."

"Ain't the same word," Zeal said.

"Maybe it is, man. Maybe she mean exactly what you do."

Billy Psalms smiled and shook his head the way he did when he was about to slap down the winning bone in dominoes.

"You can kill who you wanna kill, Ron," Socrates said. "Shoot 'em in the back if you want. I cain't stop you and I wouldn't try. I won't condemn you neither 'cause for every bad thing you done I done five. But I just want two things from you."

"What's that?"

"For you to see the hate you stir up for what it is and for you to answer the question of why you can insult my Jewish friend here when he's tryin' to do right."

The rigidity in Ron Zeal's arms released. He sat back and Darryl handed him a Dixie Cup filled with Blue Angel red wine.

"I ain't sayin' I'm bettah than him. I'm just sayin' he got it easier. An' I don't care who hates me. That's their business."

Socrates, who was still standing, looked at the angry youth and then at Leanne, whose eyes were alive with rage—then Socrates smiled. "Billy," he said, "I think it's time to bring out that cherry cobbler you made."

While the gambler moved away Cassie said, "You still haven't answered the question, Socrates."

"What's that, Cassie?"

"Why are we here?"

"We here to say what we just said."

"That's no answer," she observed, gesturing around the table with an upturned hand. "Nothing we said here tonight is going to save the world from crumbling."

"I don't know about that. I think you seen things tonight don't happen every day. Just the people at this table and the things they said make this night special. Next Thursday Billy said he's gonna put together some Texas chili make you cry. I expect to see all'a you back here again."

5.

Billy carried out a large Pyrex pan of cooked cherry filling with a dozen short biscuits floating in the red. Darryl followed him, bringing out a stack of smaller bowls while Luna collected the dishes and silverware used for the gumbo. Socrates served this time, passing the dessert around to his left.

Cassie and Antonio made coffee together.

Zeal did not partake of the desert—but he didn't leave either.

When the food and drinks were all served the talk became light again. Billy told more jokes. Mustafa conversed across the table with Wan Tai.

"Me an' Darryl take care of the dishes," Socrates was saying to Billy when the front door blew off its hinges and a dozen cops in riot gear rushed into the room.

"Nobody move!" a muffled order came.

The host turned toward the advancing army, watching the short-barreled rifles pointed at them.

Some police flanked the table in a military formation while others of them rushed into the building, moving through the kitchen. Socrates could hear them stomping on the floor above.

Amid the drumbeats and the strained faces came a tall man dressed for battle but not bearing a weapon. He was tall and slender, fair-skinned and in charge. He wore gloves and a bullet-proof vest.

Socrates stared at him and smiled.

"What are you smiling at?" the commanding officer asked.

"Everybody on the floor!" another voice commanded.

"Captain Beatman," Cassie said, coming to her feet. "What is the meaning of this?"

Socrates could see the commanding officer mouthing the words, "Oh shit."

Wheaton approached the unarmed cop.

"Counselor, what are you doing here?" he asked.

"Show me your warrant," Wheaton replied, holding her hand out.

"Everybody on the floor!" the second voice called again.

The rifles rose higher.

Captain Beatman held up a hand and the rifles came down. He handed an official looking sheet of paper to the lawyer. She read it over quickly and laid it on the table, next to Socrates.

"Drugs?" Wheaton asked.

"We saw Ronald Zeal coming to this address. We suspect him of trafficking."

"So you break down an innocent man's door?"

"Mr. Fortlow is an ex-convict."

Socrates' smile became a grin. The footsteps upstairs rumbled like thunder.

"Either kill us all or leave," Cassie Wheaton said, the waver in her voice underscoring anger, not fear.

"Morton," Beatman said.

"Yes, sir?"

"Any contraband?"

"No, sir. But we haven't performed a thorough search. With the warrant we can break out the walls . . ."

"Let's go," the captain told the man who wanted everyone groveling.

"But, sir . . ."

"Let's move."

"Everyone out!" the frustrated number two ordered.

As the attack team moved to leave Socrates stood up and faced Captain Beatman.

"You know my name?" Socrates asked.

The captain did not reply.

Socrates held out a hand to the man. For some reason Beatman shook it.

"Thank you, Captain," Socrates said. "Without you they might not have come back."

Beatman released his grip and turned away.

"Clear your calendar for tomorrow, Captain," Cassie said as the captain went out the door. "I will see you in your commander's office in the morning."

6.

At the door, when he was leaving, Ron Zeal looked Socrates in the eye.

"I ain't dealin' no drugs, man," he said. "Must be some othah niggah they lookin' for."

"Thanks for comin'," Socrates replied.

"I ain't comin' back."

DARRYL WAS IN THE KITCHEN washing the cherry cobbler casserole dish. Marianne Lodz and Luna were the last ones leaving. A driver in a late model Lincoln was waiting at the curb.

"We'll come back next week for sure, Mr. Fortlow," Marianne said, kissing his cheek. "You know how to show a girl a good time."

"Say hey to Leroy for me."

"Okay. Come on, Luna."

As the light-skinned singer waltzed toward her car her darker companion lingered.

"I won't come next week if you don't want me to," the young woman said. Her stare was almost a threat—definitely a challenge.

"Why wouldn't I want you?" Socrates asked.

"I'm the on'y one heah you didn't pick," she said. "I might not belong."

"I asked Billy too."

"So?"

"Billy's a gambler. What good is a gambler without a wild-card?"

When Luna smiled Socrates knew that he was right to hold onto her. She shook his hand, grabbing three of his fingers carelessly, and then hurried out to the car where Marianne was calling for her.

"Darryl," Socrates said as he returned to the kitchen.

"Uh-huh."

"Stop washin' for a minute."

Darryl turned off the water and brushed his hands against his already damp clothes.

"What you think about tonight?" Socrates asked him.

"It was all right I guess. For a minute there I thought we was gonna get killed." He scratched the back of his neck. "But I don't really know what it was about."

"Me neither but we both will. That's for sure."

He caught the boy in a headlock and wrestled him to the floor. Darryl struggled free and they both laughed and laughed.

TWO WOMEN

1.

Myrtle Brown lived on the fourth floor of an apartment building on Piney Court, two blocks over from Hooper. The wooden structure was painted a bright turquoise blue and edged in navy, which made it stand out almost as much as the tin-plated Big Nickel where Socrates met with people from all over South-Central and beyond talking about what was and what might be.

The zigzagging stairway leading up to Myrtle's door ran along the exterior of the house on the driveway side. Socrates could hear the wooden steps straining, sighing under his muscular weight. He stopped halfway up the last tier, not because he needed to rest but to enjoy a momentary reverie celebrating his now long ago release from prison. He did this from time to time, especially when he had something difficult ahead of him.

"They don't have me in a cage yet," he said aloud, not for the first time. He stared out over the mostly single-story dwellings and asphalt streets; over the black and brown pedestrians walking alone and in pairs; over the automobiles that stained the blue sky the way tobacco smoke does a white fiber filter.

Socrates had spent more than two-thirds of his adult life in maximum security lockdown—compliments of the state of Indiana. There he dreamed of this very moment, on Myrtle Brown's stairs and elsewhere, looking out over a broad space that he could traverse on a whim.

He felt a deep appreciation for those moments because, like almost every ex-convict, he expected to be re-incarcerated at any moment.

So what if he was headed for a showdown? He was at liberty right then and could eat a hamburger any time of the day or night. He could buy a beer or a butcher's knife—or a night with a woman.

In spite of all these potential treasures Socrates took a rueful breath and climbed the rest of the way to Myrtle's poorly painted, two-toned, matte-brown door.

At eye-level the middle-aged waitress had hung the laminated picture a young male musician who was singing into a microphone, beseeching the Infinite for love or release. The man was bare-chested except for a golden medallion that hung from a thick chain around his neck. The singer was fifteen years younger than Myrtle and he still had almost a decade on Darryl.

A woman sighed behind the door.

Socrates hesitated and then he knocked.

There was silence and then the stumbling rumble of footsteps, silence again and then a woman asking, "Who is it?"

"Socrates."

She said something else but he couldn't make out the words. There came the indecipherable tenor hum of his young friend Darryl, answering her.

"What you want?" Myrtle asked out loud.

"Darryl there?"

"We're not dressed."

"So put somethin' on." Socrates waited a moment and then added, "I just got to ask 'im sumpin', Myrtle."

There was more talk and footsteps, rustling and the sound of the lock tripping.

The door swayed inward, revealing Myrtle. She wore only a peach gown of satin that barely came down to her thighs. Socrates could see why a man would get hot over her. She didn't have a pretty face but her legs were shapely and firm and her breasts stood up well under the sheer fabric and forty something years.

"What you want wit' Darryl?" she asked.

Socrates could see the strain in her horsy features. Myrtle had big lips naturally but they seemed even larger now, swollen, almost bruised from the passion she'd had over the past few days.

"He got sumpin' for me," Socrates said, feeling regret for having barged into the teenager's life.

Darryl came up from behind the waitress wearing only black trousers. Tall and lanky, dark brown and cowed, the boy looked at the floor saying, "Hey, Socco. Sorry I didn't come by."

They stood there for a moment—the mismatched lovers and the ex-con.

"Why, why'ont you come in a minute?" Myrtle said reluctantly.

She and Darryl backed away from the door and Socrates entered the small, one room love nest. There were clothes all over the floor. The mattress of the bed was a quarter way off the frame. The radio was on but turned low. Marianne Lodz was singing "Be My Desire." The kitchen was a tiny refrigerator with a hotplate on top shoved in a corner.

The room smelled of concentrated body odors, lubricants, tobacco smoke, and incense.

Darryl fumbled around trying to pull on a dull orange T-shirt.

"How you two doin'?" Socrates asked.

"Sit down, Mr. Fortlow," Myrtle said. She was holding the lapels of her nightie with one hand to hide her cleavage. The other hand she had fanned out over her groin area.

Socrates took in a deep breath through his nostrils, grimaced and said, "Naw. I just come to get my phone."

"Phone?" Myrtle said.

"Oh shit," Darryl said.

"You forget, D-boy?"

"Yeah," Darryl said. "I mean no. I mean I got it I just forgot to bring it ovah."

With that the boy got down on his hands and knees in the clothes and blankets, pillows and papers covering the floor.

There was a single window in Myrtle's studio. It was open and the sun shone but the room was still dark. In the dim shadows Darryl was becoming frantic in his search.

"You seen my green bag, Myr?" the boy asked.

"No, baby. What bag?"

"The bag I always have. You know . . ."

"Oh . . . yeah. Uh-uh. Where'd you put it?"

"If I knew where it was I wouldn't be askin'," the boy said, his words reminding Socrates of himself.

Myrtle's queen sized bed stood high off the floor. Darryl stuck his head under to look, then he reached below, pulling out a hatbox and a small carton filled with paperback books. The books had photographs of scantily clad black women and barechested, powerful black men on the covers that Socrates could see. One red-lipped woman was preparing to kiss her man between his swollen pectoral muscles.

"What you doin', baby?" Myrtle cried. "Don't be takin' all my private stuff out from under there."

She made as if to get down on the floor but realized that her satin covering would come undone and so she just curved her shoulders and bent her knees, pleading with Darryl to be gentle with her possessions. But Darryl did not heed her. He pulled out another box that held creams and condoms, a huge anatomically correct black dildo and a strand of large red plastic beads spaced at three-inch intervals on a yard long red silken string.

"Oh no," Myrtle whispered.

"I got it," Darryl said excitedly. "Here it is."

He stood up grinning, holding out a drab green army bag.

"That's brown," Myrtle said.

"Nuh-uh. It's green. Right, Socco?"

"You got my phone, boy?" the elder asked.

"Yeah. Yeah. Right here."

Darryl rummaged through the rucksack, coming out with an open bag of potato chips and a handheld electronic game machine. Then he pulled out a clear plastic box over a bright orange carton. There was a small silvery phone and a power plug fit snugly into indentations in the carton.

"The numbah is on a strip'a paper on the back'a the phone," the boy was saying. "It's got a hundred dollars on it now and you can go into the sto' at Central an' 69th to put more money on it."

"Is it listed?" Socrates asked.

"Uh-uh. Cain't list a cell phone numbah. An' when they ask for your code for your messages or addin' on minutes all you got to say is 635-992."

"What kind'a password is that?" Myrtle asked. "How you expect somebody to remembah a numbah don't make no sense?"

Socrates was holding the box in his big hands. He grinned for the first time that day.

"That was *my* numbah in the penitentiary, Miss Brown," he said. "When I'm old an' forgot the color green I'll still know those numbers. Oh yeah. You'd have to shoot them digits out my head."

"Why'ont you sit down, Socco?" Darryl said. "We could have some lemonade."

"Yeah," Myrtle added, "sit."

"Naw," Socrates replied. "You guys don't need me around . . ." The ex-con looked at Myrtle, who was still covering herself with both hands; he had a sudden vision of the young woman he raped, bludgeoned, and strangled decades before.

"No," he said. "I got to get goin'."

He turned around, struggling to keep his equilibrium. It had been many months since he'd thought deeply about his personal damnation, his crimes that could never be washed away.

Darryl said something but Socrates didn't take the words in. He lurched out past the brown door into the smoggy sunlight. He lumbered down the stairway stiff-kneed, needing to hold onto the banister.

He was almost to the street. Someone was calling out somewhere. In the back of Socrates' mind it was a woman lecturing her child. But then a hand pulled against his shoulder. Myrtle Brown was standing there still clad only in peach colored satin; her hands no longer covering up.

When Socrates looked at her he felt a wave of nausea that was both sexual and a symptom of deep despair.

"Don't you do this to me, Socrates Fortlow," she said.

"Do what?"

"You know what," she said, tears welling in her eyes. "Darryl talk about you all the time. *Socco did this. Socco did that. Socrates told somebody sumpin' an' he back down an' run.* He'd do anything for you."

Socrates took off his army jacket and draped it around the woman's shoulders. She took the collars and crossed her hands to cover her near nakedness.

"He'll leave me if you won't even sit in my house."

"Baby, I ain't said a word against you to Darryl. He sleep where he want to. I cain't stop that."

"I love him," she said, the tears now rolling down her face.

"He's a child, Myrtle. You almost old enough to be his grand-mother."

"I love him," she said again. "There ain't a man out here twice his age treat me like he do."

"That's yo' ass talkin', honey," Socrates said with surprising gentleness. "We both know how sweet a child can be."

"No. It's somethin' else," she said. "I can see the man in him, the man you helped to make. He gonna be somebody."

"What's that got to do wit' you?"

Myrtle's head went back as if Socrates had slapped her.

"He's my man," she cried, shivering under the coarse material of the army jacket.

"He's a boy," Socrates said.

"He's man enough for me."

"He's a child, Ms. Brown. An' you know what a child will do. The first li'l girl out here flip her skirt at him and he'll be gone. You know that."

"He loves me."

"Ev'ry man up an' down this street been in love like that . . . a hunnert times."

"You 'ont understand, Mr. Fortlow. It ain't like that wit' us."

Socrates took in her words. She was right, he didn't know. He hadn't asked Darryl about the days and nights he'd spent on Piney with Myrtle. He hadn't wanted to know.

He was distracted by the meetings held at the Big Nickel, his meeting house. He'd leased the house for a dollar a year for five years and then opened it to all comers. There were treaty meet-ings between gang members that had complaints against each other, and the regular Thursday night meeting where his friends from all over discussed the world and what would be the right thing to do.

With all that talk and organization Socrates had ignored Darryl and his girlfriend.

"You right, Myrtle," he said at length. "You right."

"So you gonna come up and have a drink wit' us?"

"Not right now, baby. Have Darryl invite me and I'll come ovah. Maybe we'll go out to dinnah or sumpin' like that."

"I got lemonade right now," she offered.

Socrates saw her lips move but all he could hear was the pleading whine of the woman he'd raped and then murdered.

"I gotta go," he said.

2.

Walking down Central Avenue Socrates turned left toward The Big Nickel. He was trying to sort out the feelings that Darryl and Myrtle had unearthed in him. Seeing her nearly naked like that, with her lips all swollen and the room smelling of days of sex, had aroused his dark side. He hadn't been with a woman for two years. He wanted feminine company but the memories of his past were too strong. Sexual attraction always brought out feelings of violence and pain.

He stopped in the Bottle and Keg liquor store seven blocks from Myrtle's room. There he bought two beers with money made from his new cleaning job at Morningside Garage on 119th Street.

He was working a regular job to pay for the dinners served at the Thursday night Thinkers' Meeting.

When he was on the street again the phone rang from its wrapper. It didn't ring exactly but made a cry of escalating notes.

Through the plastic covering on the box Socrates could see a number that had the area code '310' in front of it. That was a prefix for the west side of town where Chaim Zetel, the wealthy junk man, lived.

Socrates tried to pull the plastic covering off the box but it wouldn't come loose. Finally the phone stopped sounding and the words MISSED CALL appeared on the small gray screen.

BY THE TIME HE REACHED the tin-plated addition to Fred Bumpus's lot Socrates was deep inside the question of Darryl and Myrtle. She *was* a shapely, sexy woman and Darryl needed some kind of love in his life. He didn't have parents or anyone else to show him the right way. Socrates was the only one there to help guide him.

The phone, which was still in its plastic container on the dining table, let out a loud chirp.

Socrates thought that Myrtle was too old for the boy but what did he know about love? In his entire life he'd only had one girlfriend and now they were just friends. She'd married the baker that supplied the diner she owned.

How could he give the boy advice?

The phone chirped again.

The screen now read—MESSAGE WAITING.

Again Socrates turned his attention to the thick plastic box. He searched for some kind of release mechanism but there was none. He tried the tear the container but even his great strength couldn't rip that material. Finally he got a knife from the cutlery drawer and hacked the clear covering open wide.

Below the message and the 'enter' button was the word VIEW. He pressed the button and the words VOICE MAIL appeared. He pressed the button again and the phone began to work. A mechanical voice asked him for his password. He entered his convict number and after a moment he heard Luna Barnet's voice.

"I was told that this was Mr. Fortlow's cell phone numbah," she said in her flat almost emotionless tone. "If it is, this is Luna. You should call me at my home numbah an' tell me when I could come by."

The mechanical voice told Socrates that if he wanted to hear her message again all he had to do was enter 1. He did this seven times, listening for some kind of answer in Luna's words. Finally he entered a 2 to save the message and pressed the red key to hang up.

He had her number on the sign-up sheet that Darryl passed around at the seventh Thinkers' Meeting held on Thursday nights. That was the evening that Ron Zeal brought a pistol to the gathering, which he took out and handed to Leanne Northford.

Zeal had told Socrates after the first meeting that he would not be back but he came again, and again.

"Why he still comin' if he so mad?" Billy Psalms had asked Socrates. "Man hate as much as he do cain't get nuthin' outta sumpin' like this."

"You wrong about that Billy," Socrates said. "I mean he was a long way out from acceptin' a place at this table. He was ten thousand miles from us but he traveled nine-thousand nine-hundred and ninety-nine a them miles just steppin' 'cross the threshold."

They had spent six weeks talking about black men who shot down their brothers in the street. Each week there had been a different issue. The first was about disrespect, when a man felt insulted by another's actions. After that came theft, infidelity, group (or gang) affiliation, revenge, and finally self-defense in all of its many incarnations.

The discussions went deep into the night and almost everyone had a strong opinion.

Most of the group had at least one experience to share. Even
Chaim Zetel had a story about a cousin that had murdered a
Nazi who'd escaped after WW II and smuggled himself down to
Paraguay.

"Moishe had light in his eyes before he left to avenge his parents and sister," the elderly Jewish junk man had said. "But after
he never smiled. I often thought that he was already dead but
didn't know it."

Every week Ron Zeal argued that the rest of the people were
fools.

"A man disrespect you an' you don't do sumpin' then you ain't
nuthin'," he said.

Socrates wondered out loud if children in the elementary
school should be allowed to slaughter those that made fun of
them. What about comedians, someone had asked, who make
jokes about the audience?

"And what if they are right?" Wan Tai asked.

"What you say, Chinaman?" Ron Zeal asked the martial arts
expert.

"What if you lie," Tai asked, "and then someone calls you a
liar? Is that disrespect?"

Ron returned every Thursday. Billy Psalms made a feast each
week cooking everything from fried chicken to oxtails and gravy.
Leanne Northford showed Zeal enough disrespect to get a whole
neighborhood slaughtered but still Ron was there for every meeting. Cassie Wheaton and Antonio Peron started showing up at the
same time and sitting together at the far end of the Big Table. And
Ron sat across from them, never once questioning the growing relationship between his black lawyer and the Mexican carpenter.

And then finally, a week after most of the room admitted that self-defense sometimes required deadly force, Ron came in late, pulled out a small .32 caliber pistol and handed it to Leanne.

"Take it," he said sullenly.

"What for?"

"Take it."

She took the gun from the young man's hand.

"Don't you hate me for killin' them boys?" he asked. "You they mama's friend right?"

"Yes," Leanne said.

"I ain't sayin' I did it. But you know I did. So here—kill me."

Darryl moved away from Ron's side where he'd sat at every meeting.

Leanne looked up into the killer's face, her lips twisted with dark passion.

Socrates realized then how remarkable it was that Leanne had continued to come to the meetings with Ron, the murderer of young men she'd known since they were born.

"Why?" she asked.

"Because maybe you right," he said. "Maybe we shouldn't be doin' what we doin'. Nobody could help it. Nobody could stop it. But maybe it's wrong anyway. Maybe so."

Leanne placed the pistol on the table and sat down, turning her back on Zeal.

That was the moment that the Thinkers' Meeting was set. Socrates looked down both sides of his asymmetrical table; everyone was looking at Leanne and Ron—everyone except for Luna Barnet, whose eyes were fastened on him.

"Hello?"

"Luna? That you?"

"Oh hi. You called."

"Didn't you ask me to?"

"Yeah. But I didn't think you would." Luna's voice was slow, almost lazy.

"Why not?" Socrates could feel his heart beating. This vulnerability embarrassed him, causing his pulse rate to increase even further.

"I'ont know. You never say nuthin' to me at that place."

"You're the one that never talks," Socrates said.

It was true. Luna had not once participated in the discussions about killing in the hood. She just sat there next to Marianne Lodz, the singer, and watched the people, especially Socrates.

"I don't have nuthin' to say them people wanna hear," she said. "You know that."

"What do you have to say, Luna?"

"Are you at the tin house?"

"Yeah."

"Can I come ovah?"

"Now?"

"Yeah."

"What for? The meetin' ain't till day after tomorrow."

"I wanna talk to you."

Socrates remembered his first day in prison. A man, a big man named Wendell had told Socrates that he would be on his knees to him by sunset or the dawn would find him dead.

"Yeah," Socrates said. "Yeah. Come on."

"Okay."

HE WAS SITTING ON THE PIANO BENCH on the left side of the Big Table when the knock came. It was Luna, he was sure of that. He felt her presence through the door and down into his bones. It was a fleshy, heavy feeling that weighed on Socrates' arms and legs. He felt as if he couldn't rise, that Luna was holding him down and calling him forth at the same time.

He took a deep breath and lurched up from his seat, toppling the bench as he did so. He walked slowly, not quite staggering as he approached the red door. He breathed in deeply as he pulled it open.

Like a promise Luna Barnet was standing there. She wore a coal gray dress that was approximately the same color as her skin. Her hair was teased out into five forms that appeared to be various sizes of dark flame. Two of these licks were tied with yellow ribbon. The rest stood on their own; wild and, at once, suggestive and forbidding.

"Can I come in?" she asked, neither smiling nor frowning.

Socrates stepped back and she entered the philosophers' fortress.

As he closed the door she said, "Cops out there across the street."

"Yeah. They been out there regular ever since we had them two clubs have that meetin' here."

"Why you want all them rough men 'round here anyway?" Luna asked.

Socrates smiled.

"Why you grinnin'?"

"That's just about the most words I heard you say all at once," he said.

That was one of the few times that Socrates saw Luna's friendly smile. It was a quivering at the corners of her mouth and a momentary easement from the pressure of her eyes.

"You want a beer?" he asked her.

"Naw."

"Don't drink?" he asked, trying to remember if she had ever had wine at their weekly meetings.

"Don't want to right now," she said as she strolled into the meeting room.

Socrates righted the piano bench and sat down. Luna settled into the cane chair that sat next to it.

"What can I do for you, Luna?"

"Slide down here next to me."

He did and she said, "I wanna ask you sumpin'."

"What's that?"

Luna was the second person to ever make Socrates this uncomfortable. Her quiet ways and flat, almost expressionless eyes made him feel that his innermost secrets were up for grabs. The only other person who made him feel like that was his Aunt Bellandra, the woman whose parents were born slaves; the woman who haunted his dreams for more than fifty years.

"It's kinda serious," Luna said. "Maybe you could ask me sumpin' first and then I could kinda get used to talkin' wit' you."

"All right," Socrates said, relieved that he didn't have to hear her question right off. "How come you and Marianne are friends?"

"Why?"

"You don't work together and you don't seem like you come from the same part of town. She's all fancy and particular. You look like you could live just about anywhere."

Luna chose that moment to cross her legs. The gray dress was short and so the hem rode high on her dark thigh.

"Why you lookin' at my legs?" she asked.

"You have very nice legs, Luna. Legs and thighs and eyes. You got it all, girl, and you know it too."

Luna twisted her lips, gauging Socrates' reply.

"I met Marianne after a party up in Baldwin Hills," she said. "I went up there wit' some'a my girlfriends but they hooked up and I was lookin' for a ride back down here. I was outside an' I hear this kinda like scream. You know it was like she was yellin' but someone either had their hand ovah her mouth or maybe they was squeezin' her throat."

Socrates had a familiar feeling in his shoulders and in the palms of his hands. It was the feeling of being incarcerated. He understood then that Luna's deep emptiness reminded him of himself.

"I went ovah to the side of the house an' I see this big dude tryin' to get in between this yellah girl's legs. I might'a thought it was some couple gettin' it on but he was just too rough. She was fightin' him an' he hit her wit' his fist. I call out, 'You bettah stop that for I call somebody.' An' then he jump up and I see that he had a knife in his hand. The girl was coughin' like she'd been chokin' an' he come at me . . ." Luna looked at Socrates then. She was asking a question with her eyes. He frowned and then nodded.

"He must'a been high," she continued. "He come at me fast but sloppy. You know I almost always got me a knife, my mama taught me that. She told me that a girl always need a edge. And so I stuck him in his th'oat an' he went down. Marianne put her clothes together an' pulled me ovah to her car. We went to her place up on Westwood Boulevard. She had a man keepin' her up there back then."

"What happened to the man?" Socrates asked. "The one you stuck?"

"His name was Reginald. I cut his voice box and hit a nerve in his neck. He cain't walk at all and he cain't talk. They asked him who did it but he don't know my name and he cain't read or write neither so it ain't nuthin'."

"How old are you, Luna?"

Luna got up from the cane chair and sat down next to Socrates on the piano bench before saying, "Twenty-three."

They were looking into each others' eyes.

"Why you wanna tell me about that?" he asked.

"'Cause you axed me how we got to be friends. Marianne says that she woulda been killed or at least lost her voice if I hadn't come and stopped him. She done took care'a me since then."

"But you could be arrested if I told somebody."

"You ain't gonna tell nobody," she said with a sneer, "and I never told nobody else."

"So what is it you wanted to ask me, Luna?"

"You the first full man I evah met," she said.

"Say what?"

"You heard me. You the first full man I evah met. I mean they's other men out here but they ain't for me. Fancy niggahs and fools, dumb mothahfuckahs think that a woman just waitin' to lie down and spread her legs open. And then there's men like Reginald."

"And so what's the question?" Socrates asked.

"You know."

"No, baby. What?"

Just the fact that Luna hesitated ignited a fire in Socrates.

"I want you to be my, my man," she said with barely a stammer. "I want your baby inside me."

When she put her left hand on her abdomen Socrates felt muscles in his cheeks that were unfamiliar.

"Luna . . . you're twenty-three. I'm so close to sixty I could kiss it."

"You that close to me too."

Looking into Luna's eyes Socrates saw what love could be for a man like him. It wasn't red silk and chocolates, or grins and soft kisses. The passion he now saw ignited in Luna's eyes was like that knife in Reginald's throat; that moment where survival is everything.

"Listen, girl," he said with a tone of confidence that belied his heart, "I'm old and fat."

"You look good to me. I wanna man, not some weight liftin' fool like Ron Zeal. You know I hear he take so much body buildin' drug that he cain't hardly get it up no more."

Socrates tried to think of a way to explain himself. She was young and wild but she didn't understand the darkness he came from.

"I know," she said as if responding to his thoughts. "I know what you did. Marianne told me. She said that you killed a man an' raped an' then killed his girlfriend."

The words were like every fist that landed on him while the convict Wendell tried to beat him to his knees. But Socrates could fight back against Wendell; he could fight back and win. He put that big ugly killer on *his* knees. He taught him a lesson that everyone in the Indiana State penitentiary learned.

But Luna was different. He couldn't stand up against her. The violence in his heart ebbed out of him like bad blood after the final fighter in a long-standing feud had passed on.

"I know what you did," Luna said again. "But here I am. I don't got my knife in my bag. I don't got no underwears on neither."

Socrates couldn't help but look at those bare legs again.

"You wanna see?" she asked him.

He put out his hands, laying them lightly upon hers.

"Slow down, baby," he said. "You like to give me a heart attack here."

This brought a true grin to the hard girl's lips.

"I bet you nevah said that to nobody before," she said.

"Luna, you mighta heard what I did but you can't know no shit like that. I choked the life outta that woman. I had her blood all ovah my hands. I took her and I killed her like I was some kinda wild animal. Animal."

Luna moved her wrists so that her hands were now on top of his.

"But you ain't no animal," she said.

"You cain't forgive me, girl. Nobody can."

"I don't forgive you," she said behind a steady stare. "I don't care what you did. I ain't here to give you nuthin'. I'm here to get sumpin' from you."

"What could I possibly have that you need?"

"I might be young, Mr. Fortlow, but I been around. I seen my brothah, my fathah, an' uncle all die from alcohol an' drugs. My mama turned to a old woman before I was sixteen. I seen it all. Killin's, beatin's . . . I got raped when I was twelve. My daddy killed the mothahfuckah did it."

Socrates closed his hands around Luna's.

"I'm sorry," he said.

"You'ont have to be sorry. I'm okay."

"You bettah than that. You a young woman. Smart and fine . . ."

"I ain't pretty," she said, "an' I ain't fancy. I can read but I don't know nuthin'. The only thing I know is that I want you. I knew it the minute I walked in that door an' saw you. I knew it even before when Marianne told me about how you got this place and what you wanted to do with it."

"I could be your grandfather."

"You could be my baby's daddy."

"Luna," Socrates said, feeling that he was pleading. "The things I've done . . ."

"The worst thing a man can do is not be there," the young woman said. Now she was squeezing his fingers with surprising strength. "But all somebody got to do is look at you to know that the only way you gonna leave is if you died."

Socrates wanted to pull his hand away, to stroke her hair and send her off, but Luna would not relinquish her grip.

"I'm not lettin' go'a you, Socco. I'm not playin' here."

"Baby, please," he said.

"We both done things," she said. "I stabbed that man an' he wasn't the first one. I done things wit' men. I done stole and sold drugs. We both been bad. An' you ain't that old anyway."

"Let me go now, Luna."

She withdrew her hands, clasping them upon her bare knees. Socrates enveloped the tight ball of fingers between his rock breakers.

"I'm not like one'a yo' teenagers," he said. "You got to give me a little time on this."

"You not just sayin' that so I go away?"

"I feel for you, girl," Socrates said. "From that first minute you walked in this house I wanted somethin'. But I never saw you comin'. It's like a dream I used to have in my cell sometimes."

Their restless hands kept moving. Now Luna took Socrates' big right hand in both of hers.

"What kinda dream?"

"I'd be in my eight by ten cell," he said. "There was mold growin' on the walls and bugs skitterin' all ovah in the dark, men cried out when they'd get hit and hurt. Killers be laugin' out loud and when and where it was quiet the convicts was mostly scared."

Luna was staring straight into his eyes. He could see that she could discern the truth as well as the pain in what he was saying.

"I'd go to sleep," he continued, "listening to all that sufferin', smellin' it too. And then I'd wake up because someone called my name . . ."

"Who?"

"I'd open my eyes and there'd be this li'l girl, no older than you, standing there."

"A black girl like me?"

"Oh yeah. She'd be naked an' ask me for my blanket. An' I'd get up and take that thin army surplus wool they had for us an' put it on her shoulders . . ." as he spoke Socrates was remembering this recurring reverie from another life. ". . . an' then she'd say, 'let's go outside,' and the cell do' would come open . . ."

When the tear fell from Fortlow's cheek onto Luna's hand she started slightly. Socrates wondered at his tear. He hadn't cried in as long as he could remember. That was his first lesson on his first day in the joint: no one would care about his pain or suffering or despair. He would kill himself before he cried because at least in taking his own life he'd be doing something about the pain. Crying was worse than suicide; it was worse than being murdered or raped or put down in the Dungeon for sixty days or a hundred and sixty.

This is what Socrates believed. There was no use in crying, had never been—until now. But now when Luna saw that he was a baby, and not the man she wanted, she would leave, no longer wanting him.

Another tear fell and a knock thumped in his chest like an engine choking on gasoline gone bad.

"Did you go wit' her?" Luna asked in a sweet voice that had a little music in it.

"She led me through the do'," he said. "And it was a park outside. A big park wit' trees and birds. Damn. I was even happy to see the flies buzzin' around dog shit."

Luna showed her teeth and let her right shoulder rise in an unconsciously coy fashion.

"If you won't gimme a baby right now will you at least gimme a kiss?" she asked.

"I ain't brushed my teeth all day, girl."

"You think I care about that?"

"I care."

Luna stood up, releasing his hand. She leaned over and kissed his bald head. The moment her lips touched his skin he shuddered. His hands twitched and his neck pulled back. His left foot picked up off the oak floor and stamped back down.

"I bet I could knock you off your feet if I kissed you on the mouf," she said with a sensual sneer upon her lips.

OUTSIDE SOCRATES WAVED at the unmarked police car across the street. The two black men inside the vehicle did not return his salutation.

He walked Luna to her car, a late model Lexus loaned to her by Marianne Lodz and protected by the police that were watching the Big Nickel.

She opened the door and looked up at Socrates, the dark hair and yellow ribbons again reminding him of flames.

"How much you gotta think before you know?" she asked.

They could both see the erection bulging from behind his trousers.

"You know what you just gave me in there was more than most lovers ever even heard about" he said. "It's like you hit me in the head with a three quarter inch steel pipe."

"That ain't no answer," she said.

Socrates looked at the poor child standing next to the luxury car. A hundred answers and questions, demands and declarations came into his mind. He had a whole night worth of words to say but nothing passed his lips.

They stood there like lovers whose kisses had pushed back the minutes and hours. Socrates' heart was a fist against the bars of his rib cage; his erection that steel pipe battering his good sense.

"It's like you was still up in jail, huh?" Luna asked.

"What?" Socrates said. The thoughts swirling around her mind made her words almost incomprehensible.

"It's like I when I had this boyfriend up in jail an' I'd go an' see'im in the visitor's room. He'd always be all mad an' I axed him if he didn't want me to come. An' he'd say that it just got him so excited when he see me that he get mad 'cause he couldn't be wit' me."

"What happened to that boyfriend?"

"He got out an' they shot him."

"Who?"

Luna shook her head and Socrates wondered if they weren't somehow equals on that street. He also wondered if the nameless boyfriend had gotten to be with her at least one more time before he was cut down; he hoped so.

"Kiss me on my lips and you can have all the time you want," Luna said as serious as a killer.

Socrates bent over and brushed her lips awkwardly with his own.

"Call me?" she asked.

"In just a couple'a days," Socrates said.

3.

"Hey, boy," Socrates hailed as he opened his door to the familiar, tentative knock.

It was three mornings after Luna staked her claim on him.

"Hey," Darryl said, holding his head to the side in his usual shy manner. "I went by the Nickel but you wasn't there."

"Some people comin' by tomorrow night."

"Can I come?"

"You gonna bring Myrtle?"

her nowhere," the young man said.

r girlfriend ain't she?"

said. He went past Socrates into the small

He went to the refrigerator and took out one of

ttles of supermarket cola that Socrates kept for him.

rryl sat down at the dinette table. Socrates sat across from
him and said, "When I saw you wit' her last you was her
boyfriend. An' I haven't even seen you since then."

"I left that bitch three days ago."

Socrates would not have struck the boy. He had decided long
ago that violence could not rear respect. He would never strike
Darryl—but he wanted to. Darryl could see the quick violence
rise in his mentor's eyes.

"What?" he asked in a hurt tone.

"She told me she loved you."

"That old woman nasty," Darryl said with disgust. "She do
anything I want."

Socrates stared steadily at Darryl's left ear. He didn't have to
say anything for the conversation to continue its pace.

"What?" Darryl asked again.

"Where you been?"

"Nowhere."

"You don't sleep? You don't eat?"

"I was wit' my boys. Nelson an' them."

Nelson Fabricant, Chess Peres, and Bright Conrad—Socrates
knew them all; awkward kids that didn't belong to any gang or
church, school or military organization. They got together and
joked around threatening to join the army or to go out on a ram-
page robbing banks.

"What?" Darryl asked for a third time.

"Why you break it off wit' Myrtle?"

"I told you."

Darryl finished his soda, put the bottle in the sink and got another one. He loitered by the refrigerator, hunching his shoulders and frowning at the floor.

"Tell me again."

"She always on me an' shit," the boy said. "Tellin' me t'be cleanin' up an' then she want me t'get a job. She always askin' me when I'ma get my GED."

Darryl scratched his nose and rubbed his neck, tapped on the ice box with his knuckles, and took a deep draught of the dark soda.

"What else?"

"She nasty. I cain't even say nuthin' like a joke 'cause whatever it is she ready t'do it."

Socrates Fortlow allowed himself a smile.

He thought of Darryl as a tiny dinghy that had somehow gotten lost and drifted out onto a vast ocean that was Myrtle Brown.

"What you laughin' at?" Darryl asked. "I thought you'd be happy that I broke it off wit' her. I mean you wouldn't even sit down in her house."

"That Myrtle Brown is some woman, huh?" Socrates said.

"I guess."

"I bet you sometime she get so fired up that it seem like you in a room wit' some kinda hungry animal you never even heard of."

Darryl didn't answer but his eyes were wide and passive.

"Yeah," Socrates said. "Woman get hungry it don't mattah how old she is. She be tellin' you she love ya an' bitin' you so hard that you wanna yell."

Darryl sat down.

"Did she kick you out?" Socrates asked.

"Yeah."

"Why?"

"'Cause I got mad an' told her that I wasn't gonna do what she said. 'Cause she said that I was eatin' her food but I wasn't helpin' out."

"So where you go when she put you out?"

"Ovah to Nelson's mama an' them. He let me stay there for a while."

"Then his mama kicked you out too," Socrates said. There was a wolfish grin in his chest that he kept out of his voice.

Darryl nodded.

"You know you could always stay here with me," Socrates told the son of his heart. "There's always some food and a place to sleep here."

"I know but . . ."

"But what?"

"I thought you was mad at me."

"'Cause'a Myrtle?"

"Yeah."

"You know I think she's old for a kid like you. But she like you an' she nice. An' you know you got to learn how to work an' pick up aftah yourself. You got to finish school an' do sumpin'. That's what she tell ya right?"

"Yeah. Uh-huh. But she too old for me. I need me a young woman like Shakira or Beyoncé or, or maybe Marianne Lodz."

"Here's ten dollars, D-boy. Go on down to Tibor's market an' get us some chicken. I'll make soup an' biscuits."

AFTER DINNER DARRYL FELL ASLEEP on the couch while Socrates sat in his chair reading the newspaper, preparing for the Thinkers' Meeting the next night. There were some new members and he wanted to get away from talking about Ron Zeal.

He was reading about the vice president of the United States having shot some friend of his on a hunting trip. It was an accident, the article said, and Socrates believed it. But he wondered if he could make a mistake like that and not get prosecuted, convicted, and sentenced to seven years for criminal negligence; a judgment that would come with an extra five years for being gang related due to the fact that he allowed peace negotiations to be conducted at the Big Nickel.

Socrates had begun to consider other community uses for his private university when the cell phone sounded.

"Is he there?" a sweet, bruised voice said into his ear.

"Hold on," Socrates told her. "He's right here."

"Hello?" Darryl said into the phone. He hadn't sat up, hadn't even opened his eyes. "Uh-huh. Yeah. Uh-huh. I'ont know. Okay. Okay. Yeah. All right."

He closed the cell phone and reached down to put it on the floor, then fell immediately back to sleep.

An hour later the boy sat up.

"I gotta go," he said.

"Where to?"

"Over Myrtle's."

"You comin' to the meetin' tomorrow night."

"I'll be there," the boy said. Then he took a deep breath and ran his hand over the top of his skull.

He stood up and walked to the front door of Socrates' secluded cottage.

He was about to go out when Socrates called out, "Darryl."

"Yeah?"

"Be careful, D-boy."

Their eyes met for a moment, half that. In that span something passed between them. Socrates would be there. Darryl was coming back. As the boy shuffled out the door—with his black jeans hanging down on his skinny hips and his white cross-trainers untied and careless—Socrates smiled and went back to his paper, feeling freedom in his bones.

AT MIDNIGHT HE WAS LISTENING to Ornette Coleman on the radio. The alto saxophone sounded like the freedom the aging ex-convict was feeling. He intended to stay up all night enjoying himself. He would never go to back to prison; that just wasn't possible. He was freer than any white man, freer than that howling wolf in Ornette's reed.

At half past midnight the cell phone whined its escalating cry.

"Do you have another girlfriend?" Luna asked in answer to his hello.

"Don't have the first girlfriend."

"Ain't I your friend?"

"I love you, Luna," Socrates said, surprising himself with the words. There was an ice tray cracking open in his chest. His scalp twitched but he went on, "But you're a child and I'm a old man. I wouldn't want to see my withered skin up next to yours."

"We could turn out the light."

"I'd still be sixty."

"I'm gettin' older too, you know."

Socrates laughed.

"You see?" she said. "I can talk your language. I could close my eyes in the bed."

"But what if you opened them one day and wanted someone else?"

"Then I'd get up an' go."

There was a long silence until finally Luna asked, "Can I come ovah?"

"Not tonight."

"You see?" she said. "Tonight I'm too young but later on we gonna be at the same place."

AFTER THEY GOT OFF THE PHONE Socrates went to the toilet to wash his hands. He noticed that there wasn't the feel of tacky blood between his fingers.

MAXIE

1.

Socrates sat in the right front aisle seat of a scarlet and gold colored Crenshaw bus, almost next to the driver. Someone in the seat directly behind had just taken a swig of gin. The woman sitting next to him had the smell of cigarettes coming off of her clothes.

And there were other odors.

Faint vapors of urine wafted from an elderly woman dressed in rags that seemed almost as old as she. She was seated a few rows back, across the aisle from a man with a Rastafarian hairdo who was listening to earphones with the volume set so high that everyone in the front third of the bus could sing along to the repetitive rants of the hip-hop selections he played.

The contained atmosphere of the one quarter-full bus also carried the smells of a fresh cheeseburger, lemon scented disinfectant, various perfume oils, and the clean scent of a baby suckling at the breast of a brown skinned Hispanic woman two rows toward the rear.

Socrates wondered what to make of it all. In his imagination he became a dog that could detect scents a hundred times better than a human being. But it wasn't just that the dog had the more powerful nose but that the creature was smart about what he detected.

"We smell trouble every day," the ex-convict imagined saying to the people that sat around the Big Table on Thursday nights. "But we close our eyes an' hold a handkerchief over our noses, we laugh out loud to cover the screams, we buy Egyptian incense off people in the streets to mask the smell of garbage and rot."

"What?" the cigarette smelling woman next to him asked.

"Yes, ma'am? Did you say somethin'?"

"I thought I heard you say sumpin'," she replied.

The bus driver had engaged the brakes. The hydrolics were crying out as they struggled against the hurtling behemoth.

"I was thinkin'," Socrates said. "Musta slipped outta my mouth."

"Oh," she said with a smile.

She had one tooth missing and smelled like an ashtray but her dark features were lovely, her skin so black that it probably didn't come from American ancestry.

Looking at the forty-something smoker Socrates thought about the young Luna Barnet.

"You can call me any time of night and I would come down there," she'd told him via cell phone the evening before. "I will come to you whenever you want me."

"What you think about Maxie Fadiman?" Socrates asked, partly to deflect the young woman's intensity but also because he wanted to know.

"He okay," she'd said.

"He try'n hit on you?"

"You jealous?"

"Not one bit."

"Why?" Luna asked, her quick temper rising in the early hours. "You don't think men wanna get wit' me?"

"'Course they do, girl," he said. "But I know right now I'm the one you got on the hot seat."

"Maybe I want a man let me be wit' him," she suggested.

"Has Maxie asked you anything?"

"He wanted to know if the people at the meetin' evah *did* anything about what we talked about," she said.

"Like what?"

"I'ont know. I told him all we evah did was talk, talk, talk."

"MISTAH?" a woman's voice asked.

Socrates looked up to see an elderly brown woman holding herself upright on the bars of an aluminum walker.

"Oh," he said. The bus must have stopped, he thought, and this woman climbed up step by step while his mind was wandering. He was in the handicap seat.

"Excuse me, ma'am." He got to his feet holding the canvas bag that Myrtle Brown had given Darryl to give to him: a peace offering. Before moving away from the seat he nodded to the cigarette smoker. She smiled sadly, telling him with her eyes that she would have welcomed more conversation.

Socrates took the hand of the older woman, holding the walker as he did so. When he was in the penitentiary he was once responsible for an older convict who'd lost the use of his legs and so he knew the right moves to help this woman into her seat.

"Thank you, sir," the woman said as he folded her collapsible walker. "God bless."

The bus lurched into motion. Socrates moved toward the less populated rear section. He staggered and then righted himself, tottered on his left foot and grabbed the cold chromium rod that ran overhead for support.

The metal chill on his fingers took him back over the past few moments: the sense of a dog and the scent of urine, a woman-child on the phone making him into a man, a black-skinned woman smelling of tobacco; a drunk, an infirmed woman, and music playing for a dreadlock-sporting wild man; a baby taking it all in while not having words to describe what it was feeling.

Socrates took a corner seat at the very back of the bus. From there he stared out into the passing street. It was mid-afternoon and sunny. People were walking and cars were weaving in and out. The children moved in swarms, where adults were mostly alone or in pairs.

Socrates looked at his big hands. A killer's hands, hands that had taken more than one life. He could count the deaths on five fingers, leaving one hand innocent. "Innocent of murder," he whispered to himself. "But not from brutality and just bein' mean."

"ALL I GOTTA SAY," Billy Psalms had said two nights before, at the Thinker's Meeting held at the Big Nickel, a house that Socrates used for anything from gang summits to prostitute barbeques, from poetry workshops to the meeting of the minds, "is that if we listen to the white man's words we will nevah be anything but slaves."

"We aren't slaves," the criminal lawyer, Cassie Wheaton, argued. "We have all the rights of any other American. We vote. We pay taxes."

"Chaim Zetel there is a white man," the white-bearded wiry Mustafa Ali added. "You sayin' that we shouldn't listen to him?"

"He ain't white," Leanne Northford, the retired social worker, argued.

"He's not black," Tony Peron, the Mexican, said.

"I agree with Billy," Maxie Fadiman, one of their new members, said. "White people the cause of all this shit. We got to do somethin' about them."

There was passion in Maxie's words but, Socrates thought, Billy hadn't issued a call to arms. The diminutive gambler said that Black people shouldn't *listen* to the white man.

Mustafa Ali had told the Thinkers that Maxie was a poor man who was down on his luck. He had frequented Ali's soup kitchen for the past six months. He had a high school degree and six semesters of college, but selling marijuana, a short prison sentence, and then a bout with heroin pushed him off the road.

"It's not the white man," Wan Tai, the slender Chinese, said. "It is any man or woman who teaches history or reports the news."

Tai was a Buddhist karate instructor who spoke little. His voice was strong, however, and most of the Thinkers respected him.

"That's right," Leanne Northford added. "Our enemy is the lie first and the liar second . . ."

The conversation was going along just fine. The men and women at his table were learning faster than they could in any classroom. They had good food and passable wine, a private residence in which to speak their minds and the sense of a community that was most of the time anchored in SouthCentral but that drifted into many different waters.

2.

In the back of that bus Socrates remembered what it felt like to be incarcerated. Every day you had only one thing at the front of your mind and senses—survival. There were men who wanted to kill you waiting right down the hall. They were looking for weakness in you: an injury or just a twenty-four hour bug. Every one of your possessions was up for grabs and at any moment the prison guards might come and drag you down to the Dungeon for the rules that you broke in order to survive.

Sitting on that bus life was easy. The smells and sounds, smiles and memories came on like a waterfall on a summer's day. Socrates took a deep, satisfied breath but he didn't let down his vigilance. The lessons he learned in prison served him well on the outside. He knew what to look for. He could smell the sweat on a homemade steel knife in a man's pocket—in his sleep.

On the street he took a slip of paper out of his worn wallet and looked at the address he'd scrawled.

"You sure you want this?" Cassie Wheaton had asked him over the phone.

"Why wouldn't I?" the philosopher replied. "I just wanna talk. It ain't illegal for you to gimme this is it?"

"No, Mr. Fortlow. I just . . . I just don't want you to get in trouble. You're too important to throw your life away."

THE HOUSE WAS SMALL AND WHITE. There was no razor-wire fence or video camera monitoring the grass yard. There were no gangs of convicts gathering to protect their turf.

Socrates wore a suit for the first time since the last funeral he'd attended. That was Maura Conrad, the mother of Darryl's friend Bright. The cloth was dark green. His shirt was white but not brightly so. He wore no tie and his shoes had seen every alleyway from Watts to Compton. And though much of the anger that had propelled him through life was gone there were still the vestiges of rage in his face; scars and winces, lips that hardly remembered how to smile.

"Yes?" a small, sand colored woman asked, answering his soft knock.

"Martin Truman here?" Socrates asked. He felt that his voice was too rough for such a genteel and fragile woman.

"Who are you?"

"Socrates."

"Mr. Socrates?"

"No. Fortlow's my last name. I come to ask Marty somethin'."

The woman glanced at Socrates' big hands. They were hanging loosely at his side but he couldn't do anything to disguise their size and strength.

"Are you a friend of Marty's?" she asked.

"We know each other."

"Oh. Do you work together?"

"Not exactly, but we met on the job."

"Oh."

The woman hesitated a moment longer and then closed the door. Socrates stood there wondering what the chances were of him being shot through that door as he listened to sparrows squabble and the engine of a passing car with the hot sun on the back of his neck.

A baby was crying somewhere and a butterfly had gotten trapped in a garden spider's web in a poinsettia bush growing to the right of the front door.

As the big yellow and black spider bobbed gracefully down for the kill the front door opened again. A brown-skinned middleweight stood there in black trousers and a faded blue T-shirt. The man was holding a revolver down at his left side.

"I didn't know you were left-handed, Maxie."

"What you want here, Socco?" Maxie was looking around to make sure that the killer was alone.

"I didn't know you were left-handed," Socrates said again, "but I knew you was a cop the second night you came to the Big Nickel."

"What are you doing here?"

"It was the shoes told me first," Socrates said. "They wasn't new and they wasn't old. A junkie's shoes either fallin' apart or they brand new. You had shoes like a workin' man—older than he wants but still up to the job."

"I will shoot you, niggah," Maxie/Marty told Socrates.

"Shoot me? Why?"

"You come up to *my* house and threaten my family and you wonder why I'ma shoot you?"

"You came to my house an' spied on me," the ex-con in the funeral suit said. "You took whateveah you heard to the police. Why can't I come to yo' house an' say sumpin' to you? I'm not tryin' trick you. You see exactly who I am."

"Hold your voice down, man," the police agent said.

"Hold my voice down? Here you spy on me an' threaten t'kill me an' then you want me to be quiet? What is wrong wit' you, Negro? Cain't you see that I'm the one been molested, lied to, and cheated?"

The man Socrates had known as Maxie tightened the grip on his pistol and glanced behind him. It was a quick gesture but it gave enough of a window for Socrates to have disarmed and killed the undercover cop. He considered the action and rejected it before Maxie turned back and stepped over the threshold, pulling the door shut behind him.

"What do you want, Socrates Fortlow?"

"I honestly don't know."

"What you mean you don't know? What the fuck you doin' here at my house?"

"What was you doin' at my place, Officer Truman?"

"That's police business."

Socrates smiled. There weren't many times that he could stand on equal footing with a cop.

"Is your address police business too?"

"How did you find it?"

"Do you care if I tell the people at the Nickel that Maxie is really a cop live ovah in the Crenshaw district?" Socrates asked. "Could I be arrested for exposin' a spy?"

"Are you threatenin' me?" the man with the gun asked.

"Are you threatenin' me?" Socrates replied.

"No threat, mothafuckah," Maxie said. "I will kill you."

"Maybe. Maybe you will. But that don't have to be. I ain't done nuthin' but what you did. All I'm askin' is for you to tell me why you was up in my house with my friends lyin' about who you are and reportin' what you heard to the law."

Brown veins stood out on the smaller man's neck. His gun hand began to quiver.

Socrates understood that he had never been closer to his own death. The prospect didn't scare him though. He himself was a murderer and could expect no better from life.

The door came open and the sand colored woman came out with a tiny light brown baby in her arms.

"Martin," she said. "Is everything okay?"

"Go back inside, Linda."

"Should I call somebody?"

"Go back inside."

The baby started crying. Linda took a step backwards and stopped.

"Let me help you, Maxie," Socrates said then. "You worried that I will tell where you live and that you'd have to run to stay from losin' all you got. You worried that there's gonna be a bull's-eye on you an' your family. That's a real fear there. But you know I ain't told nobody a thing about you. I did give somebody a sealed envelope sayin' what I know about you and where I went today."

"What's he talking about, Martin?" Linda asked. "Why is he calling you Maxie?"

Marty/Maxie turned, screaming incoherently at his wife. The baby yowled as the enraged cop slammed the door on them. Then he turned to Socrates, holding his gun up toward the ex-con's chest.

Socrates smiled and held his hands out to his side.

"There's a diner ovah on Avalon called Benny's Red Beans and Rice," Socrates told him. "Come ovah there tomorrow at three. Let's see if we can talk this shit out."

Socrates walked away from the man known as Maxie aware of the possibility of being shot down in the street. He was mindful of Maxie's gun and his rage while thinking about the sights and smells and sounds of the people who, for a short while, inhabited the Crenshaw bus.

3.

Socrates got to Benny's twenty minutes early but Officer Truman was already there. He was wearing his signature stained army jacket and drab green gardener's pants. Socrates had on a dark green T-shirt and white cotton pants. Los Angeles was experiencing a hot spell and he had been sweating in his bed, under just a thin sheet, the night before.

Maxie was seated in a window booth in the empty diner. Before him was a white ceramic mug decorated with blue dots around the rim.

Socrates maneuvered his way into the bench across from the policeman.

"Riot weather out there," the ex-con said.

"Say what?"

"The heat. Back in the sixties if the mercury got over ninety-two it was riot weather. Air-conditionin' is the only reason the United States didn't have a revolution in the sixties." Socrates smiled at his own humor but the man that had joined his Thinker's group only a month before was no longer interested in his ideas.

"I'm not comin' to your place anymore," he told Fortlow.

"Why not?"

The police spy was at a loss for words. He simply stared at his host.

"You want somethin' to drink, Socco?" asked a small black man in a white sailor's cap.

"You got limeade, Salty?"

"Made it fresh this mornin'," the waiter and cook said with a smile.

As Salty moved away Socrates repeated his question.

"Why you not comin' back to the Big Nickel?"

"Because I'm a cop and you found me out."

"So? Ain't nobody among us turn you away for that. And we'd like to talk to you. You the man we need to know. I mean here you are a brother and still you come in an' report us to the people standin' in our way and on our heads at the same time."

"It's not white people standin' in your way," Truman said.

"I didn't say nuthin' 'bout white people. I just said people . . ."

"Here you go, Socco," the middle-aged restaurateur said. He placed a tall frosty glass of the too-green beverage on the table.

"I called you a brother," Socrates continued when Salty had gone again, "and the ones who stand in our way *people*."

"You meant white people," Truman said. "You mean that I'm some kinda Tom workin' for white people."

"Wan Tai is a brother," Socrates said, "so is Chaim and Antonio. You don't have to be black to be a brother an' you don't have to be white to be standin' in the way."

"What you want from me, Socrates?"

"I wanna know three things."

"What?"

"Why did you come to our meetin' in the first place?"

"That's my job. I'm s'posed to get inside organizations, criminal organizations, and find out what they're doin'."

"And how'm I a criminal organization?"

"Ron Zeal," Truman said as if the name alone were proof.

"And if Ron started goin' to Holy Baptist or Alcoholics Anonymous tomorrow would you go spy on them?"

Officer Truman worked his way to the edge of the seat and stood. He took out a five dollar bill and placed it next to his coffee mug.

"Fuck this," he said, "I'm outta here."

Socrates said nothing to this. He just pushed out his lower lip and nodded. The cop looked down on him, expecting something but obviously not getting it.

"What do you want?" Truman asked again.

"For you to answer my three questions."

"And then we're through?"

"That's up to you."

"What the fuck is that s'posed to mean?"

"Sit down, Maxie. Sit down and talk to me."

Officer Martin Truman, responding to his alias, sat back upon the bench, across the table from the self-proclaimed thinker of the Big Table.

"I answered the first question."

"Not completely," Socrates said. "I asked would you spy on the Catholic Church if Ronnie started takin' mass."

"We would infiltrate any group that poses a threat to our city," the policeman said.

"The city council?"

"Of course not."

"And so because Ron Zeal comes to our meetin's they put you on us like some kinda dog on a thief?"

"You have gang meetings in that house," Truman said. "There are communists, anarchists, prostitutes in there and then you have daycare for children. It is the responsibility of the city government to protect children."

"Even the children of prostitutes?" Socrates asked, "and of gang members, communists, and anarchists?"

"Drug dealers have been seen in your Big Nickel."

"If they sold one stick in my place it would be the last thing they ever did," Socrates vowed.

"That's not the point. Police intelligence sees your place as a potential breeding ground of criminal activity and so they got me infiltrating your group."

"That brings me to my second question," Socrates said.

"You know I don't have to talk to you, Mr. Fortlow," Truman said. "I could get a group of men down at your place and beat you until you told us where that letter was."

"I doubt that, Maxie. I mean I don't doubt that you could get the manpower. I'm sure that they'd put the hurt to me. But you know there ain't a soul in this city has studied pain more than I have. I got a Ph.D. in pain. Anyway you owe me."

"Owe you what?"

"When you came out your door with that gun at your side I coulda killed you whenever I wanted. Stomped your foot and broke your neck. I could do it this very minute. And if you beat me you'd have to kill me 'cause you know I'd get you on the comeback. You know it. So let's not sit here makin' threats. You done answered one question. There's only two more."

Truman sat back in his seat and turned his head to the side.

"Did you find out we was doin' sumpin' wrong at the Big Table?"

"That's not the point."

"Ain't you there to find out if we was a threat?"

"Even if you aren't a threat right now it doesn't mean that you won't be one in the future," Truman argued. "You're a felon. You might be taking innocent people and planning to turn them into crooks."

"And did you see me doing that?" Socrates asked. "Was I tryin' to fool them people?"

"You were talking shit to them. Actin' like we could do somethin' about malaria in Africa and terrorism. Shit."

"We?" Socrates asked.

"You know what I mean."

"You doin' somethin' 'bout terrorism, Maxie, and you're just one man. One man get in with us and find all our bombs."

"That's different," Truman said. "I'm with the police."

"I'm with the brothers, Maxie. You been to my table. There's some smart people there. Honest people. Even Ron Zeal is honest. He a killer but he don't try 'n hide that. He wrong but he willin' t'learn. Why can't a man learn and then do somethin'?"

"Is that all your questions?"

"No. I got one more. I already asked you once but it's worth comin' back to."

"Hurry up. I got to be someplace."

"You mean you got some mo' po' niggahs to spy on?"

"Go on."

"Will you come back to our meetin's?"

"What?"

"Come back to us, Maxie. Come to the Big Table and tell everybody who you are an' let them talk to you."

"Are you crazy? Do you know what they'd do to me?"

"I ain't done nuthin' to ya, Max. I knew what you was and all I wanted to do was talk. I know you think what you doin' is right. But I know too that you seen what we was. And you know bettah than any other man at that table that our fears about the world are right. We talk about people spyin' on us and here you are the spy. It will help us to know you and hear what you got to say. Like I said—a brothah spyin' on his own an' he don't even know it."

"You're serious," Truman said as the truth dawned upon him. "You really believe all that stuff you sayin'."

"If you don't believe, Maxie, then you might as well give up. I learnt that in a eight by ten cell. There's no life if you don't believe in sumpin'. I was in prison for a long time, a very long time. It was possible that I'd never be free again. But I believed I'd be free and that I would get a chance to make amends for the things I did."

"I know what you did," Truman said. "I read your file."

Socrates lowered his head, thinking how many eyes had studied him and dismissed him; how many people knew of the pain he'd inflicted on those youngsters. And for a moment he almost gave up. How could he pass judgment on Maxie when he was guilty? How could he talk about doing right when he was so wrong?

"Does that make what you do better?" Socrates asked, strength flowing back through his lungs. "I did my crime. I served my time. I know in my heart how wrong I was. I don't blame nobody and I never, not even once, claimed to be innocent. That's all I'm askin' of you."

"What?"

"Come over to the Nickel and tell us about bein' a spy. And you don't have to worry, I promise I won't tell 'em your real name or where you live at. Even if you don't come your secret is safe with me."

Truman could only stare, his features distorted by confusion. He shook his head, seemed about to speak, but the words didn't come. He tried again but the amazement at this last question left him speechless.

"I can't," he said at last.

"You won't."

"I, I couldn't. I mean I been doin' this work for more than two years. You not the first people I got over on. I'd have to leave L.A."

"What if somebody saw you one day at the Beverly Center with your wife and baby, shoppin' for clothes? They might suspect sumpin'. And if they told somebody else your whole game might come to light."

The darkness that invaded Truman's features was not for the first time. But, Socrates thought, it was the first time someone had corroborated his fears.

"Are you gonna expose me, Mr. Fortlow?"

"I already told you—no. I just wanted to ask you those questions. I just wanted you to know that you not invisible and that the man you work for is not your friend."

4.

"Why don't you just tell the group about him?" Cassie Wheaton asked.

Socrates and the defense lawyer were having hot dogs at an outside stand across the street from the criminal justice building.

"Because he got a nice young wife and a baby."

"He's a spy," she reasoned. "He put them in jeopardy."

"You pregnant, aren't you, girl?"

Socrates grinned because of the rare show of surprise on the lawyer's face.

"Who told you that?" she asked.

"Nobody."

"Then how would you know? How's a man spent his whole life in prison gonna know a woman is a few weeks pregnant?"

"I was in that prison with men," Socrates said.

"Yes."

"And that's what I been looking at—your man. Antonio treat you like you'd break if he didn't pull out your chair. You with child and he the father."

"Okay," she said. "I am pregnant but what has that got to do with Truman?"

"You got people off that done wrong haven't you, Cassie?"

"They were never guilty in court," she said.

"But they killed people, they sold drugs and caused pain."

"So?"

"Ron Zeal killed those boys that Leanne knew."

"This is my job," Cassie said. "If there were no defense lawyers there'd be no justice."

"Yeah, and if we didn't have cops we'd have to carry our kids with us like kangaroos or crocodiles."

Cassie sniffed and took a bite of her hot dog.

"He spied on us, Mr. Fortlow."

"Call Maxie's boss and let him know that we seen him comin'. Tell him that we just want justice. Tell him that we'd like him to come to a meetin' and tell us why we're enemies of the state."

Cassie frowned and shook her head.

"Does anyone else know about me?" she asked.

"They know about you and Antonio. I think they were surprised by that."

"Because he's a Mexican?" she asked, ready to be angry.

"Naw. 'Cause he so short." Socrates laughed then. "They know about him but I don't think they know about your condition."

"You always surprise me, Socrates."

"That's what they tell me," the self-made philosopher said. "An' here I am just doin' what I do."

TRIFECTA

1.

"I wanna say the first words," Billy Psalms announced at the twenty-fourth weekly Thinkers' Meeting. He was standing at the head of the Big Table after having served jambalaya and collard greens, corn on the cob and a green salad.

It was early evening at the Big Nickel and eighteen men, women, and a few teenagers crowded around the odd-shaped table sitting in mismatched chairs in front of plates of every size and shape. It was often said that the dinners, always prepared by Billy Psalms, at Socrates Fortlow's Thursday night meeting were what kept many of the members coming back.

It was the custom on those evenings for someone to start out with a few words, a kind of prayer that was not necessarily or specifically religious.

THE WEEK BEFORE the junkman, son of many generations of junkmen, Chaim Zetel told an old joke:

"A man," the diminutive septuagenarian began, "prayed every morning to God. And every morning he made the same plea, 'Please, God let me win the Lottery for a million dollars.'"

Many of the men and women at the table smiled, thinking of the thousands of dollars they had spent on the same dream; or maybe the many millions of dollars that poor people paid every day on that unlikely hope.

"For many, many years this man spoke the same words," Chaim continued. "And as the years went on he married, raised a family, buried his wife and daughters, and he grew bitter. But still every day he would raise his hands to God and say, 'Let me win the Lottery for a million dollars.'

"Finally on his ninety-seventh birthday, after having made this plea twenty-seven thousand seven-hundred and forty-one mornings, God appeared to the old man. 'Jacob, please,' the Creator of heaven and earth said, 'help me out. Buy a ticket.'"

SOCRATES FORTLOW WAS SURPRISED that Psalms wanted to speak this week. He saw the inveterate gambler as a kind of sniper in the world of public oratory. He would wait until he saw an opening, a chance, and then send out a quick barb or quip or maybe even a word of support. He wasn't the type to stand up in front of a crowd and make himself known—there was no percentage in doing that and Psalms was a gambler down to his dead father's bones.

But there he stood in his black cotton trousers, black dress shirt, black undershirt and his signature herringbone jacket. It was a new jacket, Socrates noticed, which meant that Billy had been lucky at the track recently. The gambler took off his short-brimmed, dark green Stetson and rubbed a thumb over the yellow feather in the hatband that he replaced every year on the second of January.

He cracked his knuckles, then slapped his hands together and rubbed them like a hungry fly. Sensing his nervous tension the diners became quiet. Soon the only sound was of forks hitting china.

"I'm not used to standin' up and speakin' my mind," Billy said. "I'm a listener and a watcher, usually. I ah, I . . . I get worried. Not nervous mind ya, just worried because talkin' is like the roulette wheel, where it get to no one knows."

A few of the women smiled, understanding how hard it was for a man to allow himself to be exposed like that. Socrates could see the truth of this gentle care reflected in the sour, uncomfortable frowns on most of the men's faces. Ron Zeal couldn't even bring himself to look at Billy.

Luna Barnet was looking at Billy but she wasn't smiling. Next to her sat a young black man wearing a bright orange wifebeater and black leather pants. He was a good-looking boy who kept a possessive arm around Luna's shoulders.

Because she wouldn't look at Socrates he got the rare opportunity to study her. Her wild hair and world-weary expression did nothing to reduce her beauty.

"There's a thing at the race track," Psalms continued, "that most of you know. It's called the trifecta and it's the Holy Grail of race tracks all over the world and all the way back to before even the Christian church."

"Aw come on now, Billy," Mustafa Ali said. "That's just the white man's trick to get fools like you to throw yo' money away."

"These are first words," Socrates said, raising his voice more than he intended to. "You cain't argue when somebody got that flo'."

Mustafa nodded and sat back in his bamboo chair.

Socrates realized that his heart was beating fast.

Four days ago he'd told Luna that he wanted her to look for some other man. That was during their nightly telephone conversation.

"I tried to see myself wit' you," he said in even, unemotional words, "but you just a child and I got evil in my hands."

"All right," she said simply. "Bye."

They had not spoken since then and tonight she came rolling in with a greasy-haired boy who had his arm around her shoulders. Socrates couldn't imagine being jealous but there he was shouting at Mustafa Ali when Billy could have stood up for himself.

"Thank you, Brother Socrates," Billy said, "but I wanna address what Mr. Ali says. The word trifecta, Brother Ali, comes from the ancient Roman word perfecta. That's Latin and Latin's older than the New Testament."

Billy nodded and twisted his lips, daring anyone to contradict him.

"Anyway," he continued, "The trifecta is the closest thing to perfect that a gambler can have. The trifecta is why some peoples wake up in the mornin'. Three horses. That's all you need. Bet on three horses predictin' which one comes in first, second, and third. You do that and they put it in the papers. You do that and it's like a poker player hittin' a royal flush in high stakes poker game when the rent is due an' the repo man done drove off with yo' favorite red Cadillac."

Even the men could smile at that.

For a moment it seemed that Billy had finished. He turned to Socrates, who was looking at Luna with his big fists clenched.

Then Billy returned his attention to the Thinkers at the philosophy table.

"I was thinkin' 'bout the trifecta and I see that that's what we about heah," he said with striking certainty. "We wanna win all across the board. We want money in our pockets, a smile on our faces, and not a cloud of guilt in the sky as far as we can see.

"That's what we want. That's what we want. A lot of us come here sayin', 'That ain't nevah gonna work 'cause of so-and-so,' or 'the white man will stop us any which way we turn.' But the gambler's truth is that you got to keep on tryin' because you can win. You prob'ly gonna lose but you can win.

"Now I know Mustafa gonna say and Antonio gonna say and Miss Wheaton damn sure gonna say that you just shouldn't be gamblin' in the first place, that we the victim of our own vices and greed."

Socrates took his eye off of Luna and her boyfriend long enough to see Cassie Wheaton nod at Billy's estimation of her rebuttal. This allowed the ex-con a brief smile.

"That's a good argument," Billy said. "But what do I say to peoples who scared to walk the street at night? Don't go out and you won't get shot, mugged, arrested, and raped? What do I say to the young boy or girl go to a high school with five thousand other kids treated like they was prisoners with police in the hallways and bars on the windows, with metal detectors at the front door and chains on the back? Do I say don't go there and don't think about no perfecta?"

Billy rubbed his hands across his face, waited for a moment and then said, "Thank you for listenin'."

And for the first time in the short history of the Thinkers' Meeting there came applause.

IF HE HAD BEEN PAYING ATTENTION to the proceedings Socrates would have thought that the night was going well. Cassie Wheaton, self-proclaimed legal defender of the poor, said that life wasn't a gamble but a well thought out strategy against an enemy.

Leon Burns, a veterinarian's assistant from Long Beach, said, "That's like the natural strategy that animals develop to protect themselves from predators, right, counselor?"

Cassie nodded and sneered. She didn't like Burns and she was in the middle of her second trimester and so was beginning to feel discomfort sitting.

"Well," Burns continued, "I read in my boss's textbooks that the defense mechanism of rabbits is multiplication."

"You mean like in math class?" Ron Zeal asked.

"Kinda," Leon replied. "They make so many babies that no matter how many get et up there's some left over to make more . . ."

The talk continued. Now and then Luna would turn to her man friend and whisper something. Socrates didn't enter into the discussion that evening. Even when people asked him questions he just winced and shook his head.

Billy Psalms' trifecta metaphor took the evening's conversation to a higher level. People shouted, some leaped to their feet in order to make a point and all the while Socrates felt murder in his hands. He hated the boy in the orange wife-beater and didn't even know his name.

2.

"Mr. Fortlow," Luna said sweetly at the end of the evening.

People had stuck around to argue points that had not been settled during the meeting proper. It was late at night, almost morning, but two-thirds of the Thinkers were still there arguing over whether or not they had to take chances, and many losses, in order to win.

When Luna and her young man were standing before Socrates his rage leeched away. He no longer wanted to kill the boy. He didn't hate him. His arms were as weak as the smile he gave the young couple.

"This here's Peter Ford from Chicago," Luna said. "He really wanted to meet you."

"Oh?"

"Yeah, he said he heard about your Big Nickel all the way in West Hollywood where he live at."

The entire night Luna had ignored Socrates but now she stared in his eyes.

"It's a great honor to meet you, Mr. Fortlow," the young man said with real enthusiasm. "This was a wonderful evening. The people in this room make you feel like there's a real revolution in their, in their hearts. I never felt anything like it."

Peter held out his hand and, reluctantly, Socrates shook it.

"You come from Chi lately?" he asked Luna's new beau.

"Yeah. Tryin' to get into acting. But believe me you moved me tonight."

"I didn't hardly say nuthin'."

"But you made this space, you brought these people together. If I didn't know better I'd think I was transported back to ancient Greece where the first Socrates had his school."

"The first Socrates had a place like this?" Fortlow asked.

"Yeah," Ford said. "The ancient Greek philosophers started schools in olive groves and by the water and other places. That was the beginning of the first universities in the west."

Despite his jealousy, deflated anger, and sense of loss Socrates found himself wanting to know more about these ancient colleges.

"Time to go," Marianne Lodz said, coming up to the three. "The party started three hours ago and Sergio will be impossible if I don't show up."

Lodz had missed a few meetings because of a brief concert tour but she came to quite a few of the gatherings. It was because of her that the L.A. *Times* had done an article about Socrates' meeting place for gangbangers, prostitutes, and slam poets. They didn't talk much about the Thinkers' meetings or the Big Table.

"Okay, honey," Luna said, taking Peter by the arm. "Let's go."

Marianne smiled and kissed Socrates on the cheek. She had once told him in private that she valued their friendship because his strength made her feel weak inside.

"It's like a ride on a rolly coaster," she'd confided.

The three went off as Socrates watched. He felt as if he were standing in a river of molasses that came up to his neck. He wanted to go after Luna but couldn't move. Sweat sprouted on his bald head. With a great effort he took a step. He would have built up speed but Billy Psalms took his arm just as Luna had done with Peter Ford.

"Socco."

Socrates turned to Billy, was about to shake him off but then another change came over him.

Luna was gone.

That's what he asked for and that's what he got.

"Yeah, Billy," Socrates rasped and then cleared his throat of the bile and speechlessness. "That was a helluva talk, man."

"I got to talk to you alone," the gambler said.

What Socrates had always liked best about Billy was that he was almost always smiling. Billy was once playing dominoes at Socrates' home, a few blocks away, laughing and cracking jokes the entire afternoon. It wasn't until almost six when he informed his friends that he'd dropped eighteen thousand dollars at the racetrack that morning.

"How much did you win?" Comrade Jeremiah had asked.

"Seventeen-thousand eight hundred."

But Billy wasn't smiling that night at the end of the Thinkers' Meeting. His eyes were serious and he looked every one of his forty-six years.

"Can we go in the one-on-one room?" he asked.

Socrates nodded and looked over the heads of the remaining Thinkers.

"Ron," the big ex-con called.

"Yeah, Socco?" the next-generation killer replied.

"I want you to give Chaim a ride up home."

The young drug dealer and killer stared a moment at Big Nickel's head man. A dozen unexpressed thoughts went behind his nearly lifeless eyes and then, slowly, he nodded and turned his head, searching for the elderly Jewish member of the Thursday night meeting.

THE ONE-ON-ONE ROOM was the size of a large closet. It was windowless and hardly had space for the two yellow upholstered chairs that Leanne Northford donated after having buried the hatchet with Ron Zeal. She didn't forgive the street hood for killing two young men she'd known since boyhood but she gave up the hatred that the murders had raised in her heart.

Billy and Socco sat across from each other. A naked, hundred-watt light bulb blazed above them, the filament sang with the power of electricity.

Socrates sat back and crossed his legs. He had lost the youthful adoration of Luna Barnet but that was outside the small room where gang members, mothers and daughters, fathers and sons, and brothers and sisters talked out their differences.

Billy Psalms sat at the edge of his chair, elbows on his knees, hands clasped as if in prayer.

"We got a problem, Billy?" Socrates asked.

"I do."

"Wit' me?"

"You got sumpin' to do wit' it but I ain't got no problem wit' you per se."

Socrates raised his hands, palms up, inviting an explanation.

"You know I don't talk too much in front'a the Thinkers," Billy said.

Socrates nodded. He was wondering if Luna would stay with Peter Ford that night. Ford was well educated, Socrates could tell that. He wondered how, and how long before, they had met.

"But today I had to talk," Billy went on. "Sometimes somethin' come so clear in your mind that either you say it or you know you missed your chance."

Socrates felt the words but he was sure that Billy wasn't talking about him and Luna.

"I was at the track the day before yesterday," the gambler said.

"Yeah," Socrates agreed, "and I heard it said that the sun was in the sky too."

"I hit the trifecta on three nags had the odds so high against 'em that a first timer wouldn'ta bet on one of 'em to show. Ten dollar ticket on each one."

"Oh."

"Two-hunnert seventeen-thousand three-hunnert forty-two dollahs and ninety-six cent," Billy quoted. His eyes seemed to be pleading.

"Damn. Billy, you rich, man."

"Naw, brother, naw. Not me."

"Don't tell me you lost it that quick?"

"Well . . ."

"Billy. No."

"I didn't bet it or nuthin', Socco. That was so much money I couldn't even stay at the track. I went to this park I like to go to, you know, the long skinny one up in Beverly Hills run along Santa Monica Boulevard."

"Yeah."

"I went up there 'n set up shop. I had my water and a tuna fish sandwich, three bettin' papers and a transistor radio."

"You was ready, huh?" Socrates said.

"Yeah."

Billy tapped Socrates' knee with his index finger and sat back in the yellow chair.

"I spent the whole afternoon out there. Read my papers and listened to Diana Ross an' them on a old station."

"What's this all about, Mr. Psalms?"

"I was really thinkin' out there, man. Here I had a bank check for nearly a quarter million dollahs in my pocket an', an' the best win I had evah had on my mind. And that was it. That was all I could think. Here I got all this money and there was no plan in my head. If I had kids I could think about their college. Or if I had a wife I could give it to her to put away for my old age. But all I am is a gambler and all money is is the ticket for the next game. So I just sat and sat tryin' to make my mind do sumpin' else."

"So did you think anything?" Socrates asked. He was smiling now. Luna was almost a memory.

"I wouldn'ta except for this white girl."

"White girl?"

"Uh-huh, pretty little thing 'bout twenty-fi'e year old. I saw her walk by but I didn't talk to her or nuthin'. I mean I like my women dark-skinned with a li'l meat on their bones but she stopped and talked to me."

"What she say?"

"She axed me if there was sumpin' wrong. I guess I looked kinda miserable sittin' there and that sweet thing worried. She sat down and I told her that I might was gonna get a inheritance but I nevah had no money and I wasn't the kinda man to buy property or do investments. And she said was there some charity that I believed in. I told her that I didn't trust no charity or no church and she said wasn't there nobody I trusted?" Billy stopped talking for a moment.

"And?" Socrates asked.

"There's you, Socco," Billy said with the sound of wonder in his voice. "You the only rock solid man I know. I'd trust you with my money or my life."

"I don't need no money, Bill," Socrates said.

"Too late."

"What you mean too late?"

"I signed ovah all but ten thousand of my winnin's to the nonprofit thing Cassie Wheaton put on the Big Nickel. You know I had to buy me a new jacket and there's this woman I know could use a weekend in Vegas. But I put the rest in the Big Nickel's five oh one cee three."

"You did?"

"Uh-huh. Two-hunnert seven-thousand three-hunnert forty-two dollahs and ninety-six cent. I signed it ovah just this mornin'. Tax free 'cause you non-profit. Safe as it can be 'cause it's you. And I cain't ax you for none'a it back 'cause you got to spend it on the services you provide."

Socrates opened his mouth but words did not come out.

Billy had transferred the weight off of his shoulders and placed it on Socrates. The gambler smiled and took a deep breath. He sighed and shook his head as he laughed.

"That's all there is to it. You know it come to me awhile ago, right here in this house, that it wasn't the money I was after, it was the win. I knew that if I could win a big pot an' then give it away 'fore I lost it, then I'd go out of this life a winner. I learnt that from you."

Socrates heard the words. He wanted to say that it was a les-

son he'd never taught. But he could not speak. He wasn't thinking about Luna or even the riches that had fallen into his lap. He
was stunned by the generosity of his people; not Billy alone, not
black people only, but the spirit of his Big Table.

Billy Psalms got to his feet and made his way out of the small
room. Socrates sat there. After maybe half an hour he began
shaking his head.

WHEN SOCRATES FINALLY GOT UP the house was empty. As
usual the rooms were clean and the dishes washed. The chairs
around the Big Table were in disarray but he liked that, the tan-
gle of chairs reminded him of the life that had been there.

He thought about Billy's trifecta speech.

"He didn't even say he won," Socrates said out loud. "And that
was the best talk we evah had in here."

Socrates remembered Ron Zeal saying, "Billy's right. You cain't
get no honey you ain't reat to git stung."

3.

Socrates usually stayed at the Big Nickel if the meeting went past
midnight. He had a mattress upstairs on a floor in what would
have been the master bedroom of the house.

At the top of the stairs he noticed the light under the door of
the office he slept in.

He chided himself for having left the light on but then he
thought, *I won't have to take up a collection to pay the electric bill
this month*. Then the door came open. Unconsciously Socrates
shifted his shoulders, getting ready to fight or to drop and roll in
case his intruder had a gun.

Luna, dressed only in one of his old white T-shirts, came out and smiled.

"You think I was gonna take out my gun?" she said.

The T-shirt was longer by far than the dresses she wore but the flimsy material showed off the young woman's breasts and form in a way he had not seen before.

"Luna."

She smiled again.

"Luna."

"Wha?"

"I thought you left with, with Peter."

"I saw you, daddy," she replied. "You din't think I was lookin' but I saw you gettin' all hot 'cause of I had a man wit' me. You don't want me to have no man. If you did it wouldn'ta been so hard for you to shake his hand."

"Where'd he go?"

"I told him I was gonna stay and that he should go wit' Marianne an' look for some other girl."

"Wasn't he mad?"

"I don't give a shit. I don't care about him."

"But Luna."

"Daddy, come in here an' sit down on this chair."

Luna led Socrates to a chair in the center of the bedchamber/office.

"Take off your shirt," she said.

"Say what?"

"I said, take off your shirt."

"Luna…"

"Socrates," she said. He didn't remember her ever using his full first name before. "How long have we known each other?"

"I don't know . . . six months I guess, more."

"And we talk almost every day since then haven't we?"

"Yeah."

"So take off your shirt."

"Why?" he asked, almost whining.

"Because I'ma give you a shoulder massage."

"Massage?" Socrates tried to get up but Luna restrained him with a hand on his shoulder.

"Take off your shirt," she said again.

"Girl, you don't have the hands to get through my muscle."

"We'll see."

WITH HER FIRST TOUCH Socrates groaned and leaned forward, away from the pain that went down his arm and back.

"What you doin'?" he grunted.

"Usin' my elbows like I used to on my big brother before he died."

Sometimes she dug deep under the mat of muscle and then she struck out like a piston against his back.

Socrates was seeing colors, feeling sensations that he'd not known. This was his first massage. He shuddered through his neck and cried out when Luna pressed down with her elbows into the thick bands on either side of his spine. He forgot about Peter and Billy Psalms and the meeting that had been so important downstairs. He even forgot about prison and his crimes. The pain was exquisite and the release was something that he didn't know was possible.

Sitting there under the constant attack of Luna's elbows, forearms, and fists Socrates lost consciousness while sitting upright. He remembered Luna helping him up and dumping him on the mattress. He tried to say something but she shushed him and before the sound was over he was asleep.

IN A DARK PLACE he could see quite clearly. There were hard men, desperate men chained to the walls and naked women enticing them, calling them forth.

He was chained by his wrists and ankles and a woman he had only known in dreams was holding her arms out to him singing like Etta James while she got sultry and rough.

He yanked at his chains and made sounds that were not words. He moaned and grew hard but could not touch himself and she would not reach out far enough to him. A cry tore through his chest and he woke up with Luna on top of him.

"It's okay, daddy," she was saying over and over. "It's okay. You all right."

Socrates could feel the shuddering aftermath of his orgasm. Sweat covered him and her too. Luna was completely naked and Socrates was uncovered from his diaphragm to his knees. He had gripped Luna by the biceps of both arms and she kept saying, "It's okay, daddy. You all right."

He shoved her to the side and tried to stand up but his pants were around his knees and he couldn't seem to get them up or down.

His helplessness made him laugh. Luna laughed too.

"You want me to help you with your pants, little boy?"

This made them both laugh harder.

The grin still on his lips, Socrates said, "What you think you doin', girl?"

"Me?" she said. "You the one grab me in the bed. You the one kiss me first."

"I did?"

"Uh-huh. An' you know that's all I needed."

"But we didn't use protection. I been in prison, child. No tellin' what I got up in there."

"Me too," she said pressing her naked body up against his

side. "I been in the streets. I done fucked a whole lotta men. But I wanted that right there. I wanted you."

And before he could reply she said, "'But Luna' . . . that's what you always say. But, Luna, I'm too old, I'm too mean, I'm too fat, I didn't bresh my teefs. Shit. You are my man, Socrates Fortlow. Mine. I could see that when Pete put his arm on my waist. I was hopin' that you wouldn't kill the boy."

"I don't know what to say," Socrates said. "I don't know."

"What about takin' off your pants and T-shirt an' lyin' up here next to me? Or are you just gonna get some an' then th'ow a girl out in the street?"

THEY DIDN'T SLEEP. They didn't make love again but Socrates placed a hand on her thigh and one on her shoulder.

"It was the massage," he said.

"What was?"

"It got to me. I never felt like that before."

"Me neither."

LATER ON Socrates pulled the blanket up to his waist.

"I could see it through the blanket you know," Luna said. "I know you want me. But I could wait."

WHEN THE SUN WAS RISING through the window Socrates took Luna in his arms and kissed her lips.

"I guess I got to accept my luck," he said.

"Bad luck to be with a poor black girl like me?"

"Bad luck? No, baby, it's like Billy said."

"Wha?"

"I done hit the trifecta."

"How you see that?"

"Jealousy came in first, generosity placed, and then you showed me a feelin' I din't even know people had."

TRAITOR

1.

"What's in here?" the policeman asked.

"Papers," Socrates replied. He was thinking about Luna Barnet and how she had gotten around every attempt he made to keep her out of his heart.

"The worst man you evah meet got love in his heart somewhere," his Aunt Bellandra once said, many years before.

"But what if he's a bad man like mama said my daddy was?" Socrates asked when he was only five.

"Your father made you," Bellandra replied in her flat, deep, almost emotionless voice. "That's some good anyway."

"Open it up," Detective Brand ordered.

"The warrant doesn't specify this closet," Cassie Wheaton, the Big Nickel's lawyer, said. She had her right hand over her abdomen, maybe shielding the unborn child from the ugliness of her profession.

"The warrant is for a pistol somewhere on the first floor of this domicile."

"Meetin' house," Socrates said, correcting the tall white cop with the gray hair.

"Okay." Brand said. "This is a meeting house not a domicile and behind that door is an office not a closet. Open up."

Socrates put a hand in his pocket. The two uniformed police-men, who had done all the actual searching so far, stiffened.

Years of experience with the police before he was arrested and convicted for double homicide and rape and then more years under the guards in prison had made Socrates a kind of dancer. He stopped moving when the cops did, anticipating their violent response to his natural movements.

"It's locked," he explained. "I got to get my key to open the door."

The policemen gave him their full attention as he retrieved the keychain.

While sliding the key into the lock he felt a twinge of fear.

"SOCRATES FORTLOW," the voice had said on the phone that af-ternoon. The man on the other end was trying to disguise his voice so Socrates pretended not to recognize it.

"Yes."

"My name isn't important but believe me when I tell you that there's a weapon hidden in your first floor office, a pistol used in a murder in Vermont last year."

"How?"

"I just know."

"Who are you?" Socrates asked even though he knew, would have known even if he had not recognized the timbre and the way the man spoke.

"That don't matter," the man said and then he hung up.

IT WAS A SMALL OFFICE with three metal file cabinets and a wooden desk. Socrates had bought the cabinets from a used office supply store. They were red, white and blue but he didn't care. Mustafa Ali and Cassie Wheaton handled most of his paperwork before the monthly board meeting held on Saturdays. He only started locking the office after Billy Psalms had donated two hundred thousand dollars to the general fund. The officers agreed that the Big Nickel's windfall should be kept a secret.

Socrates watched as the men went through the few folders in the filing cabinets and looked under and behind the desk.

"Don't read those files," Wheaton told one of the cops, "not unless you're looking for a paper gun."

The search went on for forty-five minutes. The uniforms, both of whom were black men, pulled out the desk drawers and checked all the contents. One of them crawled underneath to make sure the pistol hadn't been taped down there somewhere.

Finally they gave up the search and gestured wordlessly to the white detective: there was no gun to be found.

"WHAT YOU WANT ME TO DO WIT' THIS, Socco?" Ronnie Zeal had asked a few hours earlier.

Socrates had traveled out to Zeal's aunt's house in Compton to drop off the pistol.

"Been used in a murder."

The young killer nodded.

"I gotta friend with a blowtorch," he said. "Aftah that I'll hit the junkyard."

DETECTIVE BRAND WAS GRIM but Socrates had no desire to gloat. He felt like a journeyman heavyweight who, after a last minute cancellation, found himself in the opposite corner from Sonny Liston. All he'd done so far was to avoid the first jab that the monster had thrown; there were ten rounds left to survive.

"This is harassment," Cassie Wheaton was telling the cop.

"We had a valid tip, counselor," the thin lipped detective uttered. "We're trying to uphold the law down here."

"Down?" Socrates said.

"Socrates," Cassie Wheaton warned, hearing the threat in his voice.

"Yeah . . . down," Brand said.

"If you think this down . . ." Socrates began. He stopped, realizing that there were no more words but only violence in his breast.

"Are you finished, detective?" Cassie Wheaton asked.

AFTER THE POLICEMEN WERE GONE Cassie sat with Socrates at the foot of the Big Table. While he ran his hand over the uneven side of the battered plank Cassie stared and waited.

After a long while they both spoke up at once.

"It's because . . ." she started.

"I expected somethin'," he managed to say. And then, "You go on."

"No, no you," she said.

"You the counselor," Socrates said. "You talk."

"It's because of the gang meetings," she said.

"Peace talks."

"That's not how the cops see it."

"Blind men don't see nuthin' noway," Socrates said.

"If I could show the police that you've stopped the peace talks this won't happen again."

"If I closed the doors and moved back into the alley where I used to live then I wouldn't have to worry 'bout nuthin' either."

"You could still have daycare for the ladies," Cassie argued. "You could still have the Thinkers' meetings."

"You sure they wouldn't call me a whorehouse if some of

them ladies used to be prostitutes? You sure they wouldn't call our meetin's subversive?"

"They wouldn't plant a pistol in your office."

"It's the drug dealers, killers and whores we got to turn around, Cassie."

"If they can't bring you down they'll shoot you down, Socrates."

2.

Three days later, at the Thinkers' Meeting, nineteen people showed up. Billy Psalms had made his ever popular chili served with basmati rice and fresh wheat flour tortillas made at a Mexican bakery just down the block.

Chaim Zetel arrived with Ron Zeal. Cassie Wheaton was accompanied by her fiancé, Antonio Peron.

Leanne Northford spoke First Words.

"I'm a Christian woman," she said and then took a deep breath. "I've been to church almost ev'ry Sunday of my life. When I was an infant at my mother's breast she took me to church and I brought her there to set her to rest.

"I'm seventy-two years old and I've heard more sermons than most of these kids out here today done heard rap songs." A few people, including Ron Zeal, chuckled at her innocent competition with the young. "But with all that I never learned forgiveness until I come under this roof." Socrates saw a few nods among the Thinkers. "I never had to face my hatreds and my pain in the Lord's house. I was safe in there. In church everybody is so nice and well dressed and smiling and singing. Even death is a party in the church. But out here in life it's not so easy. Out here is where the Lord's work needs to be done.

"I want to give thanks for Socrates Fortlow and his big heart for the redemption of a poor Christian like me."

"I BELIEVE THAT WE should form a committee," Mark Sail said at the top of the meeting. He was a broad faced dark-skinned man whose grandparents had come from Jamaica. ". . . a committee with the idea of gettin' people together all up and down these streets. Get people talkin'. Get people to feel like we do up in here."

The proposal was met by a burgeoning bank of silence. People looked around at each other as if the words spoken were in a distant dialect and could have held many meanings.

Socrates was thinking about what Leanne had said. He wondered how she had come so far in such a short time. He was thinking that the Big Nickel and the Big Table had to grow; had to. It didn't matter if he got shot down or locked up.

Maybe, he thought, different members of the original meeting could sponsor smaller meetings held on different nights of the week. But who could keep the people talking in the right way?

Socrates heard the front door open behind him. Cassie Wheaton stood up; the autumn colored bale of hair on her head made her taller than any man in the room.

When Socrates turned he was not really surprised to see Martin Truman, known to the Thinkers as Maxie Fadiman.

"Maxie." Mustafa Ali also rose, but he was greeting the man he had brought from his soup kitchen to the Thursday night meeting.

"Hi, everybody," the undercover cop said sheepishly.

"Hey, Max," Socrates said. "Billy, will you move down and let Maxie sit here next to me?"

The gambler eyed the ex-con suspiciously. No one but Socrates and Cassie knew about Maxie. People came and went from the meetings freely. Some members showed up only once; a few had never missed a week.

Billy moved down near Chaim Zetel, Maxie/Marty nodded awkwardly and took a seat. The silence from Mark Sail's suggestion turned into a hush over Maxie's odd reception by Socrates. He'd never asked Billy to move before. The little gambler had always sat to Socco's left.

While Maxie's shy gaze wandered around the room Socrates stared at him.

"What about my idea?" Mark Sail asked.

Socrates raised a silencing hand, still staring at Maxie's profile.

The quiet became uncomfortable.

In his heart Socrates praised the silence. He remembered moments when he awoke late at night in his cell and there was no sound coming from the cellblock. In those moments he almost felt free.

Maxie looked down the center of the table straight into the eyes of Cassie Wheaton.

"I haven't been here for a while," the police spy said. "In a way I guess you could say that I never was really, truly here."

"What's that supposed to mean, Maxie?" white bearded Mustafa Ali asked.

"My name ain't Maxie, Mr. Ali. My mother named me Martin but my police handlers said to use the name Maxie. It starts with the same letter and sounds a little like Marty which is what my friends call me."

"Police?" Ron Zeal said.

"Yeah," Maxie replied. "I was a . . . I am a cop. I came from outta town, up in the Bay Area, and so they made me a spy . . . "

"A traitor?" Mustafa said, all the friendliness drained from his voice.

"A traitor," Maxie agreed. "It was my job to join in with people and to report to the police who was the bad apple."

"Why?" Leanne Northford asked.

"Because he's a Benedict Arnold," Mark Sail said.

Socrates wondered then if it was Mark who planted the gun in his accounting office.

"Because I thought it was right," Maxie said. "I thought the same thing you talk about here. I wanted to stop the gang-bangers and drug dealers and thugs from runnin' the streets. I thought that the police were meant to protect honest people and so I . . . I spied on you."

"And so then you saw that you were wrong and that's why you left?" Darryl asked.

Socrates smiled at the son of his heart. It was one of the few times that the boy articulated a full thought that was also a question. It didn't matter that he was wrong.

"No," Maxie said. "No. Socco sniffed me out and found where I lived at and came to my house. I quit because I thought that *he* would betray *me*. I was afraid of what he'd do so I took my family and left Los Angeles. I went to another city and kept on being a spy."

Maxie lost steam and brought his hands to the table. Everyone, even Luna Barnet, was staring at him.

"Why did you come back?" Chaim Zetel asked.

"Because . . ."

It was then that Socrates understood the Thinkers' Meeting had gotten away from him, and not just tonight. He had wanted a place of safety where men and women of all kinds could come and say what was heavy on their hearts. They could complain and plan and see themselves as important. But what he got was the opposite from what he wanted. Leanne was right. The room he created was as dangerous as a prison yard. Every word brought them closer to action. And action in this world went hand in hand with pain.

Socrates hoped that Maxie would maintain his silence, stop with a confession, but he knew this was not to be.

"Because I remembered somethin' that Socco said to me before I, before I left."

"What?" Wan Tai asked.

"I moved to San Diego," Maxie said. "I told them that I wouldn't do any more political work and so they put me with drug dealers. One day they said to tell this guy who was about to leave the business and go to Morocco that they had one final buy for him. I did what they asked and then, the night I was supposed to go to the meet, they called me and said that it had been called off.

"Robert, that was the drug dealer's name, Robert had told me that he was tired of the life in the street. He told me that he was gonna get away from it. He had a girlfriend from Morocco. They were gonna get married and he was gonna have a new life in a new country.

"In the morning the radio said that Robert had been shot down on the corner where the meeting was supposed to take place. There was no mention of the police. The cops that came said it looked like a drug buy gone bad.

"After that I remembered that Socco had said that I should come here and tell you what I was, what I did for a livin'. He said that you'd learn something from my experience. Hey . . . maybe he's right."

Socrates had no questions for Maxie, neither did Billy, Ron Zeal, or Cassie Wheaton. But many of the members of the Thinkers' table had never realized that they lived among people like Maxie. They had questions that went way into the night.

Had he committed crimes in the name of the law? *Yes*. Had he framed people innocent? . . . *Yes*. Had he tortured men, sold women into prostitution, taken drugs, robbed honest people, lied under oath, lied to criminals, killed men who he might have saved? *Yes, yes, yes, yes, yes, yes, yes*.

He explained each situation, named names and even gave dates and places.

"I thought I was doin' right," he said whenever someone would ask why. "I was the law protectin' my people from themselves."

Mark Sail's idea hadn't made it to discussion that night. Maxie and his confession dominated the talk. Some people shouted at him; others shook their heads. Maxie said that he and his wife were moving again. This time they were leaving the country.

"I cannot atone for my crimes," he said. "And there is no court for me. Just talkin' here tonight might get me killed when the word gets back to the others."

"You got a spy in here wit' us now?" Ron Zeal asked.

"Maybe not at this table tonight but they got people watchin', people comin' in. They want Socco to go down. Nobody wants the gangs to get together. Nobody wants the peoples down here to unite . . ."

3.

Socrates asked Luna to go back to her place with Marianne Lodz that evening.

"No," the young beauty replied. "I'ma stay right here wit' you."

"I thought we had an agreement?"

"We do. I'ma go home when you need me to. When you need to be alone or wit' Darryl. When you need to take care of business. But tonight you need your woman wit' you. I cain't be leavin' when I know that there's police spyin' on you, tryin' to bring you down."

Socrates didn't want to laugh but he couldn't help it. There was no humor or good will to his hilarity but something deeper, something darker but not bad.

"My woman?" he said, still laughing.

"What else am I if not yours?"

The question cut off his humor like a faucet slammed shut.

Luna stared at him and he looked back, blankly. His heart was gripping like a fist on a tennis ball in the prison yard from early morning until the horn blew.

"They been tryin' to kill me for more'n half a century, girl."

"An' now they got to go up against the both of us."

Nothing in his years of dark defiance had prepared Socrates to resist this claim. He had thought that it was the flattery of a young woman's body that broke through his defenses, made him prey to her desires, and his. He thought that she would lay with him awhile and then move on to another man who better suited her needs.

He thought that this affair was just another way for him to learn what he needed to know to bring out the truth from his soul—but he was wrong on all counts.

"Socrates," Luna said.

"What?"

"Why you just standin' there?"

"Uh . . ."

"Socrates."

"What?" he asked, almost shouting.

"You gonna talk?"

"Where did you learn how to do that?" he asked.

"What?" she asked. "I mean how to do what?"

"How to jerk my head around when I'm tryin' my best to look the other way."

"What you talkin' about, Socrates?"

"They separated us, girl."

"Who?"

"Them. The slave masters."

"Slaves? Slavery over, Socco."

"It is and it isn't," he said, recalling the nervous feeling in his toes the first time he wandered to the far end of the public pool. The ground was no longer beneath his feet and suddenly he forgot how to swim. "But that's like Iraq."

"Iraq? What's Iraq got to do wit' us?"

"Everything. The war's gonna be ovah one day, right?"

"I guess."

"An', an', an' when it is that's what people gonna say, 'It's ovah.'"

"All right," Luna said. She reached out gently and touched his bulging forearm with three fingertips.

"But what if somebody you knew had been walkin' patrol the day before the pullout? What if he stepped on a mine and lost his left leg and lost his left arm?"

Luna moved close enough to kiss the fabric of his blue work shirt. She gazed up and his arm came around her shoulder blades.

"I guess his war wouldn't evah be ovah," Luna said.

"They separated us," he said again. "They made sure that slaves came from different tribes and spoke different tongues so they couldn't plot against 'em. That's how we learned to be black people—alone, even in a crowd."

Luna blinked.

"And then," Socrates said, "and then you come up just as easy as you please an' say, 'now they got to go up against the both of us.'"

"So?"

"Don't you see? I only know one way."

"Ain't you nevah had a woman before?" Luna asked.

"Not really. I been in prison. They ain't no women in there."

4.

Just before he awoke, on some mornings, Socrates got the notion that he was still in prison—locked away and forgotten. When this thought entered his mind his heart would skip and he'd jolt into consciousness with the electric feeling of desperation in his hands and feet.

That morning Luna Barnet was sound asleep next to him; mouth open and hair wild. She was wrapped up tightly in the sheet.

Socrates thought that she was like an island that a lost ship found itself next to in the early morning after days of nothing but flat seas and no rations. Not just an island but a great sheer cliff that dwarfed his small ship and its journey.

He had been lost and now he was somewhere with no idea of how he'd gotten there. There were no breadcrumbs or footprints behind him in the shifting sea; no possibility of any landmark, or footpath, not even any clear memory of passage or arrival.

Everything seemed far away except for Luna and the Big Nickel and the light coming in through the window.

"WHY DIN'T YOU WAKE ME UP?" she asked hours later when he was almost finished making breakfast.

"I like to watch you sleep."

"You wasn't watchin' me." She wore only a T-shirt because she knew how much he liked to look at her legs in the morning.

"Oh yes I was," he said. "I could see you through the ceilin'."

She was going to continue the banter, but the woman inside, and the child too, drew her into his arms.

"WHERE ARE YOU?" Luna asked in the early afternoon when the sun shone on the other side of the meeting house.

They were two spoons in the bed.

"Inside you," he said.

"Where?"

He didn't answer, didn't even consider saying the word.

"Do you wanna make a baby up inside me, Baby?"

There was nothing to say; not yes and not no and not that he didn't know.

"'Cause if you don't you bettah move back."

"I love you," he whispered so softly that she did not hear it.

THAT EVENING HE MADE FRIED CHICKEN and an avocado, onion, and tomato salad. They sat at a small table in the kitchen because Luna didn't like to eat at the Big Table.

"I always feel like we got to be talkin' 'bout sumpin' important at the Table," she said. "An' you know sometimes I just wanna eat."

"They prob'ly gonna try'n kill me, girl," Socrates said at the end of their meal.

She twisted her lips and shook her head.

"We ain't at the meetin' table," she said.

"This is serious, Luna."

"I know."

"I cain't be upstairs tryin' t'make babies when people down here wit' knives and guns."

"Who better'n you?"

"What if I die?"

"Ain't no *if* to it, honey. We all gonna die one day."

Socrates was reminded of the great cliff of his early morning vision. He smiled and shook his head.

"Don't die," she said. "Don't let 'em do that to you."

HE DIDN'T TELL HER ABOUT THE NOTE he found shoved under the office door in the early morning. Maxie must have put it there before coming into the meeting the night before.

> Dear Mr. Fortlow,
>
> I am the one who called you and said about the pistol in your office. When they told me about it I knew right away that I had to warn you. I came back to L.A. after Robert was killed. I pretended to be on their side but I wasn't. I thought that I could watch over you and in that way make up for the wrong I had done. But I was wrong.
>
> The man in charge of your case is named Telford Winegarten. He has an office at the municipal building on Alvarado. He's got an office but he's acting like he's not a cop.
>
> By the time you read this I'll be gone to Canada. I'd appreciate it if you'd tear up this letter.
>
> Maxie

Socrates tore the note into tiny pieces and then flushed them down the toilet. Then he waited for the tank to refill and flushed it again.

THE NEXT AFTERNOON he got on a bus that deposited him three blocks from the Alvarado Municipal building. He went through the metal detector and presented his identification to the freckled Hispanic woman at the front desk.

"Do you have an appointment?" the receptionist asked.

"Tell them it's Socrates Fortlow."

"HOW DID YOU GET HERE?" Telford Winegarten asked as soon as Socrates was admitted to the secret policeman's office.

His outer door had a small removable plate fitted in its name-slot that read: TELFORD WINEGARTEN—COMMUNITY RELATIONS.

Winegarten was of medium height and build, maybe forty-five and well groomed, if balding.

"Took the bus," Socrates replied. "Mind if I sit down?"

Winegarten nodded with neither fear nor confusion showing on his face. But Socrates knew he had upended the white man's plots and schemes. He knew that Winegarten had used the fifteen minutes Socrates waited outside, across from the pretty young secretary, to hide the maps and flowcharts he used to decipher the information they had to bring down the Big Nickel.

Sitting across from each other the two men gathered themselves.

"What can I do for you?" Winegarten asked.

"Just answer one question."

"What's that?"

"Why you wanna frame me?"

"I don't know what you're talking about."

"Okay."

"Is that all?" Telford allowed himself a smile that showed no teeth.

"No . . . I mean in a way it is."

"I don't understand."

"I'm what you call a reformed killer, Mr. Winegarten . . . or should I say Captain Winegarten of the LAPD?"

The policeman said nothing, made no gesture.

"I got to get this right now," Socrates said, pressing two fingers of his left hand against his brow. "Cassie Wheaton is filing papers against the LAPD that name you, Captain Harvey Jamal, and Lieutenant Jerry McCann for violating my rights and the rights of everyone in my organization."

"What?" It was the first honest word uttered by the cop.

"We gonna put it all out on the table," Socrates said, using the words that had been spoken many times at the Thursday night Thinkers' Meeting. "Your spies and plants and conspiracies. We gonna put together a petition to get you up off'a us and we gonna bring every one of your secret agents into court."

The shadow over the policeman's face came from inside.

"You're threatening me?" he said.

"No, sir. No threat here. I used to be like that. I used to bully and intimidate. But now I just lay it out. Let the courts and the newspapers know what you doin' an' what I'm doin'. Let'em see in the light'a day what's what."

"I could crush you like a bug," Telford said.

Socrates could remember using the same words in the prison yard when someone questioned his authority. He smiled, recognizing this affinity with the offensive man.

"Not right now you couldn't, boss," Socrates said. "Later on maybe, when you're miles away and your hatchet men come up from behind. But right now you couldn't lay a hand on me."

Telford Winegarten sat back in his chair and laced his fingers. He wore a tan suit and a dark green shirt. His tie was golden with a metallic sheen. The shadow lifted from his countenance and he nodded and smiled. Behind his eyes were a general's calculations. He was weighing his opponent and maybe even enjoying the process.

"What do you want?" the policeman asked.

"Nuthin'."

"We all want something."

"Oh? Tell me, Captain, what do you want?"

"I'd like to know what the gangs are saying. I'd like to hear about the prostitution ring being run out of Compton."

"I don't know nuthin' 'bout that."

"What do you know?"

"What I said, Captain. You are my nemesis, you and all your spies and agents. Like you said, I'm a bug compared to you. But this bug is goin' to federal court.

"Now if you wanna talk to gangbangers and street walkers I'll ask 'em to meet ya. If you wanna come down an' find out what's happenin' I will make the room. There ain't secrets. The gangs want peace. The street walkers and call girls and call boys want peace. Damn, the whole United States wants peace. It's you don't see it, Captain."

"I don't want this court thing, Fortlow."

"I know. And believe me I don't want it either. When it come to me that I was gonna sue a cop I almost shit my pants. My lawyer's scared and you know Cassie Wheaton ain't scared'a nuthin'. But we are goin' to court."

"If you've already made up your mind then why are you here?"

"There wasn't nowhere else to go, Captain. I'm the kinda man wanna stand up to my enemy and say where it is I stand. I ain't no drive-by shooter, no hit man come up behind your back. I'm a fighter.

"I come here to tell you that I'm comin' for you. You could frame me or beat me or have me shot down dead in the street.

But I'm still comin' for you. The papers are in the court's hands and in the newspapers' hands. Marianne Lodz talkin' to a entertainment magazine about it right now and Leanne Northford tellin' all of her friends down at social services.

"I come here to tell you that I'ma come down on you like a ton 'a mothahfuckin' brick. That's why I'm here. I'm here right in front'a you. I'm here to tell you that I'll be in my house and at the Big Nickel, with my girlfriend and maybe even I'ma bring a life into this world. And I ain't runnin' or hidin' neither. I come here to let you know that I know and to see if you ready to fight a man who see you as good as you see him."

Socrates stood up. He felt the veins pulsing in his temples.

Telford Winegarten sat back further.

"You're making a mistake," the policeman-in-disguise said as Socrates blundered out the door.

On the street he took a deep breath and exhaled through a grin. He thought about Luna, about how she would have been proud of him, about how she would love him even though he was frightened and foolish.

5.

"I evah tell you what I always thought the Big Nickel was?" Billy Psalms asked Socrates that evening at the philosopher's one-room home behind his patron's house. His small garden house was more of a retreat than a domicile these days. He spent so much time at the Big Nickel meeting with community people and lawyers that he only made it home a few nights a week.

Socrates had told Billy everything, even about the revelations he'd had with Luna.

"No, man," Socrates said. "What's that?"

"That it was like a slave ship only in reverse."

"How so?"

"When they took us off the ship they separated us like you said. But now, all these decades and centuries later you done gathered us up and put us back on the boat. We leavin' an' the boss man don't know what to do."

Socrates sipped his red wine from a crystal goblet that Leanne Northford had given him. He stared at William Herrington Psalms III and shook his head.

"Why ain't you at the track today, Billy?"

The gambler laughed at that answer to his deep thought.

"You know, Socco," he said, "the more I hang out with you the less I feel the need to take a chance."

"You a fool, Billy Psalms."

"What about you then?"

"I'm right there with you."

BREEDING
GROUND

1.

"Socrates," a voice said somewhere up ahead, maybe around the corner at the end of the corridor.

He was on his way down the long hall, flanked by Hennie Brown and Bertrand Sawman, two guards who he'd known longer than any other person-not-a-convict. They hadn't told him where they were taking him but his hands were shackled and his ankles were chained together. This circumstance filled the convict with glee but he didn't show it.

Brown had been nineteen years at the prison. Sawman had seen twenty-one birthdays come and go since donning the gray-green uniform. But Socrates had them both beat. He was at the twenty-seven-year mark and counting.

He was happy because the chains on his feet meant that he was going to see the warden. That walk unnerved many a hardened con but Socrates wasn't worried about the punishment he might receive. He only wanted a glance out the window.

"Socrates."

For eight years Bearclaw, Socrates' third warden, would call convicts to his office in order to discipline them. The offender would be made to sit in an oak chair before the oak desk where, through the window behind Arnold Bearclaw, he would be able to see a small valley where there was a power line and a stream. For more than half the year the window was open and errant sounds would come in. Birds and the sound of cars from an unseen parking lot below. Terry Blanderman swore he once heard a woman singing—a real woman, he'd said.

Socrates would have shanked a man if it meant that when he'd go before Bearclaw for discipline he could be sure that the woman would be singing. It would be worth a hundred and eighty days of darkness to hear an actual voice of the opposite sex.

"Socrates."

According to custom the guards secured the left ankle manacle to an iron eye in the floor before the warden entered. That way the prisoner had no chance of jumping the head man before the guards could club him down.

This too made sense. A great many cons spent entire days writing letters to the warden or painting pictures of him. They talked about him and loved or hated him like they did the father who abandoned them or beat them or their mothers. The warden, whoever he was at the time, was an unhealthy abscess on the minds of many convicts. But Socrates only cared about that window.

He was forty-eight years old and had spent more than half of his life in prison. He would never be free, never be free . . .

"Socrates, wake up."

"Life," Judge Arrant had said and life he would spend without complaint or appeal.

He had killed and that was his punishment.

Socrates never claimed he was innocent, never bragged about his crimes. He didn't hate the warden or his own father but he wanted a look out of that open window and hear a car parking and maybe a woman humming some popular song.

THE WARDEN WAS TALL, big boned, and black. He'd been a soldier, a police captain, and now he was boss of seven thousand felons.

Beyond him was the window. It was open maybe a foot and a half. Outside the sun shone between gray clouds. There was rain falling in the distance.

A bird called and Socrates had to concentrate in order to stifle his smile. You could never show a man what made you happy because then that man had full power over you.

Socrates concentrated on his stern expression, exulting on the inside when another jay cried out an answer. He could smell the rain and feel a slight breeze between the various loops of iron and his exposed skin.

"... granted," was the warden's last word.

It was the only word the convict had heard. He tried to figure out the sentence that it came from but could not and he wasn't about to ask.

"Did you hear me?" the warden asked.

"Socrates, wake up," Luna said.

"I said . . . has been granted . . ."

". . . it's Darryl," Luna said.

He opened his eyes. The dream had stopped mid-image not because of the name but the tone in Luna's hard young voice. The dream was gone and sleep was too. All that was left was the fear he'd felt when the warden, uncharacteristically, repeated his sentence.

"Your petition for release has been granted," he'd said.

The birds stopped singing and the rain reached the prison.

Sawman closed the window and Socrates stopped breathing for a long span of seconds. It had been the most frightening moment in his life.

"What about Darryl?"

"He been shot."

2.

It was 1:06 A.M. but Leanne Northford was already at the emergency room; she and Cassie Wheaton, Ron Zeal, Billy Psalms, and even Chaim Zetel, the septuagenarian Jew from the west side of town.

"Socrates!" Myrtle Brown cried.

She came running at Socrates, throwing her arms around him, throbbing with hysteria and sobs.

Myrtle was forty-something, more than twice Darryl's age, but she was his woman. Socrates had expected the relationship to founder but Darryl kept going back and she did everything in her power to hold onto him.

"What happened, Myrtle?"

"I don't know."

"I'm the one that called her, man," Ron Zeal said.

The powerful young killer stared at his elder with less emotion showing in his face than Socrates had offered up to the warden when he was sent there to be punished.

"One'a my boys called me when he heard about it. He knew I had put out the word to let Darryl alone."

"Who?" Socrates asked.

"I'ont know yet, man. But I will."

A white man with gray hair and a white smock came through the swinging doors behind Zeal. The man walked up to Socrates.

"Are you the guardian?" he asked.

"I HAVE TO ASK YOU about the insurance," the doctor said when they were seated in a tiny, cluttered cubicle away from the bustle of the late night tragedies of the emergency room.

"Why?"

"We have to know how this is being paid for."

"That gonna change how he get treated in here?"

"Doctor," Chaim Zetel said. He had come up on them silently. "I have given my credit card to the admitting nurse. It has a high limit."

"Darryl has been severely wounded," the doctor said, business behind him. "He's been shot twice. In the hip and chest."

"He gonna make it?"

"Maybe not."

"But you want to make sure I can pay even before you let him die."

"Mr. Fortlow," Chaim said.

"What?"

"Will you, will you let me speak to the good doctor alone for a moment please?"

BILLY PSALMS HAD FOUND an all-night coffee shop and bought coffee and plenty enough doughnuts for everyone, even people who had nothing to do with Darryl.

There were three gunshot wounds brought in that night; batterings and car accidents and people suffering from ailments who didn't belong there but they had no doctors or insurance and so when symptoms flared they came to see some stranger to give them medicine and advise them to find a physician of their own.

Myrtle cried on Socrates' shoulder and more and more members from the Thinkers' Meeting showed up. Socrates had other friends but the Thinkers had a call sheet and everyone associated with the Thursday night meetings knew how to get in touch with the others.

Socrates was like a dusky spider at the center of a web that went all over the city. He sat patiently at that midpoint thinking about Bearclaw's window and how lovely it was.

One man had been stabbed but he said that he'd fallen on the knife. A woman who had two swollen eyes swore that she'd tripped because she was drunk.

A baby died from an inexplicable asthma attack. A twelve-year-old girl gave birth to twins.

"SOCRATES?"

Myrtle was asleep on his shoulder and his people were all around him. Chaim Zetel had put his small and powerful hand on Socrates' free arm.

"Can I speak to you alone?" the old tinkerer asked.

When the ex-con moved Myrtle woke up.

"What is it? What happened?" she cried.

"Nothing, Miss Brown," Zetel said. "He's on life-support. Nothing has changed."

"Where you goin' then?" she exclaimed. "I'm comin' wit' you."

"Wait here, Myrtle," Socrates commanded softly. "Just sit here an' I'll be back in five minutes."

"I'll sit wit' her," Luna said as she lowered into the vacated chair. She took Myrtle's hands in hers.

OUTSIDE CHAIM TOOK A CIGARETTE from his pocket and lit it.

"You smoke?" Socrates asked.

"I have one every day," the small man said, looking up, smiling. "Benson and Hedges. My wife tells me it will kill me and I tell her that she will kill me with her worries."

"How is Fanny?"

"She sends her love for Darryl and you."

"What you got to tell me, Chaim?"

It was nighttime on the street. Few cars passed and there was no ambulance coming or going at the moment.

"There is a doctor named Laird in West Los Angeles," the old man said. "I am told that he is the best for operations like the one Darryl needs."

"How much?"

"They are coming for him now. Dr. Laird told me that he has a busy week but he could do the operation at five."

"How much?" Socrates asked again.

"I have a grandson who studied under Laird," Chaim said. "The doctor knew your name from the court case in the papers. He thinks like us."

"You ain't gonna tell me?"

"I didn't ask."

DREAMING AGAIN. In chains again. Sitting in that chair with no one in the room and the window open wide. Socrates watched a bank of clouds move excruciatingly slowly over the hills, toward the sun. There were a thousand birds singing and Diana Ross too.

He opened his eyes mid-dream. No one had called his name. This was a tactic he'd developed in prison. He'd wake up now and then—a sneak thief on consciousness.

Chaim was sitting next to him in the pleasant waiting room. The air-conditioning was on. Classical music was playing. There were tasteful magazines, with smiling white women on the covers, strewn across the coffee table before him.

"Where'd Ron go?" he asked.

"Up to the shop," Chaim said. "I have some children coming in this afternoon. He's seeing to them."

"Ronnie's workin' for you now?"

"Yes."

"How did that happen an' I didn't even know it?"

"You are a busy man, Mr. Fortlow. You don't have time for everything anymore."

"Busy man? I used to spend all day walkin' around collectin' bottles then spent the night drinkin' wine an' playin' dominoes wit' my friends. 'Fore that I was up in prison countin' the days, hours, minutes, and sometimes even the seconds."

A door next to the nurse's window opened and a white man, colored copper by the sun, came out. He wore a white doctor's jacket and alligator shoes.

Dr. Laird's cornflower blue eyes clashed with his tan. His smile was brilliant and his grip strong enough for Socrates to feel.

"He's going to live, Mr. Fortlow."

He was back in Warden Bearclaw's office being given his freedom, only this time he felt the joy rise up in his chest like a big red balloon.

"You know what, Doctor?"

"What's that, Mr. Fortlow?"

"I need to sit down."

Chaim Zetel, Dr. Laird, and even the small Asian woman behind the admitting window smiled at his words. Socrates stumbled over to the chair and slumped down. He pressed his left palm hard against his forehead and groaned.

It was three o'clock in the afternoon and the doctor had been cutting all day.

"He's breathing on his own and the bullets are out," Laird was saying. "His lung should heal up just fine. You're lucky your friend brought him here to me."

Socrates smiled. "You the best, huh, Doc?"

"I was today."

3.

". . . an' that old white lady come ovah ev'ryday wit' cakes and'a puddin' made outta noodles an' raisins," Darryl was saying to Socrates from his hospital bed. "She said—"

"Fanny," Socrates said.

"Huh?"

"That old white lady, her name is Fanny, Mrs. Zetel, Chaim's wife."

"Yeah, yeah right. She Jewish huh?"

Socrates nodded.

"They got funny names."

"More'n we got?"

"Naw. But different."

"Chaim an' Fanny are good people."

"They wanna take me in for a while till I get bettah."

"What you think about that?"

"That'a be good I think. You know I cain't even walk yet."

Socrates smiled at the boy's survival.

"People been comin' ovah ev'ryday from the Thursday night meetin'. Miss Wheaton an' Marianne Lodz come. Luna here ev'ry othah day. I like her. She easy to sit wit' 'cause you don't have to be talkin' the whole time."

"What about Myrtle?" Socrates asked.

Darryl glanced away at an imagined fly buzzing past.

"What about her?" the boy asked.

"She come by?"

The young man rubbed his nose with the back of his hand. Socrates thought that he would have turned his back if it weren't for the bandages and straps holding him in place.

"I wish I was like you," Darryl said.

"Old and fat with no children and not a nickel to my name?"

"You got the Big Nickel."

"Or it's got me."

Darryl blinked, thinking about his mentor's comment. He blinked again.

"When I told her that I was goin' to stay wit' Chaim for a while she said that I should come home wit' her. I told her that she work an' I couldn't even get out the bed for at least two weeks."

"What she say to that?"

"That she get friends to stay wit' me when she weren't there. I told her that was stupid an' that Chaim's wife was already home an' she had a lady to help her with the housework. But Myr got all mad an' left an' haven't called me since."

Socrates' mind brought him back to the day he crossed the road in front of the prison. He stood there waiting for the bus to come. This was one of those potent moments where he was between one place and the next. Darryl, he thought, was at a moment like that.

"You makin' the right choice, D-boy."

"How you know?"

"Somebody shot you three blocks from Myrtle's house. You don't know who it was. You cain't go back there till we get this fixed."

A shiver went through Darryl's fragile frame.

"I'll talk to Myrtle," Socrates said. "I'll tell her to leave you be till you can carry the weight."

"You ain't gonna tell her I'm scared?"

"Naw, man. I'm'a tell her that you smart."

"Socrates."

He opened his eyes and was transported from an Egyptian desert to his upstairs bed at the Big Nickel. Luna leaned down over him and handed him the cell phone that Darryl had gotten him months before.

"Yeah?" Socrates said into the receiver, fear clutching at him.

"Come on down an' meet me at Florence an' Central," Ron Zeal said. "I'll be at Denver's Diner right near there."

Zeal's phone disconnected and Socrates folded his shut.

"Make love to me, Daddy," Luna whispered.

"I got to meet him."

The woman-child sneered and sucked her tooth. "He ain't gonna be as much fun as me."

Socrates stood up and lurched toward the chair where his clothes were folded and hung.

When he was dressed and headed for the door she said, "I'm pregnant, Daddy."

He swiveled his head and met her eye.

"Congratulations," she said and smiled.

As Luna rose to her feet Socrates lowered to his knees. He pulled her naked body into a tender hug and breathed in deeply.

"Ooo," she moaned, "you bettah no do too much'a that or poor Ronnie gonna have to wait for the twin."

"I don't know what to say," he whispered through her sex.

"Talk is cheap," the young mother-to-be replied. "You already did the important part."

"Hey," Ron Zeal greeted Socrates as came up to the booth.

He sat across from the young killer and grunted.

"You see ovah there across the street?" Zeal said.

A group of young men were standing around smoking and talking loudly, judging by their gestures.

"What can I get you?" a woman asked.

"Coffee and some bread."

"English muffin, toast, bagel, or cinnamon roll?" she asked with well-worn monotony in her tone.

"Toast."

She was a brown woman with lots of Negro blood in her, Socrates could tell, but she was most probably from one of the Spanish speaking nations.

"The big one the one shot Darryl," Ron said when the waitress was gone.

"The one with the gut?"

"The tall one with the gold-plated chains. His name is Tim Hollow, the homeys call'im Hollah."

"Gang related?"

"No one'll get mad if you take him down. Darryl ain't done nuthin' to nobody an' this fool is nobody."

"Where he live at?" Socrates asked, his voice working on its own.

"Two blocks from here."

The toast came with a tray of jellies and jams. Socrates sipped his coffee and nibbled at his bread.

I'm pregnant, Daddy.

"I got a piece here in a bag on the flo'," Ron said. "I got a car don't nobody own up the street. I'll drive if you want."

The laughter that came from Socrates surprised him. It was a happy laugh followed by a satisfied hum.

"How long you been workin' for Chaim?" he asked.

"What?"

"How long?"

"Month."

"How come you decided to do that?"

"Miss Wheaton said it'a be good if I get a job."

"I bet you yo' mother told you that every day from the second you turnt sixteen."

"My mother?"

"I'm just sayin', Ron, that you didn't get no job because a woman told you to."

"So?"

"So why you workin' for Chaim?"

"He offered me a job pay twenty bucks a hour. He said that I could help him wit' the kids come from the street. An', an' at the same time I could learn the trade myself."

Socrates smiled broadly.

"What?" Ron asked.

"You still on trial for murder, Ron. Beat them charges and keep your job. You don't have to be runnin' these streets killin'. You got a way out."

"But what about D-boy?"

"You evah go up against a man that was bigger, stronger, an' meaner than you and you ain't got no gun or knife?"

Ron's lip curled but he didn't answer.

"I have," Socrates said. "And I'm still here to tell ya that I ain't scared'a no mothahfuckah on God's green earth. Not a soul. I went up against the LAPD, got in they face an' spit in their eye.

"I appreciate the information but don't evah think that you gotta do my business. I know what to do. Now the only question is do you?"

Ron Zeal was struck silent by the words that could have come from his own lips. He watched Socrates for a moment, then nodded and rose to leave.

"I love you, brother," Socrates said.

Ron frowned, appeared to be younger for an instant, then walked out of the diner.

4.

Socrates savored his toast and had three refills on his coffee. The waitress was named Lupe and she was born in the Dominican Republic. She'd come to L.A. with her parents when she was seven.

"You the one got that big metal house, huh?" she asked him as he watched the young man nicknamed after a scream through the window.

"Yeah," he said. "We, some of us, were so smart way back when that we changed the world over and over. But now we don't know it. People come to the Big Nickel so they can see what they are, remembah where they come from."

"So it's like a school?"

"No, baby. It's a place where we come together an' share ideas. It's a breeding ground and a last chance."

Lupe frowned. Socrates could tell that she was groping for the right question to ask.

At that moment Hollah rose to his feet. He started saying good-bye, banging fists with and giving faux hugs to his friends.

"How much I owe ya, Lupe?"

"Nuthin', Mr. Fortlow. It's on the house."

"Why?"

"You our hero down here," she said, her eyes glinting with

Caribbean light. "Marianne Lodz talked about you in a magazine. I saw you in the paper too."

"Come on by to the meetin' house sometime, girl. Somebody there almost every weekday mornin'. So many people want to come to the Thursday night meetin's that we got to screen 'em but there's somebody there almost every day.

"Excuse me but I just saw somebody I know."

Lupe touched his arm and smiled at him as he moved past her.

He was thinking about Lupe's gift while following Tim Hollow down the street. For a block the young man was accompanied by another guy. The friend went into a doughnut shop and Tim turned off the avenue onto a side street. Two blocks down he came to a salmon pink apartment building and went in.

Standing outside, across the street from the apartment building, Socrates wondered at the fate that brought him to that juncture. There were children playing on the sidewalks, spilling over into the streets. There were mothers and older sisters, sullen teenage boys and girls who somehow seemed much older. Music came out of passing cars and apartment windows, and there was a general drone in the air.

Socrates closed his eyes and tried to imagine forgiving Tim Hollow, of walking down the street and letting sleeping dogs lie. He tried to overcome the spirit of vengeance that lay like a hot blanket over his soul.

In prison you had to hit back and hit back hard; that's what all young convicts learned. They brought that knowledge back to the streets and turned the hood into a vast prison yard.

But Socrates had a Ph.D. in revenge; he was a master of the art. Most of the young men in the street confused killing with style or importance. They didn't know how to get to the point and get out. Ron Zeal understood but he was unusual.

"Aren't you that man?" a male voice inquired.

He was a regular-looking kind of guy; brown-brown skin and short hair. There was a red tattoo of a Chinese symbol on his left forearm and a faded blue image burned into his neck. Other than the body art he seemed to be an everyday working man. He wore jeans and a white T-shirt with a few small holes here and there. His cap had a long visor and the brown leather belt cinched tight around his waist had a cowboy buckle of nickel and brass.

"What man?" Socrates asked.

"The one run them Thursday night meetin's."

Socrates nodded and wondered if he should wait for later to exact his justice.

"Yeah. That's me."

"I wanna shake your hand, brother," the everyman said. They shook and he went on talking, "Pat Simmons my name. You know I been down here for years waitin' for somebody to start us talkin'. I mean real talk. The kinda talk that sumpin' gotta come out of. When I told my wife about you and how I was waitin' for sumpin' just like that she said, 'Why din't you do it yo'self?' And it hit me that what I been sayin' bad 'bout people not gettin' together was true about me too.

"So I went through my phone book an' called all my friends who know sumpin'. Tanya, that's my wife, she cooked dinner and we all got together an' talked. We been doin' that for six weeks now. Next week my man Bernie gonna have us ovah his place.

"We been talkin' 'bout gettin' a place, either buyin' or rentin', an' callin' it the Safe House; you know like the cops an' robbers do. Anyway our safe house be for kids to go do their homework and be calm an' quiet an' shit."

"That's a good idea," Socrates said sincerely. "It's a snappy name too."

"Tanya come up wit' it. She good about things like that."

"She sure is."

"You wanna go grab a drink, Mr. Fortlow?"

"I'm busy right now, Pat, but here." Socrates took a plain white business card from his wallet. "Call this numbah and tell the answerin' machine your name and number an' say I said, light bulb man."

"Light bulb man," Pat Simmons repeated.

"Now you got to excuse me, Pat. I got some business to take care of."

THE MAILBOX GAVE Hollow's apartment number. It was on the fourth floor at the far end of the hall. Socrates took the stairs three at a time and strode down the long hall like a screw making his rounds at the Indiana State penitentiary.

At Hollah's front door he did not hesitate. He knocked, not too loudly, and waited.

"Who is it?" a male voice said with a slight quaver.

"Jim Beam."

When Tim opened the door Socrates clocked him with a blow that would have killed a smaller man. Tim fell backwards and onto the floor. Socrates strode in swiftly and looked around for friends of the doomed boy.

He kicked open the bathroom door and yanked the curtain from the cheap fiberglass shower stall, making sure that they were alone. When he was back in the main room of the studio apartment Tim Hollow was halfway to his feet. Socrates hit him with an uppercut so vicious that it tore a cry from the young man.

He slammed the front door shut and turned to his kneeling victim. He lifted him and delivered two body shots, let him fall, lifted him, hit him twice more and let him fall again.

Socrates lifted him from the floor a third time.

"Please stop," the helpless young man wheezed. "Please . . ."

Socrates slammed his hard fist into the side of Tim's head and the boy went silent, falling to the ground like a two hundred pound sack of grain.

Breathing hard from his effort the ex-con grabbed a piano stool that sat at a single-stalk table obviously salvaged from a dump or demolition site. Socrates sat down hard, catching his breath before executing his final design. He reached into his pants pocket and came out with a folding hunter's knife.

Unconscious Tim Hollow didn't seem a day older than his twenty years. He was bulky with masculine muscle but had a child in his face.

Socrates opened his knife, revealing the gray, notched blade.

He got to his feet and searched Hollow's clothing for a gun. He raised the knife for the killing blow and then retreated to his stool.

He remembered seeing Darryl in the ICU at the emergency room; tubes in his nose and mouth and three needles in his arms. He looked dead.

Socrates went to Tim again, raised his knife again, and then he went back to the stool.

"I'm pregnant," Luna had said. "Congratulations . . ."

And there was the waitress who'd touched his arm and the man with the tattoos who shook his hand. And there were others; people that stopped him on the street and in the supermarket. For a short while, while he worked at the garage, he was approached every day by men and women who wanted to touch him and ask questions. The garage owner, a man named Gramsci, finally had to let him go because of the number of non-paying customers who came to see the Watts philosopher.

"Please don't," Tim Hollow whispered.

Socrates roused from his reverie.

Tim was looking at him, hugging his ribcage.

"Don't kill me," he begged.

"You tried to kill Darryl. You shot my boy down in the street. He ain't nevah done nuthin' to you. He laid up right now, cain't even walk right 'cause'a the way you shot him."

"It was a mistake, man. I didn't mean to hit him. It was this other dude I was aftah. He ripped me off, man. I was aftah him."

The killing fever was already gone; with its departure Socrates was suddenly aware of a foul odor in the room. He didn't know if it was the boy himself or some piece of rotting food but it was rank. Suddenly Socrates wanted to get away from that smell.

But he didn't go. He stayed in his seat gripping the knife and staring into Hollah's eyes.

"I know who you are, boy."

"I'm sorry."

"Don't make no mistake about me, Hollah. Don't be fooled by this big gut or bald head—I will kill you if I have to."

"It was a mistake."

When Socrates stood up Tim flinched and then cried in pain from the movement.

"Don't let me see you again, Tim."

"I need a doctor, man," the boy whined. "Call 911."

"Crawl there," Socrates said and he left the room unsatisfied and discontented.

5.

That Monday Socrates stared at the cardboard box that Myrtle Brown had left at his private backyard doorstep.

A note was taped to it. It was Myrtle giving Darryl back his clothes and his life.

"'Bout time that ole heifer let up on D-boy," Luna said. She was holding Socrates by the hand as they sat side by side on matching maple chairs.

"If she a old heifer then what am I?"

"You are my man and the father of my baby."

Socrates knew better than to argue against those words.

"You love me, Daddy?" Luna asked.

"Love?" he said. "Damn, girl, if you was to leave me it would be worse than if somebody hacked off my good leg."

Luna smiled and Socrates snorted.

"I'd kill for you, Baby," she said and someone knocked on the door.

Ron Zeal was standing there in the afternoon sunlight reflecting off of the lush green vegetation.

"Hey, Ron."

"Talk to you a minute, Socco?"

As Socrates closed the door behind him he noticed that Luna had already turned away; a woman giving her man the space to do his business. In that brief moment, before he turned back to deal with Zeal, Socrates thought of how perfect he and the child were together. He was more than twice her age, he was older than her father would have been if he were alive but he never felt superior to her, not for one moment.

"Tim Hollow's dead," Ron said as the door shut.

"Dead how?"

"Somebody beat him up pretty bad an' his friends come ovah

to take him to the hospital. On the way he told 'em that you the one beat him and then he told 'em why. I guess it got out that he shot D-boy an' you know you got friends all ovah this town. They kilt him comin' outta his girlfriend's house last night."

"You had anything to do with that, Ronnie?"

"Uh-uh. Matter'a fact, when I heard about the trouble, I went ovah to Hollah's friends an' told them to tell him to leave. Either they didn't tell him or he didn't listen. One way or the othah it ain't got nuthin' to do wit' you or me."

IT WASN'T UNTIL FRIDAY that he went up to Chaim's house on Lorenzo Drive in Cheviot Hills. It was a small place set up away from the street. Chaim was at work, he knew. Rosa, the house-keeper, answered the door.

"Mr. Fortlow," she said, trying to hide her fear with a smile.

Socrates could see in Rosa's eyes that the domestic didn't like him. She could probably tell, he thought, by his walk and mien that he was a killer.

"They in, Rosa?" he asked gently.

"Come in."

"Mr. Fortlow," Fanny Zetel said in greeting.

She was coming from the hallway that led to the bedrooms wearing a turquoise dress suit and maroon shoes with modest heels. She was short and slight but her face carried both dignity and the certainty that comes with it. Her makeup was minimal and her eyes were cut from blue-gray quartz.

Fanny was in her seventies and, with Rosa, ran a perfect little house. The next day's breakfast table was set with butter and a covered pot of air-dried beef the night before. The floors were swept every day. "She even got all hers shoes and Chaim's in little silk bags in the closet," Darryl had told him.

"Hi, Fanny," Socrates said.

"He's coming," she replied, beaming at the powerful man.

Darryl came in slowly, using a cane that Chaim had from a knee operation a decade earlier.

"You men sit in the living room," Fanny said. "Rosa, bring them coffee and a soft drink."

THEY SAT FOR A WHILE. Darryl went into a story about how the man across the street, a Mr. Stegner, had a swimming pool that he let Darryl exercise in.

"I just walk from one end to the other ten or twelve times and then I get out."

Rosa was no taller than Fanny, the color of burnished copper. She bore fancy freckles and had done her best work many years before. She put down the tray with their drinks and left without speaking.

"You evah hear of a boy named Tim Hollow?" Socrates asked, interrupting Darryl's new line of thought about how he and Fanny had gone to Santa Monica to see the ocean.

"Uh-uh."

"He the one shot you."

Darryl blinked and his mouth twitched.

"Somebody killed him," Socrates said.

"Good."

"I wasn't me, D-boy. I kicked his sorry ass but I couldn't kill him. Not no more."

Darryl thought about this a moment and then he nodded.

"Myrtle left all your stuff in a box at my door."

"Yeah. She said she would."

"It's ovah?"

"I'ma move in a room Chaim an' them got out back," the boy said. "I'ma get me a old car an' go to Santa Monica City College."

"Since when?" Socrates asked.

"You mad?"

"Naw. I ain't mad. You know I been tryin' to get you to go back to high school an' now you say you goin' to college."

"They got a program get your GED an' start college at the same time."

It was Socrates' turn to be quiet.

"It's like you told me, Socco."

"What?"

"When sumpin' bad happen you nevah know, it might be for the best."

Socrates wanted to say something but felt as if he'd already said it.

"Luna's havin' a baby," he said at last.

"I know. She been comin' ovah ev'ry othah day. Congratulations."

"How are you two doing?" Fanny asked from the hall.

"I think we both be ready for long pants soon," Socrates said. "Why'ont you come on in an' join us. I'm about to be a father and Darryl here 'bout to be a man."

RED CADDY

1.

They had been talking all night, Luna and Socrates. She was telling him about an apartment she lived in that was also a drug factory, distribution warehouse, and store.

"My daddy worked there and my mothah and brothahs too," she said. "It was at the back of the first floor apartment of a small buildin'. We had a steel door with sixteen locks. I was thirteen an' my boyfriend, Darien, was thirty-six."

Socrates stroked her wild mane and laid his left palm over her still-flat belly.

"I nevah cried," she said, "not when they shot Darien down in the street, not when my daddy died from poisonin' hisself wit' alcohol an' drugs. One'a my brothers was dead an' the other was on the run when they arrested my mama an' I was still only thirteen. I lived on my own after that."

Luna put both her small hands on Socrates'.

"I wanna tell you everything now we like this together," she said. "You know I did the things that a woman do when she on the streets alone. I sold myself to old men and women too. I sold drugs an' I even was with some men when they killed somebody one time."

They were lying in the bed of his small cottage behind the big house in Watts. She turned to him and he kissed her gently next to her severe mouth.

"What do that mean?" she asked.

"That I love you, Luna."

"Then why don't you kiss my lips?"

He did so.

"You don't have to stay wit' me if you don't want," she said.

"Luna."

"What?"

"When I first met you you wouldn't say more'n three words at a time. Even when we got together you didn't talk much. But now everything I say, even what I don't say, you got some comment. An' usually you either think I'm lyin' or that I said sumpin' I didn't.

"What do you want from me, girl?"

She smiled and turned on her side to face him.

"I was in a juvenile detention center when my mama died. They had me in there for prostitution an' because I was wit' those men kilt that othah man. I run away and then, a long time later, I saved Marianne an' she got me a lawyer that cleared it with the court for me."

"Uh-huh. I figured that," Socrates said.

"Do you love me, Mr. Fortlow?"

"Yes I do."

"An' you don't care about what I did?"

"Not one bit. Not for one second."

"Then why you got to be goin' out in the middle'a the night an' stayin' away for days?"

Socrates laughed and Luna slammed her fist against his chest.

"Don't laugh at me."

"I'm just surprised, girl. I nevah thought in a million years that a pretty young thing like you be jealous of a old man like me."

"That ain't no answer."

"Billy an' me goin' to San Francisco, that's all. He got these people up there he want me to meet, says they could help out the Nickel. I ain't nevah had a vacation in my whole life. It's just me an' him."

"An' all them hos up in Frisco."

"You the only woman in my life, Luna. I ain't lookin' for nobody else."

She pouted and hit him again. It was just a tap this time.

"What's goin' on, L? You know I ain't no hound. You had to chase me down just to get me to look you in the eye."

She smiled. "That's 'cause I was so young an' you thought they was gonna put you in jail."

"You not that young," he said. "Anyway, you know me better'n that."

"Look at me," she said.

He did.

"You sayin' you don't see trash from the street?" she asked.

"That ain't the right question."

"Huh?"

"The question is, do you see yo'self in my eyes an' see trash? You know what I think an' you don't care what nobody else think. You done taken the leap, let yourself be pregnant and be with a man. You know I love you. You know where I'm from. But what you don't know—"

Socrates didn't finish because Luna put her hand over his mouth.

She crawled up on top of him. They were both naked in the night.

Luna hugged his big, black, bald head to her chest with all of her considerable strength. He brought his powerful hands to her sides as if holding her in place.

"You meet all kindsa women now that they know about your place," she said, her voice muffled by the embrace. "They all want to be wit' you now."

"If I was another kinda man I might give 'em a tumble too," Socrates admitted. "You know some men need it day and night. But that ain't me, L."

"You gonna be on that TV show and at that breakfast at the mayor's mansion. What are they gonna think when they find out that yo' woman's a ho?"

"I'ont know what they gonna think, Baby. I'on't know what they gonna say. But . . . if you gonna be my woman then I don't care. You gonna have my baby. You gonna hold me an' want me to be wit' you. That's heaven for a man like me don't even deserve to be free, not really."

Luna raised up and brought both her fists down on his chest.

"Then why you leavin' me?" she screamed.

"I'm just goin' away for a few days with my friend," he said. "You right about the TV an' the mayor. I need to get away an' clear my head. I ain't runnin' aftah nobody an' I sure'n hell ain't runnin' away from you."

"You leavin' in just a little bit," she said. "You leavin' me alone wit' my baby inside me."

"You got the key to this cottage an' the key to the Big Nickel. You got most'a my money and all my friends' numbahs."

"But I ain't got you." There were tears in her eyes. Socrates had not seen Luna cry before.

There came a knock on the door of the small garden house. Socrates got up from his bed and went to the door. He cracked it open and spoke in a deep tone. Then he came back and took his pants from the closet.

"Don't go," Luna said.

"I got to, Baby. I already made plans with Billy."

He put on his T-shirt and then a long sleeved blue work shirt.

He was tying his shoes, shoes that were older than the girl in his bed, when she said, "If you go I won't be here when you come back."

It was the old Luna talking, the girl he had met on the first night of the Thursday meetings, the child who could cut a man's throat and leave him bleeding in the street with no mercy or guilt.

"That's okay, Luna. You could be somewhere else if you wanna be. But believe this—I will come and get you, wherever you are. You can put money on that."

2.

"Where you get a bright red 1969 Cadillac look like it just come off the showroom floor?" Socrates asked Billy when they were on their way at 3:00 A.M.

"You," Billy Psalms said.

"Me? I'm the one got your money, man."

"Yeah," Billy replied, a conditional tone in his voice. "Yeah you do but you still bought me this car. This automobile, these clothes, my new apartment, and even my new job wit' Sheryl Limon."

"What?"

"Yeah," Billy said as if that one word explained everything.

They both went silent as Billy drove his big red Caddy toward the ocean. They would pick up the Pacific Coast Highway and drive all the way north beside the vast Pacific listening to old soul music and breathing the salt air.

Two hours later they were a dozen miles north of Santa Barbara and the sun was only a threat behind the coastal mountains to their right. A James Brown compilation of greatest hits was pounding out rhythm on the CD player and the windows were open wide.

"What you mean me?" Socrates asked as if Billy had only just spoken.

"It's hard to say, Brother," Billy replied.

He turned down the volume on the Godfather of Soul. "You changed my life but I cain't put a finger on it. I cain't point to this or that an' say this is it."

"But this car cost money," Socrates said. "Hard cash. You could say where that come from."

"Oh yeah," Billy said. "That's for sure. I got the money in Gardena . . . playin' cards."

"Now how the fuck am I gonna have anything to do wit' you winnin' money out in Gardena?"

"That's just it, Socco. I don't know. I mean you the first person evah in my life I trusted. That ain't no lie. That's a fact. An' once I give you that money I made on the trifecta I was free."

"Free from what?"

"Just free. I wasn't worried 'bout a mothahfuckin' thing. I haven't been to the track more'n two three times since then. And then about a month ago I went down wit' my girlfriend to Gardena 'cause her mother live out there. I sat around wit' the old girl for a while but they wanted to be alone so I went and found me a bar. There was a casino next door so I sat down to a poker game. You know I don't like poker but I can play.

"Shit. I play like a mothahfuckah that day and night and the next day and the next night too. Denise come to take me outta there but when she see that big pile'a chips I had she went back home to her mama to wait and see if I hit it rich or went bust."

"Billy."

"What, Socco?"

"What do I have to do with you plyin' your trade?"

"I don't know but you do. You see I used to get in a sweat when I gambled. I had to win or my heart would sink. But out there in Gardena I didn't care anymore. I just kept playin' as long as I was winnin'. When the tide turned I laid them cards down. That's you right there. You ain't addicted to money, sex, or alcohol. You don't even care if you live in a box next to the railroad tracks or a penthouse in the hills. Man shove a gun in your face an' you shrug. I seen it. An' if you see sumpin' then you know sumpin'. That's God's honest truth right there."

The ocean was beginning to appear under the spreading light of dawn. Socrates was smiling and frowning at the same time.

"How much you win?"

"Eighty-six thousand dollars. Paid my taxes, bought this here car, rented me a real apartment, and put the rest in a checking account. Called Sheryl Limon an' asked if I could be a cook at her caterin' service. Told her I could work whenevah she want as long as it wasn't on a Thursday night."

For the first time that early morning Socrates thought about Luna. He wondered where she was and how she was feeling.

"That ain't me, Billy," he said. "It's you."

"That's why I like you, Socco."

"Why?"

"Because you a lotta different men. You could sit in front'a all them people ev'ry Thursday, real people who done lived a lotta life, done seen everything men an' women could know. They been in wars an' schools an' traveled round the world. But you stand up in front'a them an' they sit up straight like kids in a classroom. They listen to you an' learn sumpin' else ev'ry minute.

"But that's not what I like most about you."

"No?" Socrates asked, the smile winning out over the frown.

"Naw, man. What I like is that you the smartest man in the room but you push so hard that you could be wrong too. Like when Ron Zeal was talkin' 'bout fightin' for what's ours an' you gave the flo' to Wan Tai. He said he could kick anybody's ass in that room but he believed in passive defense. You knew Wan could say it better.

"An' sometimes you get worried an' sometimes you just wrong."

"I nevah said I was perfect," Socrates said.

"Naw. But we all act like you are. But even though we do you nevah take the bait. You still talk from your heart and get suckered by life like all the rest of us."

"Billy, what are you sayin', man?" Socrates yawned then. He realized that he had not slept at all.

"I could see how much you wanted to stay away from Luna Barnet but that girl set her sites on you and you just a man."

Socrates raised his hand. Whether this was a threat or some kind of agreement he did not know.

"Or like when you tell me that this Caddy is because'a me," Billy continued. "You know better but you haven't worked it out. You seen me before the Big Nickel an' you see me now. You put me to work, Socco. An' the more I worked the more I changed. Me an' Darryl the only two you pulled outta the domino game an' brought ovah to the nickel."

"I don't have anything against our old friends, Billy."

"But why you drag me along? I could see wit' Darryl, he's like your son but you nevah even liked me all that much."

"But I knew that you brought sumpin' to the table," Socrates said. "You gotta sharp eye."

"You can say that and you still gonna sit there an' tell me that you didn't buy me this Caddy?"

Socrates wanted to reply, to deny Billy's claim. He wanted to say that the gambler was his own man and that he couldn't, he shouldn't claim that someone else was responsible for what happened to him. He wanted to say these things but sleep came up on him like a huge crocodile coming out from under a day-dreaming bather.

HE WAS ASLEEP but at the same time he was still aware of the world he passed through. He could feel the great, ancient ocean rocking next to them and the wind coming in from Billy's open window. Sunlight warmed his right arm and music played softly on the car speakers. Speakers. The word, though unspoken, echoed in his chest and mind. The motor was humming to him, pulling him down from a scaffolding of thoughts and ideas. He tumbled peacefully through an air of unconsciousness. The fall would not hurt him, nothing would.

Luna was crying somewhere, she had to be. She had gone too far and now the pain had gotten to her. She didn't know how to let go for even a few days. She didn't know how to trust a man that she also loved.

"Socco. Cops," he heard Billy say and was immediately awake, his dreams forgotten.

The red Caddy swerved to the side of the highway. Socrates squinted in the bright sunlight.

They were no longer next to the ocean. The landscape around them was comprised of green rolling hills with a cluster of cows here and there, and now and then a solitary oak.

Through his side-mirror Socrates could see the highway patrolman coming toward his door. The ex-con went cold inside. His mind emptied itself of all contents. There never was a Big Nickel, a Thursday night, a Luna Barnet.

"Please step out of the car," the cop on Billy's side said.

"Here we go," the gambler muttered under his breath.

Socrates opened his door. When the patrolman saw his size and strength he took a step back and unholstered his gun. His brown eyes opened wide and for a moment he was speechless.

"What are you doing here?" the cop asked once he had regained his composure.

"Passin' through," Socrates said. He had already shown his state issued identification.

"Is this your car?"

"No."

"Who's is it?"

"My friend's."

"It's an expensive car."

"That's how Billy rolls."

"Are you carrying drugs or guns?"

"No."

"What would I find if I opened up the trunk?"

"Trunk? I'ont even know what you'd find in the glove compartment, man."

THEY OPENED THE TRUNK and the glove compartment. They looked under the seats and the white carpet that Billy had specially installed. They used a breathalyzer to make sure that the men weren't drunk and they had Billy touch his nose and walk a straight line. They checked the men's pockets and had them take off their shoes. And when they found nothing they arrested Billy and Socrates on suspicion of drug trafficking.

At the station they separated the gambler and the philosopher. After a long spell in a locked room two men in suits came in to talk to Socrates. One suit was brown and the other green but the men were both white, middle-sized, mid-age, and sour.

"What are you doing here in Loma Linda?" one cop asked.

Socrates was thinking about his head being cradled against Luna's breasts. He'd used his one call on her but she wasn't answering.

"Did you hear my partner?" Brown-suit asked. He had a whitehead pimple on the tip of his nose.

Socrates made his face into a visage of innocent ignorance.

"We can be polite or this can turn ugly," the tow-headed green-suit said.

Socrates laughed.

"What's funny?"

"Cain't get no uglier than this, man. Arrested for drivin' down the highway with no contraband. Damn. I might as well live in Russia."

The cop in the brown suit stood up. Socrates wondered if he was about to get slapped. He decided without even an elevation of his blood pressure that he would kill this man if he so much as laid a hand on him.

The door to the locked room came open and a group of men and one woman walked in.

There was an officer, maybe captain, in a very neat uniform, two lower ranked officers, a small man in a dapper gray-silk suit, and a tall white blonde wearing a peacock blue dress that was both careless and sexy.

"Mr. Fortlow," the dapper man said.

"Yes?"

"My name is Tinheart. Mason Tinheart."

The name was familiar to the ex-con. "You the man Billy wanted me to meet."

"Yes." Tinheart gave him a lawyer's smile, noncommittal but intense. "Billy called us and we drove down to get you out of here."

The captain looked angry when he said, "Let him go Billings," to the man in the green suit.

"Okay, Captain," the inquisitor said.

It struck Socrates that the cops weren't bothered; that they were just doing their job. Tomorrow they wouldn't even be able to remember who it was that they had interrogated.

The white woman was smiling at Socrates.

"Mr. Psalms doesn't want to press charges for wrongful arrest," Tinheart was saying. He was both short and slight but there was an ease to his bearing that befitted a tall man. "Would you like to file a complaint?"

Socrates smiled, thinking that Billy was following an unwritten, centuries-old code that said you never challenged a lion in his lair; and that black men in America were always strangers in the lion's den.

"Who are you?" Socrates asked the ranking officer.

"Captain Stillman," the officer said after a moment's delay.

Socrates rose to his feet. He was the biggest man in the room, and the baddest by his own reckoning.

"Why your men arrest me? Why they take all my belongings and lock me up?"

The Captain's frown was meant to be an answer but Socrates wouldn't let it go.

"I asked you a question, man. Least you could do is answer me aftah keepin' me bunged up in this room for the last six hours."

"There was a report that two men, two African-Americans, were supplying drugs to underage children in the community."

"And?" Socrates nudged.

"And what?"

"The only reason you arrested me and Billy was that we was two black men goin' down the road?"

"You fit the description."

"Can I see that?" Socrates asked.

Tinheart gave a real smile then.

"That's police business. We don't share that kind of information with suspects."

"That's it? No more explanation?"

"I'm not answerable to you, Fortlow."

"Absolutely, Mr. Tinheart," Socrates said. "I wanna press charges. I wanna know in this man's court why he can arrest two black men for bein' black men together."

The white woman's mouth opened into an unanswered kiss.

Socrates wondered where Luna would be sleeping that night.

3.

"Ron Zeal asked me where was Wan Tai at the seventh Thursday night meeting," Socrates was saying in answer to Brigitta Brownlevy's question, "that's when I knew the Thursday night meeting was workin' and that it was gonna last."

"It's so wonderful," she said, "like the ideal Athens rising up out of the shit."

Their eyes met across a round table at the hotel restaurant. San Francisco was only an hour's drive from the Loma Linda jailhouse. Socrates took the time to fill out a complaint against the officers that arrested him and also the Captain who supported their actions.

"What are the plans for your university?" Tinheart asked.

In private Socrates had thought of the Big Nickel as a kind of college, a place of learning able to make that knowledge something real, but he'd never heard anyone else make this claim; no one except Peter Ford, the temporary boyfriend that Luna had brought by to make Socrates jealous. The boy had spoken about ancient Greek universities but there were other things going on in Socco's heart that night.

"Try'n make it a part of the life down there. Maybe make other places like it in Richmond and Oakland, Compton an' maybe even East New York."

"Like a fast food burger joint," Billy Psalms said.

He winked at Brigitta but she was watching Socrates.

And he was looking at her too.

"We're having a social justice meeting in Berkeley tomorrow," Tinheart said. "I had asked Billy to bring you, just for you to see what we're doing here."

Billy had told Socrates that Tinheart was a serious gambler. They had met once years before at a Vegas poker tournament and Billy had kept the lawyer's card.

"But after what I saw and heard today," Tinheart continued, "I was hoping that you could speak a few minutes to our member-ship. We . . . we need to hear something new, something else."

"I ain't a minister, Mason."

"We don't need a sermon," the lawyer replied. "Maybe just a few words. A minute."

After the dinner Tinheart took Socrates and Billy Psalms to an elevator that led to the forty-first floor of a downtown San Fran-cisco building.

"They got this many rooms?" Billy asked Mason on the way up.

"No," Tinheart said. "The first thirty-six floors are offices. The hotel only uses the top of the building."

When they got out Tinheart led them down a hall. Half the way to their rooms the walls on both sides became windows that gave a nearly 360° view of the city. There was the bay and the

Golden Gate Bridge, and faraway mountains in the gathering gloom with almost iridescent fog flowing down like thick slush.

"Damn," Billy said.

Socrates looked around in wonder.

"So this is how the other half live?" he said.

"More like the other one percent," Tinheart replied.

WHEN SOCRATES GOT TO HIS ROOM the first thing he intended to do was call Luna. But he was distracted. The ceiling was low and the furniture all had an Asian cast but the windows went from floor to ceiling and he could see almost half of the beautiful city. The nighttime city was a carpet of electric lights.

"I'm not here," Luna's answering machine told him once he had made the call.

A knock came on the door.

"Hey, Socco," Billy said as he entered the posh room. He opened the bar and said, "Look here, brother. They don't have them li'l bottles but whole fifths up in here."

Psalms brought out a bottle of cognac and poured them both a generous four fingers.

After a few sips Socrates relaxed. He and Billy talked like they did in the days before there was a Big Nickel or a Big Table or cops that wanted to bring him down because he frightened them with his words. The ex-con philosopher and the gambler laughed for two hours before Billy yawned.

"That was a long mothahfuckin' day, man," Billy said. "I need some shuteye."

WHEN BILLY LEFT Socrates called Luna again.

"I'm not here," the taciturn recording said.

After that he sat in the sofa chair and watched San Francisco's darknesses and lights.

When the knock came on the door he started awake and glanced at the digital clock. It was 10:30.

Opening the door he expected to see Billy again. The gambler was a light sleeper and probably couldn't keep his eyes shut.

He was surprised to see Brigitta Brownlevy dressed in a kimono-like robe of shiny red silk that barely made it down to her thighs; surprised but not bothered. Brigitta had shapely legs and a smile that was an invitation to a closer inspection.

She hesitated a moment and then found her resolve.

"I was going to tell you that I was locked out and could I use your phone but. . . ." She shrugged. "Can I come in?"

"Where's Mason?"

"I told him that I had a headache. I live north of here so he got me the room."

Socrates took a step back, almost stumbled on his own feet. He felt a foolish grin invade his stern features. Brigitta smiled going past him. She placed a hand against his broad chest for a moment and then pulled it away.

She took a seat on the small upholstered chair that stood next to a loveseat.

"Can I get you a drink?" Socrates asked, remembering his manners.

"Seven-Up and vodka please."

Socrates took another four fingers of cognac after pouring the nordic beauty's glass. When he sat down she crossed her legs. His brows knitted.

"What's wrong?" she asked.

"Those are some nice legs you got there, girl."

Brigitta smiled and leaned forward to take her drink from the jade colored coffee table. Her cleavage was impressive too.

"I want to come spend the night with you, Mr. Fortlow," she said.

His breath became as shallow as a man slowly dying from emphysema.

His lips parted and his tongue clove to the back of his front teeth. A sound escaped his chest that was both deep and animal.

Brigitta's smile broadened.

Wonderment was there next to lust in the ex-con's heart. This was the first time in nearly forty years that a chance meeting with an attractive woman hadn't called up the wrenching guilt for the violence of his past crimes.

Brigitta sat back in her chair, twisting to the side so that her robe opened even further.

Time came to a still-point for Socrates; it stopped mid-heartbeat and hovered in the air like Judgment Day or maybe just the day he'd die. There were no deep thoughts to accompany this paralysis. The room was silent. The light, he noticed, was low. Brigitta's smile faded into something more sensual and urgent but Socrates couldn't even take in a full breath.

"Should I take off my robe and come sit on your lap?" she asked.

"No."

This small utterance took his full strength.

"What do you need?" she asked.

"I . . ." he said and stalled. There was a vast ocean underneath him, a depth so great and crushing that he was exhilarated by its power and slow certainty.

"What?" she asked confidently, seemingly aware that she was the power in his mind.

"Uh," Socrates grunted. It was the sound of a moose rutting in the deep forest where men had rarely gone.

"Is something wrong?"

"Brigitta?"

"Yes."

He shook his head.

"Have I done something?" she asked, her hand closing the bodice of the sexy garment.

"Oh yeah," he said. "Damn."

"Should I go?"

"No. No, no, no, no. It's just that sumpin' like this haven't happened to me since I was ten years old."

Sensing a story Brigitta tucked her calves up under her thighs and huddled down in the chair.

"My Aunt Bellandra once took me to Iowa to visit her friend lived on a farm out there. She told me, before we left, that I ain't nevah had no real pork roast before. But I told her that my mama made a pork roast on the first Sunday of ev'ry month, when we could afford it.

"Her friend, his name was Ira, slaughtered a pig the first mornin' we was there an' he cooked the roast the next night. He used rosemary he grew in his garden and garlic that he harvested too. I took one bite and was amazed. I had never imagined that a pork roast could taste that good.

"Bellandra was always tryin' to teach me sumpin'. It took fifty years for me to see it an' here tonight I'm still learnin' my lesson."

"What lesson?" Brigitta whispered.

"That there's somethin' better out there. That I don't have to settle for what has been or what people told me would be."

Brigitta wanted to ask another question, Socrates could see it in her face, but she kept silent.

"I never just met a woman and wanted her and didn't feel like I was wrong."

"It's not wrong," she said.

"No," he said, making two replies in one. "But you know I got a li'l brown girl down there in Watts would cut my throat if I did what I wanna do wit' you."

"We don't have to tell her. It's just us here tonight."

"She's here too," Socrates said. "You the light shinin' in my eyes, Brigitta, but Luna done opened up the window shade. She the one pult me outta the shell. And if I do this with you I'd be goin' right back in."

The blonde woman's blue eyes shifted and once again Socrates was reminded of the ocean.

"Thank you," she said.

"For what?"

Brigitta smiled and then looked up at the ceiling, a little dramatically, Socrates thought.

"I am a pretty girl," she said. Her mouth curled into a smile around the last word. "When I go places men want me. Rich men, after knowing me for only a few minutes, offer to take me to beautiful places. Once a man I didn't know gave me a four karat deep green emerald gemstone because, he said, he wanted to show his appreciation.

"I never really understood them until I met you in the interrogation room. I wanted you like those men wanted me. I could feel it in my chest and in my sex."

"I ain't no beauty, Brigitta."

"You are too beautiful," she said, "like a mountain or a bear or maybe a fresh pork loin."

She stood up, allowing her robe to fall open for a moment. She looked at him before tying the sash again. She smiled, enjoying his restraint.

"Can I be your date at the dinner tomorrow night?" she asked.

"I thought you was with Tinheart?"

"Not tomorrow night."

"I'm not here," Luna's answering service said. "Leave a message or call me back."

4.

He called her sixteen times between that night and the next. Luna was not answering her cell phone, at least not when Socrates called.

He spent the day walking around San Francisco with Billy. They shopped at Gumps, a posh department store where he bought Luna a teddy bear. They ate fish and chips at Fisherman's Wharf and saw Lombard Street, *the crookedest street in the world.*

"You that man right?" a middle-aged black man in a well worn gray suit asked Socrates at the entrance of the art museum.

"I know you?" Socrates replied.

"Naw, naw. My name's James Tippton. I live in Oakland but I read an article in the *Chronicle.* They had a picture looked just like you. Aristotle right?"

"Socrates."

"Yeah, yeah, that's it. I told you it was him, baby."

A taciturn fifteen-year-old girl tried to smile but only managed a sneer. At first Socrates thought that the man had found a child to make him feel young in bed but then he saw that their eyes and cheekbones were the same.

"I read that article three times, man," James Tippton was saying. "You know I'm a social worker. I go down in the hood an' meet with teenage single mothers, gangbangers, dope addicts, winos, and just plain crooks. I do it all, brother. All of it. They get AIDS an' they come to me. They get put in jail an' they call my number. You know I thought I was the shit. I was the man who was trying to make a difference. But I read that article and I knew that I was just another sold out brother makin' a paycheck."

Socrates often ran into men like Tippton; confident and inse- cure, fifty but holding himself as if he were twenty years younger, both bold and restrained. These men wanted to talk but rarely felt that there was anyone to talk to and so when they met Socrates the dam broke open and all he had to do was stand there and listen.

"You the real deal, man. You live it and you makin' a differ- ence too."

"Amen to that," Billy Psalms said.

"I decided aftah readin' 'bout you that I needed to quit social work. Either I should make some real money or do sumpin' mean sumpin'."

"James?"

"Uh-huh."

"No disrespect but I'ma ex-con, man. They wouldn't hire me to flip burgers in one'a these fast food restaurants. I do what I do 'cause I am what I am. That's all. You made this child here. You give people a phone number an' answer day or night I bet. We together in this. It ain't no race."

The girl was staring at Socrates as he pulled a card from his work shirt pocket.

"Here, man," Socrates said. "When you down in L.A. come out to the Big Nickel. Ask for Billy Psalms here. He'll remember you. He remembers everything. You spend a day there wit' us and you'll know that it ain't no competition. It's just you an' me an' all the rest of us."

THAT EVENING BRIGITTA came to his door to get him. She was wearing a mid-thigh tight green gown that came nowhere near her shoulders. There were diamonds in her ears and she smelled like the ocean with a hint of something sweet buried deep within.

"How do I look?"

"Like a mountain climber on vacation."

Her laugh nearly broke him.

"WE'VE COME HERE this evening," Mason Tinheart was saying, "as we do each year, to raise money while raising awareness for the plight of our fellow citizens that have the good life dangling in front of them like a carrot in front of beast of burden . . ."

Brigitta drove them to the hotel in her two-year-old silver Jaguar. Billy rode with Tinheart. Socrates had his phone with him. He had not turned off the ringer.

"But tonight we have a special treat. A great man, a teacher, has come to us from the southland. This man has had a hard life and has turned not only his life around but he has also helped his entire community to come together and transform.

"On his way here to us in Billy Pslams's beautiful red 1969 Cadillac the police stopped them for being black. They searched the car, found nothing, and then arrested them for being black . . . literally."

Gasps and other sounds of protest rose from the round dinner tables that filled the hotel ballroom.

"You thrill me, Mr. Fortlow," Brigitta Brownlevy whispered into his ear. She shoved her hand into his pocket and squeezed his thigh under the table.

Before this interruption Socrates was thinking that Tinheart was competing with him on that stage, though he probably wasn't aware of it. It wasn't because of race or class. It was because Tinheart could see the desire in mistress's eyes. She was hungry for Socrates' violence and desperation.

". . . I'm talking about Socrates Fortlow, the new conscience of SouthCentral, Los Angeles."

The applause was loud and long. People rose to their feet, following Brigitta Brownlevy's cue. They cheered him all the way to the podium, while Mason Tinheart shook his hand and then hugged him.

Socrates squared himself behind the microphone not knowing what he was going to say. He perused the crowd of faces; there were Asians and Latinos and some black people too but mostly there were white faces, people in tuxedos and gowns. They were concentrating on him while he had Luna standing silently at the back of his mind.

"I fount out a few weeks ago that I was gonna be a father," he said.

He did not expect the renewed applause. The women were smiling more openly now.

"That's a natural thing for most people," he said when the clapping died down. "Most of you have had kids, or will have. And all of you been children. Maybe you had a happy childhood and maybe not. But you most likely had parents that ooed and cooed when you were in the bed. My mother wanted to love me but couldn't because I was the product of a rape . . ."

Socrates had not ever uttered these words and wasn't expecting to.

"I was the result of violence and the child of unhappiness," he said. "I only evah had one woman that cared for me when I was a boy. Her name was Bellandra and she had a life so hard that she didn't know how to love straight forward like most folks. We were made for each other, me and Bellandra. She told me stories about real people and she told me the truth.

"I learned her lessons but it took a whole lifetime. In between then and now I murdered and raped and murdered again. I lived twenty-seven years in a prison that would kill a normal man in ten minutes flat. I done things would make you so sick you wouldn't evah sleep right, evah again.

"That's the man you clappin' for. Not no hero on a white horse. Not no victim but a man that preyed on his victims. Not no innocent man but a man did the crime.

"And so I nevah thought about bein' a father. I nevah dreamed I could be that kinda man. These hands so rough I could wash 'em with sandpaper. What right I got to stand here in this fine hall or to have some child call me daddy?

"That's why I started the Big Nickel and the Thursday night Thinkers' Meeting. I don't care 'bout them cops stoppin' me or takin' me to jail. They looked at me and saw what they thought they saw. I don't give a fuck about them. They the cops and I'm the killer. That's why you rich people pay taxes—so that I don't get too close and do to you what I did to my own people.

"You cain't th'ow sugar on shit and call it chocolate cake. You cain't clap away a man's sins. Ain't nobody can turn that train around."

The hall was silent. No one was smiling. Socrates had finished his speech but he didn't know how to get down off the dais.

Brigitta came to his side then and led him away by the hand. He didn't look up and so had no idea if people were watching him leave. He felt the way he had when he'd been stabbed by a man named William Haddon. The wound was bleeding and gave him a sharp pain.

On the car ride back to the hotel he stared out the window at the lovely city. He didn't speak and neither did his beautiful date.

She walked him into the lobby and took the elevator with him to his floor. She walked him to the door.

"I had it all planned you know," she said as they stood there not knowing what to do with their hands.

"What's that?"

"I was going to walk you to the door and say that after all my makeup and chauffering that I deserved at least one kiss."

"That's an awful lot for a kiss," he said. His voice could have come from a corpse.

"It was going to be a great kiss," Brigitta Brownlevy said. "It was going to be so good that you'd have to invite me in and throw me down on the floor."

Socrates felt a shock go through him. Suddenly his depression turned into lust.

"What changed your mind?"

"I have never seen the truth before," she said. "I didn't know it until you started speaking. You, you were standing there talking to us but finding yourself. They wanted you to be one thing but you didn't care."

They came together in a gentle embrace. She kissed him, lightly at first and then with fierce determination. Socrates pressed his body against her and she pushed back, moving from side to side, pressing her thigh against his erection.

They grunted together and then Socrates' phone sounded. The ring went through one cycle and he kept kissing. It went through another turn and still he pressed. But in the middle of the third ring he moved away and took the little phone from his pocket and flipped it open.

"Yeah?" he said in a thick voice.

"I wake you up?" Luna asked.

"No," he intoned. "I was just thinkin'."

Brigitta moved away to give him room to talk.

"'Bout what?"

"'Bout when you was gonna return my call."

"I was waitin' for you to call me twenty times before I was gonna answer. You only did nineteen but it was gettin' late an' I thought if I didn't call, you an' Billy might fall into some wild couchie up there."

"Is that it?"

"Did you?"

"Did I what?"

"You know what."

Socrates looked up and saw Brigitta Brownlevy getting into the elevator down the hall.

"Naw, baby. There was this one girl wanted it but I told her that you'd cut my throat if I did."

"Hm."

For some reason Socrates put his hand in his pocket then. It was the place where Brigitta had stroked his thigh earlier that evening. There was something there, something small and hard.

He pulled it out and saw that it was shining green stone, an emerald of some size.

"Don't be mad at me, baby," Socrates said. "If I knew you needed twenty calls I would have called you thirty times. I'll call you back right now if you want me to."

"Do you love me, daddy?"

"I love you and I need you."

"You need me for what?"

"For me to be a man."

THE APOLOGY

1.

Donations were pouring into the Big Nickel, the nonprofit school and social center. The center was run by its president, Billy Psalms, and the board director, Socrates Fortlow. There were pottery classes taught by an old ceramicist from a production pottery down in Guadalajara named Angel Diaz, and instruction in the martial arts were presented by Wan Tai, a founding member of the Thursday night Thinkers' Meeting.

Cassie Wheaton, though she had a full time law practice and was eight months pregnant, ran three weekly meetings of the Dispute Resolution Workshop where gang members and others came to solve their problems hopefully, without resorting to violence.

The Big Nickel was affiliated with another community center called the Safe House, a place where children could come to study in peace and safety. The Safe House also held classes at the Nickel to teach adults how to read.

Billy Psalms' kitchen, except for Thursday afternoon and night, was transformed into a sandwich shop food line. They had put in a window and all day long volunteers from around Los Angeles came to make sandwiches and pass them out to people that lined up down the block. James Tippton, a social worker from the Bay Area, had quit his job and moved down to

L.A. to manage the food line. He had turned in his threadbare suit for a canvas apron and worked day and night organizing volunteers and greeting his thousands of clients.

"I love this job, Socco," the ex-Oaklander said just about every time they met.

"An' the job love you," Socrates would reply.

THE BIG NICKEL WAS BEING SUED for various zoning and health violations, and for brainwashing and unlawful restraint. One man, whose wife had left him and used the Nickel childcare center to keep her child while she went to work, had charged Socrates himself for kidnapping.

A man named Ben Wiggam, who lived five blocks away, had filed a complaint that the cult called the Big Nickel had sent its agents to spy on him when he was sleeping.

In turn the Big Nickel board was suing the city for police harassment on a conspiratorial level and the celebrity lawyer, Mason Tinheart from San Francisco, had agreed to take the case pro-bono.

For a spate of time early on the police busted the center every chance they could. If a fight broke out on the sandwich line the police would come into the house itself *looking for evidence*. If a neighbor called and complained about noise a SWAT team would descend on the tin plated house in full riot gear. But a federal judge, a professional acquaintance of Cassie Wheaton, put an injunction on the LAPD and the invasions stopped, almost completely.

SOCRATES HAD HIRED and appointed mostly founding members of the Thinkers' table to run different aspects of the fast-growing institution. Leanne Northford was in charge of counseling and social services while her one-time nemesis, Ron Zeal, supervised security when security was needed. Antonio Peron oversaw any structural changes that were necessary for the building. Marianne Lodz, the rising pop star, made most of their public announcements and hosted fund-raising parties.

MOST MONDAYS Socrates boarded a bus bound for the Westside of the city. He made three transfers and got off at the Santa Monica Pier. There he met Darryl, the boy that he had saved and who, in turn, had saved him, and together they would fish in anonymity from the farthest end of the quay.

When they got together Darryl would talk and talk, which would have surprised any of his friends or schoolmates because with most people he was a sullen young black man who had little to say and rarely expressed an opinion.

"School is hard," he said to Socrates before their bait hit the water.

"Hard how?"

"I'ont know. It's just all these questions and answers, you know? I study 'em an' a lotta times I'm right but it still don't make no sense."

"You ask Chaim to help you?"

"Yeah. Mr. Zetel's real nice too. He sit down wit' me but a lotta times he don't think like the textbooks and the teachers. And he so smart that he know the answer wit'out figurin' the way they do. My best help come from Luna."

"Luna?"

"Uh-huh. She still come up twice a week an' we sit an' go ovah my work. What she do is get out a pencil an' some paper an' tell me to show her how to do it. That way I teach myself kinda. An' you know Luna talk like I talk. She real nice."

It was a Monday like any other. They caught fish that Fanny Zetel would later make some delicacy out of, ate at a fried fish stand, and walked along the beach barefoot.

"How come you so quiet?" Darryl asked in the late afternoon.

"Am I?"

"Uh-huh."

"I guess so," Socrates said. "It's just funny is all."

"What is?"

"Me an' you standin' here on this beach barefoot and at peace as far as it go. We both done been to the bottom of the barrel an' here we are up near the top. I try but I cain't explain it. I mean you know the board done approved my salary at ninety thousand dollars a year."

"Ninety thousand!"

"Uh-huh. But you know that don't even mean a damn thing to me. I mean, I'm happy to make money for Luna an' the baby when it get here but I don't care 'bout no money. Shit. I know drug dealers pullin' down ten times what I'm makin' but that don't mean nuthin'. You could have a million dollahs but this beach here an' you an' me walkin' down it, now that's sumpin'."

"You gon' marry Luna?" Darryl asked.

"I axed her."

"What she say?"

"Nuthin'."

"Nuthin'?"

"Not a word. She just sat there quiet for a while an' then axed me what I wanted for dinner."

"Damn. What that mean?"

"I don't have the slightest idea," the big man said. "It'd drive me crazy if I wasn't already used to it."

"You think she mad acause'a that lady?"

Brigitta Brownlevy had come down to Los Angeles with

Mason Tinheart three times and even though she was with the lawyer she showed Socrates a deference that was unmistakable.

"Luna told you about her?"

"Yeah. I think she's jealous."

"She never said it," Socrates answered. "An' you know L will tell you how she feel if that's the only thing she say all day."

Darryl laughed happily and said, "You know that's right."

Socrates put a hand on the boy's skinny shoulder.

"How's Myrtle?"

"Mad."

"Mad about what?"

"If I don't call her or if I do. If I say, 'okay we broke up,' or if I ask her if she want to get some coffee. But mostly she mad 'cause I'm livin' in Mr. and Mrs. Zetel's guest house an' I'm not goin' back down to the hood."

"You nevah comin' back?"

"I'ont know, Socco. You know when I got shot like that it made me scared."

"But it was a mistake an' the boy that shot you is dead himself."

"But that's just it," Darryl said. He stopped walking and gazed at his mentor.

"What's it?"

"I mean if somebody shot me 'cause I did sumpin' to him then that would make sense. I could protect myself or at least I'd know why. But he shot me for no reason an' then he got shot for no real reason. I even think about walkin' around down there and I get scared."

Socrates lowered himself down onto the sand into a half-lotus position. Darryl fell to his knees, head bowed like a penitent glowering at gravity.

"You mad?" he asked.

"Naw."

"Then why you stop?"

"'Cause you knocked me on my butt, that's why?"

"Huh?"

"You, Darryl. It's like Tim Hollow killed the boy and the man rose up out the dead body. Before Hollah took aim you was like a plastic bag in the wind, just floatin' any which way the breeze blow. But now you like some kinda goddamn hero."

"Hero? For runnin'?"

"That's right. You know they ain't one young man in thousand got the courage to leave all he know an' go out on his own like you. Ain't one in ten thousand really do it. You right, Darryl. What happened to you is crazy. Only thing crazier is if you see it happen an' you don't do nuthin' 'bout it.

"Big man, almost twice your size, come up outta nowhere an' shoot you with goddamn elephant gun and then when somebody come to you and say, 'oh, I made a mistake.' That is crazy."

"That's what I'm talkin' 'bout," Darryl responded.

"I accept everything you say, son, but I want you to do me a favor."

Darryl smiled at the appellation *son*.

"What's that?" he asked.

"I want you to come down wit' Chaim on Thursday nights. You be safe at the Big Nickel and you can either stay the night or go back with him. We don't need you to risk your life, brother, but we need you to be there and help us understand."

"Okay," Darryl said quickly, decisively.

The sun was beating down on them but a small breeze cooled their dark skins. The boy's nostrils opened wide to breathe in the salt air and the man scowled.

"What's wrong?" Darryl asked.

"What I said is true but it ain't the whole truth."

"What is?"

"I want you there for me, Darryl."

"Like how?"

"I wouldn't be there if it wasn't for you, boy. I'd still be in the streets collectin' bottles or more likely I'd be in jail for killin' some fool think he could mess wit' a man in the street.

"I got things to do, Darryl, an' if I see you at the table that's gonna make it a lot easier."

2.

Chaim and Darryl showed up early that Thursday night. The elderly Jew preceded the boy into the room. He smiled at Socrates and shook his hand.

"Chaim," Socrates said. "Darryl."

"Hey," the boy said. He smiled.

"Hello, men," Billy Psalms called from the kitchen door.

"What's for dinner, Mr. Psalms?" Chaim asked.

"Pasta and meatballs with stuffed eggplant and baked milk for desert," the gambler said loudly.

"Baked milk?" Darryl said in disgust.

"Taste so good you be beggin' for seconds 'fore the night is through."

Everyone greeted Darryl gladly. It was the first time he'd come to a meeting since he'd been shot down in the street. And though every one of the Big Table thinkers had been to his bedside it was different to see him at the meeting itself.

"We need youngbloods like you here," Mustafa Ali told him. "Without young men there won't be a future."

"And young women," Cassie Wheaton interjected. "Ain't no young men wit'out young women."

Mustafa didn't reply. He just took a deep bow and came up with his right hand flat against his chest.

There were twenty-one members at the table by 8:00, all but two of the original Thinkers plus two young gay men, partners they called themselves, one white and the other black, both named Robert. There was also a young political activist named Kelly Beardsley. He had formed a lunch program that involved a cart taking sandwiches from the Big Nickel window and distributing them among the homeless that could not or would not come out for food.

The two members that had not come were Marianne Lodz, the singer, and her sometime companion, Socrates' lover and soon to be the mother of his child—Luna Barnet.

For the past ten days, ever since Socrates had asked Luna to marry him, she had been staying with Marianne. She said this was because the singer was going through a rough breakup with a movie star boyfriend and needed the company.

It was Luna's absence from that night's meeting that caused Socrates to let go of her in his mind. With Darryl in West Los Angeles and Luna away for more than a week Socrates felt lonely for the first time since he was a very small boy. That time his mother left him at an illegal daycare center for nine days while she went to Detroit to stay with her auntie. He'd cried for three days and then his Aunt Bellandra came to take him in.

"Cryin' won't bring her back, child," Bellandra said on his second day with her. "An' cryin' won't keep her out of your heart neither."

That was when he stopped crying and stopped being a child. He wasn't a man, not nearly, but he would never cry for his mother again. After she returned they lived in the same house until he drifted away. They saw each other from time to time until he was convicted of double homicide and rape. They didn't communicate after he was sentenced.

He'd dropped Luna the same way he'd dropped his mother, or maybe in the way his mother had never held on to him. Ten days gone and they hadn't even talked on the phone. That, in Socrates' mind, was forever. He stopped taking her calls.

THE MEETING STARTED, as usual, with a few words before the meal. Antonio Peron rose to speak his words to the assembly.

"I have only missed one meeting since the first day Mr. Fortlow asked me here. That was because my brother was killed in Compton and I had to make the arrangements. But you all came to the funeral and . . ." he stopped for a moment. "I met the woman I love here. And my words for you this evening are that Cassie and I would like to be married on a Thursday, in this room with you. We want Socrates to be our justice of the peace."

Everyone rose to applaud and endorse Antonio.

While he clapped and smiled Socrates saw Marianne and Luna walk past his right to seats at the far end. Luna tried to catch her lover's eye but he looked away.

"Let me propose a toast to Tony, one of the best men I evah met," Billy Psalms said, raising his Dixie Cup of Blue Angel red wine, "and to Cassie Wheaton who never once let me get away with a thing."

The people all raised their cups and glasses and mugs in toast.

Congratulations were heaped upon the couple and there was a general hubbub that was unusual for the blessing-like First Words.

Socrates was looking at Cassie and she was smiling at him and neither of them, nor any others at first, noticed that Luna Barnet had gotten to her feet.

Slowly a silence settled on the slight, dark, lovely and six months pregnant woman. She stood erect but her head was hanging down. There was an entire story in the way she was standing so in a few minutes the celebratory mood had shrunk down to profound silence.

When everyone was quiet and looking at Luna she lifted her head in pain and looked at the host.

"I know that it's common for just one person to say first words, Mr. Fortlow," she said. "But I have something important to say and I hope you will let me speak."

Socrates was thinking that it was improper to make such a request. He wanted to say that anything important could wait for the general meeting, but looking into her eyes he knew that he was being petty and cold and so he nodded.

"You all know who I am," she said, "but you probably don't know me too well. I haven't said much to many of you and I've never talked out at your conversations. I listened and learned too but I nevah spoke because that's not how I learned to be."

Luna looked around at the various faces, receiving nods and smiles.

"The only reason I come here the first night," she continued, "was because Marianne wanted me to. And from then on," she said, looking down at the battered Big Table, "I kept comin' back because I couldn't keep my eyes off Socrates."

The lovers looked at each other, flanked by two lines of faces that were trying to figure out where this talk was headed.

"I nevah felt like I had anything to say to you people. I ain't no thinker, I don't have no deep thoughts. I know how to survive in these streets but that kinda knowledge ain't made for public conversation."

Leanne Northford hummed and said, "Amen, child."

Luna took a deep breath.

"But I have fount somethin' that I need to say to y'all," Luna said. She seemed to be struggling with her words as if they were too large for her mouth. "I got mad at Socrates awhile ago. It wasn't nuthin'. I was just mad like I get sometime. Just mad. And he didn't pay no attention, he just went right on doin' what he was doin' like he should'a done."

A few laughs rose from the throats of those that had come to know the hard-minded felon.

"But later on that day he called me and I got all spiteful and didn't answer and didn't call back. And then, must be two weeks later, Billy told me in passin' that they had been arrested and dragged off to jail and that he called me wit' his one call from jail. And there I was . . . a black woman lettin' down her man."

Socrates experienced a pain in his body that he couldn't quite isolate. It might have been in his chest or his jaw or his head. He winced and wished that he could get away from that room with its bright lights and bright eyes.

". . . a man who would die for me," Luna said, "a man like all these other men be dyin' a little each day an' I couldn't pick up the fuckin' phone." Luna looked out among the assembly and they all stared back at her.

Socrates rubbed four powerful fingers against his chest and wondered if he was dying.

"Here's a man willin' to cross a mountain of pain to be wit' me," Luna said, "an' here I cain't answer the fuckin' phone."

She didn't cry or shake but there was a tremble in her voice.

No one spoke.

Two minutes had gone by when finally Wan Tai rose to his feet and said, "I think we've done our work tonight, brothers and sisters of the Big Table. Why don't we take this home with us and think about it."

3.

Everyone left except Marianne Lodz and Luna Barnet. Darryl had gone back to Cheviot Hills with Chaim, and even Billy Psalms, who had taken to staying after the meeting to discuss the talk with Socrates, had driven off in his red Cadillac.

Socrates went up to his office/bedroom and closed the door. He sat there in his favorite chair watching the wall and pressing the thick fingers of his right hand alternately against his jaw-hinge and chest.

The knock was soft, almost contrite.

"Yeah?"

"It's me," Marianne Lodz said through the door.

Socrates smiled in spite of his pain because if it had been Luna he would have sent her away, told her that he wouldn't be embarrassed into taking her back into his heart. But Marianne was another case.

"Come on in."

The door opened and the light-skinned singer entered.

She went to the chair across from the bed and sat on the very edge.

There they sat, she watching him while he regarded the floor at their feet.

He was sullen and aching and she was the light breathing of a world that feared his mood.

"You have to take her back, Mr. Fortlow," she said after a very long time. "She's gonna be the mother of your child and she didn't know you were under arrest."

"That's not what this is about," he said, his gaze still earthward. "I don't expect nobody to come get me outta jail. Either I get out on my own or I don't. I ain't called her to help me."

"Then why?"

Socrates looked up and Marianne leaned back out of reflex.

"She ain't called me in ten days, more. That hurt me more than I could tell you."

"She was with me."

"I don't care where she was. I care where she wasn't. She didn't call me. And when I asked her to marry me she didn't even have the decency to say no. She just went away. Okay, okay fine. I don't need her. I been on my own for longer than anybody you know. My own mother wouldn't love me so I can just go on doin' what I been doin'. I don't need her or anybody."

There was fear in the young singer. Socrates' voice had gotten low and deadly. She heard the danger in a register below the deepest bass.

"You got to get over it," she said, her voice quavering slightly. "Luna couldn't help what she did any more than how you felt about it. You got to forgive her."

"Why?"

"Because that child you made will not survive without the both of you. Alone you both too hard and too sensitive. That baby need the mother to be held up by the father and the father to be held up by his wife."

At first Socrates heard what she'd said without understanding. It was just a bunch of words but they seemed to sink into his skin. *Child* and *baby, mother* and *father, held up*. Then the ideas came into being as if they were somehow his own thoughts.

They transformed into his past and experiences; his mother telling her boyfriend Beaumont that Socrates would not be going on vacation with them, Bellandra making him little cupcakes to cut the pain.

"Well?" little Marianne Lodz asked bravely.

"Take her home wit' you, Marianne," he said. "Tell her that I will be at your place at noon tomorrow. Straight up noon and I won't be late. If she wanna see me then she'll be there."

"Don't you wanna go down and tell her yourself?"

"No, baby. Uh-uh. You done your job. Take her home. Tell her what I said."

"You got my address?"

"It's in our mailing list. I know how the buses work."

"I could send a car to get you."

"I move under my own power."

Lodz hesitated a moment and then she stood.

"You know that we all love you," she said, looking down.

"You keep on talkin' an I'ma drop dead right here on the floor."

AT 11:58 THE NEXT DAY Socrates Fortlow walked up to the concierge desk at the Pacific Rim Condominiums on Wilshire Boulevard in Westwood. It took him two and a half hours on three buses but he only had to walk five blocks to get there. On the way he met a woman whose husband had beaten her and she didn't know what to do.

"He drag me out in the yard an' slap me in front'a ev'rybody but when the police got there I told 'em that it wasn't nuthin' but a argument," she said from behind big sunglasses.

Socrates hadn't invited her confession nor did he ask her why her husband had done what he had done or why she hadn't pressed charges. He knew that there were no sensible reasons behind his violence or her protection. He didn't ask her why she changed seats to sit next to him when the Asian woman who had occupied that seat had gotten off the bus. She knew who he was, many people did. At least she knew his face and name. Very few people outside of the Thinkers' table really knew what Socrates stood for or what he would do and what he wouldn't.

"He beat me all the time but I cain't fight back an' I cain't leave," the nameless and bruised black woman said.

Socrates regarded her but did not speak.

The bus stopped, its brakes hissing and complaining in a high whine. Socrates wanted to get out and wait for another bus but that would have made him late for his appointment and he prided himself on being a man of his word.

"Can you help me, Mr. Fortlow?"

He couldn't make out her age because of the scarf wrapped around her head and the dark-lensed sunglasses. Maybe she was twenty-five, maybe thirty.

"No," he said thickly.

"What?"

"I said no."

"But what am I gonna do?"

"There's only three choices," he said.

"Wha?"

"Either you wait till he sleep and you kill him, or you let him keep on beatin' on you till one day you dead, or you transfer from this bus to the bus station downtown and go back home to your mama or daddy and try to get some knowledge 'bout why you let a man beat on you like that."

The woman took off her glasses to get a better look at the man talking to her. She was younger than he thought, not yet twenty. Her right eye was swollen and raw, barely open at all.

"What kinda help is that?" she asked.

"It's not help, sugah, it's the truth. Either you leave him or one'a you be dead. That's all there is to it."

"Cain't you people take me in an' protect me?"

"No."

The bus was slowing to a stop.

"What's wrong with me?" she asked, anger thrumming under her words.

"You didn't press charges. You didn't leave a man treat you like a punchin' bag."

The brakes began their perennial complaint. The bus lurched forward on its chassis and Socrates said, "This my stop."

"You just gonna leave me like this?" she asked.

"It's the way I found ya. Only way you change is if you do what you blamin' me for."

"MAY I HELP YOU?" the concierge asked.

A young black man sitting on a chair in the sun-drenched lobby raised his head.

"Luna Barnet in Marianne Lodz's place," Socrates said.

The young man rose to his feet in Socrates' peripheral vision.

The concierge, who was wan and white and thin, smiled, his young face looking like an unspoken lie. He was wasting time, waiting for the muscular man to make it to the marble podium.

"Hey," the black youth said.

Socrates turned to regard him. His strength was from exercise with weights. On his throat there were four dark blue Chinese characters tattooed in a vertical row.

"Hey," Socrates replied, pretending that the young man was speaking in greeting.

"What the fuck you want, man?" The tattooed youth's right hand lifted up to his chest.

"Touch me and your mama will bury you this weekend," Socrates said, replying to the gesture not the words.

The young man threw a punch with all the slowness of a body builder. Easily Socrates grabbed his wrist and with one downward thrust forced the young man to his knees.

"This ain't no play yard, baby," the ex-con told the boy. "Just 'cause you in this white boy's neighborhood don't mean you cain't get killed just the same."

Socrates released his grip and the young man bounded to his feet. He took half a step back, looking for a way to regain his pride.

"She's coming down," the concierge said, his voice hysterical and high. "Miss Barnet knows him, Craig."

Craig's eyes opened wide in rage and fear.

Socrates' smile turned into a sneer.

"What you laughin' at, man?"

Socrates waited a moment before saying, "I cain't smile up in here? You gonna tell me what to do wit' my face?"

"Ain't no niggah gonna laugh at me, man," Craig said with wild courage.

"I ain't laughin' at you. I ain't laughin' at all. I just come up in here an' ask a man to ring a numbah. If they don't wanna see me then they don't have to."

"I kick yo' ass mothahfuckah," Craig warned.

Again Socrates paused. He pretended to be watching the youth's face but really he was aware of the boy's hands. If he reached for something it would be his last grab.

"Hey, baby," Luna said from some unseen corner.

"Hey," Socrates replied, not taking his eyes from the young, tattooed black man.

"It's okay, Craig," Luna said as she came into sight. "This is one'a Marianne's best friends."

Craig began to shiver, which made Socrates laugh audibly.

"What you laughin' at, man?" Craig shouted, aggressive fear lacing his words.

"Nuthin'."

"Craig," Luna said. "Craig, do you hear me?"

"What?"

"Marianne want you to go get Tina and bring her to the recordin' studio. She need her makeup."

The powerful young man slowly shifted out of his deep concentration on Socrates.

"You should show some respect, brothah," he said after a long moment of introspection.

When he turned to go Socrates stifled a grunt. Luna put her hand on his forearm.

"Let's go upstairs, Baby," she said.

MARIANNE LODZ'S APARTMENT was the penthouse of the Pacific Rim Condominiums. There were windows on all sides of the split-level living room and a brilliant skylight in the ceiling. Through sliding glass doors she had a sundeck that was almost as large as the lot on which the Big Nickel stood. There were chaise-lounges and a round table with a huge red umbrella opened to shade it.

Luna led Socrates to the table and he sat.

"You thirsty?"

"After almost three hours on the bus you better believe I am."

While she went into the apartment he looked out over the green Westside of Los Angeles. There were hills and beyond them mountains. This was a paradise compared to where he came from. It was no surprise that Darryl wanted to stay in this part of town.

"Marianne's cook made this lemonade last night," Luna said as she placed a large and frosty tumbler before him.

"Fresh?"

"I think so."

She wore short red pants that opened wide just below the knee and a yellow T-shirt. Her belly was round but not that large and the rest of her was as slim as ever.

"What you lookin' at?" she said.

"You never dress like that down at my place."

"Your place?"

"Yeah. My place or the Big Nickel neither."

"Ain't it our place no more?"

"Luna, you haven't called me in a week and a half. You said that you was wit' Marianne and that was it."

"You could'a called me."

"I stopped callin' you after Frisco with Billy."

They were both silent for a spate of minutes. Socrates sipped his lemonade, which was delicious, and watched helicopters as they patrolled the city like huge mosquitoes sniffing for fresh blood.

"What if I say that I won't never do that again?" Luna said, her eyes squinting against the sun.

Socrates turned his palms upward and gazed at the light on them. Someone had once told him that sunlight had weight like any other thing in the universe but that it would take the sun shining on a whole city block to make up something he could feel pressing down; and even then it wouldn't be heavy.

Then he remembered Craig and how he had sneered at the boy and the nameless woman on the bus.

"What's wrong, Baby?" Luna asked.

"What? Why?"

"You look sad."

A story that his Aunt Bellandra had told him came into his mind. It was a tale about an old man, burned black by the sun because every day it was his job to carry the huge ball of fire from the east to the west, "rain or shine."

He considered rushing to the edge of the twenty-story patio and leaping off the side. Suicide was a common companion to the lifelong prisoner.

"What is it?" Luna asked, seeing something of his mood. She pulled her chair next to his.

"I met a woman on the bus told me that her husband beat her."

"Uh-huh."

"I was cold to her. I told her that she needed to move away from him."

"That's the truth you told her, baby."

"And I threw Craig down on his knees for tryin' to do what he thought was right."

"So?"

"We ain't supposed to treat people like that."

Luna watched his face a minute and then took two of his fingers in her hand.

"What else can you do sometimes?" she asked gently enough to surprise him.

"We need to ask each other that question every day, Luna. Even if it take all week to understand we got to ask ourselves that and we got to see."

Luna kissed him on the lips and leaned back to gauge the effect.

"You could'a told Craig that you was a friend'a Marianne's and that you had a meetin' wit' me," she suggested.

"And I could have taken that woman's hand and said what I said in a gentle voice. I could have taken her for a coffee and explained what I said."

"And I should have called you . . ."

DETAILS

1.

"This is our community," Leanne Northford said at what should have been the midway point of the next week's Thursday night Thinkers' Meeting. "We are colored people and we need to think like that."

She was responding to a comment made by "White Robert" the partner of "Black Robert."

White Robert had said, "It's time to move out from the oppression that all people, both black and white, put on themselves. When Robert and I look out of our window in Venice we see every color and it doesn't make any difference who we are."

"Excuse me," Socrates said before Ron Zeal could jump into the conversation. "But I would like to table this discussion for next Thursday."

"Why?" Black Robert asked. He was a handsome young man who wore black pants and a rose colored T-shirt.

"I want every Negro member of this meeting to come back here tomorrow night at seven," Socrates replied. "We need to have a conversation among ourselves before we go on with this talk."

"That's racist," Minna Pope, a red-headed Irish girl from Bellflower said. "I thought this meeting is for all of us."

"That's two things you said, Miss Pope," Socrates replied in his mildest tone. "To answer the second I'll tell ya that I want to have the special meetin' Friday so it won't be this meeting.

"The first thing, the one about racism, is that, yes, it is racist. We are all racists here. You, me, the baby inside'a Luna and the one on Cassie's lap. In this country you born in racism, bathed in it every day of your life. But the reason I wanna meet with my black brothers and sisters is to go ovah how we talkin' here in this room on this night. We sayin' things that we never think about, not really. I wanna go ovah that so that at least all the racists be talkin' the same language."

"I don't understand what you're saying," Minna said.

"But I ask you to trust me anyway," Socrates countered. "I wouldn't be doing for this if I didn't think it was right and if I'm wrong I will apologize."

"WHAT'S THIS ALL ABOUT, Socco?" Billy Psalms asked him after the Thinkers went home.

This was the second week in a row that the meeting was cut short. Ron Zeal and Mustafa Ali complained audibly while others simply looked confused.

"We not just a bunch'a black people on wood crates in the alley, William," Socrates said. "We got a responsibility in here."

"What kinda responsibility?"

"To see open and clear, to make a mark in the world that don't have to be a black mark."

Psalms frowned at his mentor but he did not argue. He just hunched his shoulders and said, "Okay, Brothah. You lead and I'll follah. At least as long as I can."

"I ain't no leader," Socrates complained.

"Oh is that so? Now you sound like a real convict."

"What's that supposed to mean?"

"I ain't nevah been in prison," Billy said, showing his dark smile, "but everybody I evah met in jail, on the way to trial, always said that they was innocent. It's like the man whose wife come home an' find him in bed with another woman, humpin' away."

"What he say?" Socrates asked.

"He look his bride right in the eye an' say, 'Baby, the lights was out an' I thought it was you.'"

Socrates' laugh started out mild but before Billy went out of the door his chuckling had turned into a roar.

AT HOME THAT NIGHT the big man lay next to Luna stroking her tight belly with his killer's hand.

"What you thinkin' 'bout, Baby?" she asked, snagging one of his restless fingers.

"My people."

"Black people?"

"Them . . . and the others too."

"What others?"

"Luna?"

"Uh-huh?"

"Do you love me, Baby?"

"It hurt me how much I love you, Daddy," she said. "I mean I feel it so deep that it's way down in the ground under my feet. Like a, like a earthquake."

"But I'm right here," he said.

She tugged at his fingers until his hand was over her breast.

"That's where you is," she said.

"But what if you got mad at me again?"

"That ain't nuthin' an' I done told you, I will never be deaf to you again."

"But what if I said somethin' to you that you didn't like?"

"Like what?"

"I don't know . . . like you smelled bad or sumpin'."

"Do I smell bad?" she asked.

"No."

"But if I did would you tell me?"

"I guess."

"If you did then I'd feel bad for a minute and then I'd get in the bathtub an' have you wash me where it smell."

She sat up and kissed his lips.

"You wanna make sure our baby got a nice broad nose, Mr. Fortlow?"

He reached out and turned off the lamp.

"What you do that for?" she asked.

"So if my wife come in I could tell her it was dark."

2.

Almost every black member of the Thursday night Thinkers had come. Billy and Ron and Cassie Wheaton and Darryl, Black Robert and Leanne Northford and Mustafa Ali, the political activist Kelly Beardsley, and a dozen others. Black men and black women filled out the ranks of the Big Table that Friday night.

Socrates realized, looking out on the congregation, how many had come. They were there for him and here he didn't even have one word planned.

Billy couldn't cook because of the food line but he passed out sandwiches and placed bottles of wine along the middle of the table.

Luna was sitting in Chaim Zetel's chair next to Socrates. People were talking softly and eating the Big Nickel's free food.

There were no First Words that evening; this wasn't the regular Thinkers' Meeting. Socrates just stood up at the given time and started speaking. It was as if he were continuing with a conversation that the group had been having for many long days and sleepless nights.

"Are we all agreed that we are black men and women sitting at this table?" Socrates asked.

"'Course we all black, Socco," James Tippton, the social worker from the Bay Area said. "You said you only wanted black people."

"That's what I said, Jimmy, but that don't mean we, all of us here, is black. Maybe some people passin'. Maybe there's spies here among us."

"I know you're talking about me, Socrates," Weldon Marshal said. He was sitting three-quarters of the way down the left side of the table. A very light skinned man, he had the sour, uncomfortable look of someone who was expecting an insult.

"No, Weedy," Socrates replied, using Marshal's nickname. "I ain't speakin' to no one person. I just wanna talk about bein' black."

"Why?" Mustafa asked. "We all black. We all know it. Why I wanna sit around and talk 'bout sumpin' I've known since the day I was born?"

"So you think we all black men and women in this room?"

"Yeah."

"Does everybody else here agree?" Socrates asked, his eyes moving from one person to the next.

"Not everybody got black skin can call himself a brother," Ron Zeal said.

"What's the difference between a brother and a black man?" Socrates asked.

"Him," Ron Zeal said, gesturing his head toward Black Robert.

"Bob? What about him?"

"He's a faggot," Zeal said on a sneer. "And a punk ain't no man. He might be a black woman if he want."

An odd wave of unspoken response went through the room. Some turned away from looking at either Ron or Bob, some seemed as if they wanted to nod in agreement. Darryl turned to Socrates and Socrates glanced at Bob.

"I wasn't going to say anything," Black Robert, whose real name was Carter Jones, said, "but as long as we're talking here I don't think that Mr. Zeal qualifies as being black."

"You better watch yourself, punk," Ron threatened.

"Don't worry, Bob," Socrates said. "Ronnie ain't gonna do nuthin'. Tell us why you don't think he's a black man."

"Because he preys on black men," Robert said, fear reverberating from his chest. "He's a gangbanger that made his living off of drugs and violence. He's on trial right now for the deaths of those poor boys. He's been in prison. A lion is not a lamb and if black women and men are victims of men like Zeal then how can he be one of us?"

"So am I a black man?" Socrates asked.

Robert looked at the head of the table but he didn't speak.

"That's right, faggot," Ron said, his upper lip and right nostril flaring.

"Oh come on now, Ron," Socrates said in an avuncular manner. "You an' me been in the joint. We know what men be doin' up in there. Either you somebody's punk or they yours."

"Why the hell we here, Socco?" Ron said in retaliation. "Why we here?"

"The first time you sat in that very seat," Socrates answered, "you told me that you was mad that there was other than just black people here. Now you mad that they all black?"

"You just tryin' to make us mad," Ron said. "You playin'."

"No, Brother Ron, I ain't playin' wit' you. Not even a little bit.

But I do have somethin' to say. Last night Leanne ovah there started talkin' 'bout colored people and how we should think and how we should be actin'. But you know there's all kindsa colored people. There's Wan Tai and Antonio Peron and even Chaim Zetel—"

"Chaim's a white man," Mustafa Ali said.

"I grant ya he look like one," Socrates said. "But when they killed his people in Germany they killed 'em because they wasn't white like all the rest."

"What do we care what the Germans did?" Cassie Wheaton asked then.

"I'm just sayin', Cassie," Socrates said in a slow measured voice. "There's all kindsa races and colors. Everybody in that room was a colored person so what Leanne was about to talk about was somethin' that we don't even understand . . . but we think we do."

"So you even gonna call that white girl, Minna Pope, colored?" Luna asked in a rare show of interest in this world of the Table.

"She Irish," Socrates answered.

"Irish is white as you could get," Luna replied.

Billy Psalms was smiling then, his teeth showing.

"What you grinnin' at gambler?" Leanne Northford said.

"Socco reminded me of sumpin'," Psalms said.

"What's that?"

"I used to go down to the races with a guy named Shorty, he was six foot five," Billy said in such a way that brought smiles to many of the hardening faces of the group. "Shorty was a Swedish dude loved to bet the longshot. He liked boxing too. He told me one time that any race that boxed was not white."

"That's just some shit there," Mustafa said. "One time all the boxers was white boys."

"The Jews," Billy said, nodding in agreement. "The Irish and Italians. They look white to us but they wasn't treated like whites by everybody else. The real whites would spit on those Irish boys and the Jews."

"But they white to us," William George, a butcher for a Southern California supermarket chain, said.

"Georgie got it there," Socrates said then. "Here we was about to start talkin' 'bout colored people an' we don't even know what that mean. The only thing I figure we could talk about is bein' black but you know it don't seem to me that we even agree on what that is."

"No we don't," a voice replied in an emotional wavering tone.

It was Samson Fell, a carpenter who worked for Antonio Peron on his various charitable works. Samson was five nine and well proportioned. His skin was black like charcoal and his features pronounced. His lips were thick and red where they met and his nose was like a shield across the middle of his face. His hair was nappy and his head had a sidewise oval shape to it.

Samson was staring at Socrates. There was anger, maybe even violence in that look.

"Yes, Brother Fell?" the ex-con asked in a serious tone, "are we missin' somethin'?"

"I'm the only black man in *this* room," Fell said. "The rest'a you is just mulattoes and half-breeds ashamed'a where you come from."

"The fuck you say." That was Ron Zeal.

"I ain't no man's mulatto," Weldon Marshal said loudly. He stood up.

"Sit down, Weedy," Socrates commanded. "This is just a talk, that's all. Samson has a right to speak."

"But he cain't insult us like that," Reena Thorn, a young woman from Compton, said.

"What color are you, girl?" Samson asked.

"I'm a woman," she replied.

"What color woman?"

All eyes turned to Reena. She was a plain young woman, somewhere in her thirties. Her skin was nut brown, neither deep or light. Her eyes were large and her thick hair straightened.

"Brown I guess," she said. "But that don't make you more black then me."

"But I am blacker. People all up these streets call me the dark-skinned one. Any room I'm in they say that. If I straightened my hair like you, woman, I'd look like a fool. But you do it 'cause there's a lotta white in you and your hair can be any which way. I'm only one way. I don't have good hair, they call me liver lips and real niggah an' most women, so-called black women, don't even give me a second look."

Reena averted her gaze then.

Samson stood up.

"You know what I am, Socrates?"

"No, brother. What?"

"I'm the bad dream that all the othah niggahs tryin' to wake up from. I'm Africa. I'm slavery. I'm what they think is stupid and ugly and just plain wrong. I am the conscience of guilty men and women. They see me and they remember where they come from. They remember but they wanna forget."

"I don't feel like that, like you say," Cassie Wheaton said.

"That's not what this is about, Ms. Wheaton," Billy Psalms said. "It's what Samson Fell feel an' he the only one among us live in that skin. Maybe he's too sensitive but how many times you hear women talkin' 'bout good hair and niggah lips? How many times do we say dark-skinned? And you got to admit this brothah heah look like Africa, deep Africa, a long time ago Africa that come ovah on the slave ships in chains."

Billy's little speech sat Samson back in his chair. The people in that room looked around at each other, wondering about the gambler's words.

"And so I ask you again," Socrates said. "Are we agreed that we are all black people here in this room?"

"That's not the right question," Deacon Saunders said, speaking softly but still making himself heard.

SAUNDERS' GIVEN NAME was Deacon but he was also a real deacon at Third Baptist of the Burning Bush on Avalon. Twice Saunders had questioned the structure of the Thursday night meetings. He thought that someone other than Socrates should lead the meetings and the direction of the Big Nickel in general.

"I mean no disrespect," he'd said to the assembled Thinkers, "but Mr. Fortlow here has come from our lowest place in society. In order for us to rise up we must be led by the best educated and high-minded."

The only thing that kept Deacon from being shouted down was Socrates, the only thing that kept Saunders from being excluded from the Table was Socrates backed up by Billy Psalms.

The good deacon tried once more to restructure the leadership but no one else could imagine the Nickel without its leader. They didn't care about Socrates' past or his crimes, his gruff ways or the fact that he was a target of the police.

Socrates himself appreciated Saunders and his attempts at a coup. Every time the deacon spoke up the people of the table expressed their acceptance and love of the ex-convict. Because of this Socrates had developed a fondness for his self-ordained opponent.

And so when Saunders spoke up Socrates smiled. He knew that this challenge would be against not only what Socrates was saying but who he was. This, he believed, was important for the spiritual health of the Big Nickel.

"What's that you say, Brother Saunders?" Socrates asked.

"I said, Brother Fortlow," the deacon replied, "that you are asking the wrong question. Of course there are differences among African-Americans. Some are dark or light, gay or straight, some are even Republicans but that does not mean that we don't recognize an African-American when we see one.

"It's a good point you bring up about Hispanics and Jews and maybe even the Irish and Italians, but the Negro people are one people even if we have many differing kinds and colors."

Saunders was in his fifties and had a degree from UCLA. His skin was a bright, highly polished and then oiled, brown. But for all of his qualifications it was clear that this particular congregation was not impressed by his fine words or grammar.

"I don't know, Deacon," Socrates responded. "I ain't never been to Africa and because of my criminal past I doubt if the government will grant me a passport but I will say this—I don't believe that our people back in Africa ever called themselves one race. I think they had families, tribes, and nations that defined them as men and women.

"And I'll go you one further—if you get down to the nub in any man or woman in this room they don't think about themselves as black people."

"What?" the deacon said, looking around at the faces in the room as if this was the proof of Socrates' inability to lead them.

"What do you see when you look in the mirror, Mr. Saunders?"

For a moment the deacon was without words, the question obviously seeming to him like it had come from nowhere.

"What I mean to say," Socrates continued, "is do you see a black man in the reflection or is the first thing you think, 'that's me in the glass'? There ain't no black men and women, no African-Americans in this room, there's just people with names and ages and features. Samson might think he's dark or Weedy might think he's light but somebody else might see their mother's features in theirs or maybe they look in their own eyes and remember somethin' that they done thought or heard. Irish and Jewish people and the minister of your own church think the same thing.

"You use the word Hispanic but my friend Vasquez down at the corner store says that he's a Mexican. He don't want you to think he's from Salvador or the Dominican Republic.

"Samson over there thinks that it's other black people keep him out of the world. Weedy and Bob and even Ronnie there think the same thing from time to time. A lotta times you hear black women talk like the only problem they got is black men and you know there's not a black man anywhere don't think that about our women.

"We spend way too much time thinkin' 'bout hair and color and what we look like to who. But you know and I know that the black man, the man they want us to be, is just a cage dreamed up by the white man. He the one made up the countries of Africa. He the one brought us here and called us ugly. He the one taught us in school that there was no history for us. He the one put us in chains and then threw us out in the street callin' it freedom."

"But, Socco," Billy Psalms interjected. "If you say that even the Jews and the Irish and the Italians ain't white people then who the ones did all this?"

"What I said was that it was a dream, Billy," Socrates answered. "They dreamed up a cage for you an' me an' Vasquez on the corner and in doin' that they dreamed up a cell for them too. We all locked up away from each other and from ourselves talkin' 'bout I'm this an' he's that. But when we look in the mirror the cell come open. The lock break and all that bullshit go right out the door."

"But," William George said, his voice tentative, even a little frightened, "are you sayin' that there's no such a thing as a white man or a black man?"

"What I'm sayin' is that if someone ax me who I am I tell 'em Socrates Fortlow from Indiana. I don't say a black man from Indiana. George Bush don't say that he's a white man from Texas."

"So you sayin' the reason we here is 'cause of a dream somebody had?" Luna asked.

"Then why are we here together at the Big Nickel?" a woman named Harriet Williams asked.

"That's the right question right there," Socrates said. "And let me tell you people I don't nearly have no answer. I know that deep down I'm just one man for good or for evil. I know that somebody dreamed up a prison for me and as long as I believe in his dream, and my nightmare, I ain't nevah gonna be free. I might feel safe. I might feel like I know my four walls. But I will nevah be free until I wake up."

"So you sayin' that bein' black or believin' you black is like some kinda security blanket?" William George asked.

"Absolutely," Socrates replied. "Bein' black is what explains everything to us—why we get love or don't, why we made it through a bad time or why we don't make enough money, why our chirren is sick or our friends get killed. Good or bad we got a explanation. But you know it was all made up in a dream they havin' right now. An' it's not just us, baby. It's Jews and Arabs, Christians and Buddhists, gays and straights, tall men and short ones. Some of 'em get together and some run away. Black people, it seems like to me, do both. We love ourselves and hate each other, we fight to the death for the number one spot in the white man's dream and then we congratulate the winner."

"But, Socco," Mustafa Ali said. "If there ain't no black people really and they ain't no white people then how come you still usin' them words?"

"Because them words is still usin' me, Brother Ali. They usin' me like a mothahfuckah."

THE DISCUSSION WENT ON until the next morning. At 5:00 A.M. not one person had left the Big Nickel. The argument went round and round and no one claimed to have an answer.

Darryl was asleep in his chair and Antonio Peron had called Cassie Wheaton twice to make sure she and their six-month-old daughter, Remi, were okay.

Luna pulled her chair up next to Socrates and rested her head on his shoulder.

By six everyone had departed except Socrates, Billy, and Luna. She had gone up to bed.

"So Socco it's the next mornin'," Billy said, "an' everyone is tired and none of 'em is black. You either a genius or the devil."

"Shit," Socrates said. "Why cain't I be both?"

3.

In the weeks that followed many of those who attended the unorthodox Friday Night Meeting approached Socrates at odd hours. Samson Fell thanked him.

"For what?" Socrates asked.

"I look like my mother," he said simply. "I been lookin' in the glass for my whole life an' ev'ry time I seen my mother in there but I nevah paid attention. I loved my mother, man, and she loved me sumpin' fierce. And now I know when someone wanna make fun of how I look I know it's just them makin' a mistake."

Whenever someone wanted to talk to Socrates about the meeting on race he took the time. Some were angry, others relieved. But no matter the reaction they all acted differently in the Thursday night meeting. It wasn't that they gave up the terms of their race but, Socrates could see, that there was a struggle not to use their color as a reason or an excuse, a sword or a shield.

For three weeks Deacon Saunders did not attend the Thursday night session. Socrates noticed his nemesis' absence and so one Sunday he headed over to Third Baptist at 2:00 P.M. when the services ended.

He stood out in front of the big double doors of the stone and plaster building at the bottom of the stairs.

There he waited as the members of the congregation passed by eyeing him with both trepidation and curiosity. It was a sunny blue day and hot. Socrates was dressed only in a T-shirt and khaki pants. The fancy clothes of the men and women made him stand out like an escaped convict at a garden party.

"Can I help you?" a young man wearing a lavender jacket and black trousers asked. He was backed up by two other young men in similar uniforms.

The words *Christian soldiers* came into Socrates' mind.

"No, sir," the ex-convict said.

"Then move on," the young man of medium height said.

"I'm on the sidewalk, corporal," Socrates said. "It's a free country and I'm a free man."

"You disturbin' the congregation," the young man told him.

"I'm just standin' here waitin' on a friend."

"What friend?"

"Not you, Brother."

"Hiram," Deacon Saunders said from the top of the stairs.

The young man turned as the church officer approached. Saunders was wearing a white jacket and black trousers, a higher rank among the Baptists.

"This is Socrates Fortlow," Saunders said as he neared. "He's an acquaintance of mine."

The young men moved, almost in unison, shaking off the violence that had been building in their shoulders and arms.

"Brother Fortlow," Saunders said, moving into the space between the men at arms and the felon. "What can I do for you?"

"I was thinkin' that maybe we could grab some coffee."

"Come on up to my office," the deacon offered.

"I had another place in mind."

THERE WAS A RESTAURANT six blocks from Third Baptist. It had been a house but now it was a breakfast café for people in the neighborhood. It was populated by Spanish-speaking brown people and blacks of various hues. The furniture was catch-as-catch-can and there was no name anywhere to be seen.

"Mr. Fortlow," a dark skinned woman with straight black hair hailed as he and Deacon Saunders entered. All the tables that could be seen were occupied by families or couples.

"Hey, Zelda," Socrates said. "You got room for two hungry men?"

"I always got your table, Mr. Fortlow."

The hefty woman led the convicted felon and the officer of the church through the kitchen to a hall that came to a small room with a table that could easily seat six.

"The usual?" she asked Socrates, who nodded. "And what can I get for you, sir?"

"You got waffles?"

"You want fried chicken with that?"

"Um, okay."

After Zelda had gone to get their food Socrates and Deacon Saunders sat with one chair separating them.

"I never knew this place was here," the deacon said.

"Yeah. Zelda told me that she got about two three hundred people know about the place. 'Bout sixty or so come each day. Breakfast is cheap and it's home cookin'."

Saunders nodded with little concern about the words.

"What can I do for you, Socco?"

"Why you stopped comin' to the meetin's?"

"After that last travesty I couldn't see where it would do anybody any good."

"Travesty?"

"Either that or a sham," Saunders said. "Here you are tryin' to tear apart what little community we have and nobody there will listen to reason as long as you're at the head of the table."

"And that reason is you?"

"I'm an educated man, Socco. You can't become a deacon at Third Baptist without at least a BA. I have a Master's Degree in psychology and social work. So when I see an uneducated ex-con pulling the wool over my people's eyes I try to talk reason. But at your house there's no one who will hear me."

"Okay, but where's the travesty, Deacon?"

"You don't really want to know."

"Oh yes I do."

"Two waffles and fried chicken for the man in the suit," Zelda said, coming into the room with two plates in one hand and a platter on the other, "and a glass of grapefruit juice and a hard-boiled egg for Mr. Socrates. A pitcher of water and syrup on the table. Call me if you need anything else."

She moved out of the room before either man could thank her.

"You are tryin' to tear us apart with your unconsidered crack-pot ideas," Saunders said.

"What ideas?"

"All that nonsense about us not being black."

"Nonsense? Do you look down on your kids and say to your-self, 'look at that little black boy and girl'?"

"Of course not. But that's not the point. We have to work to-gether to get out of where we are. And if people like you tear down the one thing we got then we won't have a thing."

"Except ourselves, Brother."

"The white man will squash us one by one."

"He already been doin' that, man. Look at the high schools, gangs, police, and army recruitment offices. We killin' each other, robbin' each other, passin' 'round disease like it was Christmas candy and here you say *he* will squash us."

"I think that your way is worse," Saunders said.

"No you don't. What you think is that you can protect your li'l congregation from people like me. Your wives and your kids and your friends with their degrees. And you know damn well that people comin' to the Nickel lookin' for pride and a way to make their lives bettah."

"They would be better off at our church."

"How they gonna get in? You got yo thugs standin' at the back door keepin' people like me off the street."

"You have your beliefs and I have mine," Saunders said.

Socrates waited a few moments for the churchman to eat a little.

"Why do you care if I don't come to your meetings anyway?" the deacon asked after biting into a chicken thigh.

"You never understood us, Brother," Socrates said in way of answer. "We not like you people settin' rules for everyone in the room. We just askin' questions. We just wonderin' why."

"You don't need me for that."

"'Course we do. I ain't looking for everybody to agree with me or to go out and do as I say. I like you there because you make sure I don't get lazy. And you should want to be there 'cause you think I'm wrong."

"You think I'm wrong," Saunders replied.

"So what if I do? You the man with the degree and the church title."

"But everybody follows you."

"But, Deacon, what if your long ago Christians felt like that about the Romans? What if they were afraid that a little ole lion would get in the way of the Lord?"

"You got a tongue like the Devil, Socrates Fortlow."

"And the Devil, Deacon, is in the details. That's what I'm talkin' 'bout on Thursday nights. Every man, woman, and child in that room has a different part to play. But they all think they the same, at least they talk like that. You might wanna think I'm the devil, Mr. Saunders, you might wanna run from me. But the details, the words we speak, will go on with or without you. You could sit up in that church with your degrees and fancy clothes but the world still goin' on out here, brother. The guns and heroin and prostitutes and all the hatred we can muster."

Socrates drained his glass and put the uncracked egg in his shirt pocket. Then he stood up.

"I expect you to come back an' keep us straight, Deacco. 'Cause you know you cain't save a soul and run away from it at the same time."

AFTER THE
WEDDING

1.

Cassie's and Antonio's daughter, Remi Raphaelita Wheaton-Peron, was born seven months before her parents' wedding at the Big Nickel. She was carried down the aisle by Luna Barnet; the baby alternately crying and cooing while waving her arms. Socrates was the best man and Deacon Saunders presided. There were more than a hundred people in the Thinkers' room. The Big Table had been moved into the backyard. Cassie was smiling while Antonio grinned broadly. There was a room full of presents locked away and a feast made by Billy Psalms was served in the backyard on the odd-shaped table that had been resurrected for the purposes of ghetto philosophy.

The service was short and only a reflection of the civil ceremony held the day before. After that the partiers ate and drank and danced to the music of Marianne Lodz and her small band of musicians.

"What we have here is the first child and the first union born of the Big Nickel," Billy Psalms said in his toast. "We have a beautiful baby girl and she has a real family and a place that has a history even though it's only about a year old."

"We have innocence and forgiveness under one sky," Chaim Zetel said when he lifted his glass. "All of us have been on both sides of the scales. We have done wrong and tried to make things better. And today we have a child and she has parents who love her and they have a community that loves them. I drink to life."

Dozens of toasts were made and congratulations heaped upon the couple. Some wondered quietly at the union of a Mexican carpenter and a black woman lawyer, some worried about the child of such a marriage. But on the whole people were happy and they celebrated into the night as police officers, parked in unmarked cars on the street outside, sat watching and waiting for some opportunity to take action.

But there was no violence, nor were there any complaints about the noise. The police were brought out food and water. The area councilwoman came by to make sure her constituency was well treated.

"You takin' a honeymoon?" Socrates asked Cassie toward the end of the evening.

"We just want to stay home with our baby, Mr. Fortlow. Tony finished building our house in Silverlake and we just want to spend a few weeks alone with our child." She took his left hand and brought it to her lips.

"Thank you," she said.

"For what?"

"I wouldn't have any of this without you. I've been working to create a place like this for years and one day you just wake up, put on those old shoes, and go out and make it. You made this life for me, for all of us, and even if it all falls apart tomorrow at least we've seen that it's possible."

Socrates watched them leave the party in Antonio's old Dodge station wagon. He didn't feel happy like the others. There was something eating at him about the celebration. It made him think about prison; feeling once again what it was like to wake up every day knowing that he didn't have the freedom just to go out and walk, or fall, under his own power.

"THAT WAS SO NICE," Luna said to him late in the night. They were in bed in his garden house about half a mile from the Big Nickel.

"Did you like it?"

"Uh-huh."

"I knew Cassie and Tony would get together from the first night," Socrates said, rubbing her tight belly. "She need a quiet man who's strong too."

"What about us?" Luna said, laying her hand on top of his.

The question brought about a hollowness in Socrates' head and chest. He felt as if there were no inside to him at all. He couldn't even think about thinking about an answer to her simple question.

"Um," he said after a long span of seconds.

Luna sat up and leaned over to kiss his lips.

"You don't have to answer right off, baby," she said. "Just think about it, okay?"

"O-okay," he stuttered, feeling so light that he had to wonder what was holding him down.

2.

At noon the next day Socrates Fortlow walked into the Black Bear Bar, a small, rough place off of Crenshaw. The walls were painted black and the dark brown ceiling was low. Socrates went to a stool at the bar and ordered bourbon with soda—something he hadn't done in years.

The bartender was a youngish black woman with a broad face and wide shoulders. One of her eyes was dead and the other burned brightly as if from fever.

"You that man ain't ya?" she asked when serving his order.

"I'm *a* man."

"No, uh-uh, you that dude with the house where ev'rybody go to meet at."

Socrates downed his drink and said, "One more."

"HEY, SAILOR," a woman said when Socrates was on his seventh drink.

She was young and light-skinned. Maybe he wouldn't have thought she was pretty if there was less alcohol and more sense in his blood.

"Hey."

"You wanna buy me a drink or sumpin'?"

"Sumpin'? Like a sandwich?"

She wore a short dress of shiny golden material, gold rings on at least eight fingers, and three golden necklaces. There were many hoops in her ears and she had on glasses that were tinted a rose color.

When she smiled at his joke he noticed that none of her teeth were edged in gold.

"What?" she asked, seeing something in his gaze.

"You have a nice smile."

"What can I get for you?" the bartender asked.

"She wants a pastrami on rye," Socrates said.

"Sangria please, Dorothy," the girl said.

"What's your name?" Socrates asked.

"Lana."

"Lana what?"

"Just Lana."

Socrates nodded and lifted his drink.

Dorothy brought a tumbler full of red liquid and set it in front of Lana.

"What's your name?" Lana asked after Dorothy left.

"Go away, girl," Socrates said.

"What?"

"Take your party wine and find somebody else to talk to. I'm here to drink."

With that Socrates held up his glass for the bartender and then put his big hands on the oak bar.

He thought about the year since he started the Big Nickel, about Luna and Billy and the others: prostitutes and gang-bangers, church women and the homeless. He was still under the spell of weightlessness. It felt that he was being dragged along like a plastic float marking the place where a fish was fighting somewhere far below. That fish, he thought, was what he was trying to get at, something he needed. But he knew that he would never get down that far.

It seemed as if he'd been dragged along his entire life by one force or another—hunger or incarceration, rage and sometimes despair.

With a gesture he ordered another drink.

In prison they told him when to wake up and when to go to sleep, when to wash his body and what and how much to eat. They would have read his mail if he ever got any. They were his tailor and shoemaker and even told him if he was sick or not.

They could have held him forever but instead they let him go—like a child who tires of a blue balloon and releases it to see how far it rises before the pressure of the atmosphere causes it to explode.

"Marron."

Socrates glanced to his left and saw that the young woman was still there. Or maybe she'd gone away and returned.

"Excuse me?" he asked.

"My last name is Marron. Lana Marron. I'm from Kansas City, Kansas."

Even on that barstool Socrates could see that Lana had curves, nice ones. He felt the breath coming out from his nostrils. It was hot and he was much younger. There was no Big Nickel or Luna or even Darryl. It was many years before and he was that bull in the china shop everyone was always talking about.

"Ain't you gonna say nuthin'?" Lana asked.

Socrates scanned the room then. There were maybe twelve men and women here and there at tables and the bar. They were talking and smiling if they were together. The solitary ones were more somber.

"Somebody after you?" Lana wondered.

"How old are you, Lana Marron?"

"Twenty-seven."

"And what are you doin' here?"

"You know what I'm doin'."

"And why you come back to me after I was so rude?"

"I'ont know. Maybe I felt bad that I didn't say my name."

"It's a nice name," he said. "Sounds like it comes from a good family with a high white porch and lemonade in the summer when the weather get hot."

Something shifted in the young woman's eyes. Socrates noticed this and wondered who he was in those eyes.

"I got a room down the street," she suggested.

"How much?"

"Depends on what you want." She turned so that he could see her legs and body in the sheer garment. When he was silent she said, "I could suck your dick or you could fuck me on my knees."

"That's not what I want."

"I could do anything," she offered.

"What I need is for somebody to hold me down so that I don't just drift off and disappear."

"Huh?"

"Dorothy," Socrates called to the bartender, "could you bring me a pencil and a piece of paper."

She came over with what he had asked for.

He took the scrap and pencil and wrote something and then signed the bottom. This he handed to Lana. She took the paper and read it.

"I don't get it," she said.

"What's it say?"

"IOU two hunnert an' fifty dollahs an' it's signed Sosh-sumpin' Fortlow."

Socrates nodded. He felt his head bobble as if he had just awakened or maybe was about to fall asleep.

"So if I give you this you gonna pay me?"

"Yes."

She offered him the paper and he exchanged it for a roll of bills from his pocket.

"You wanna come wit' me now?"

"No, baby. You go on without me. I'ma sit here and drink."

"You could come wit' me," she said, trying, and almost managing, to sound friendly. "You could spend the night if you ain't got no place to go."

"I thank you for that, Lana. But I don't need company."

"But you need somebody to hold you down."

"Yeah. Yeah I do."

3.

There was a light rain awaiting him when Socrates left the Black Bear Bar. He had fond thoughts of Lana Marron. She had written her phone number down on his IOU and returned it.

He walked for hours in the rain but the whiskey kept him stoked. It was a long while and late at night before he got to the abandoned furniture stores. The space between those two buildings, where he had lived for nearly four years, had been boarded over but he tore down the two-by-fours and shambled into his old makeshift home.

The next door building's electricity still flowed into his old place and there was even a lamp with a live bulb that he could turn on.

The furniture and most of his other belongings were gone. Soot and dust were everywhere but Socrates sat on the damp floor in the dim light and felt like he was home for the first time in years. Not home like his garden house or Bellandra's little place. This was the place that he'd discovered and built with his own hands.

He leaned against the wall feeling heat rise in his body. He'd had fourteen drinks and felt every one of them as he huddled up next to the splintery wall and closed his eyes.

"We all niggahs up in here," Giant George Riley had said on the yard of the Indiana state penitentiary many years before. "Niggahs so stupid they spend ten years in jail ovah a ten dollar robbery. You know a man that dumb deserve what he get."

Nobody argued with Giant George. He was the only man that might have cut down Socrates if he wanted. But Socrates and George were friends in the joint. They watched each other's back and over the young boys that got placed in their cellblock. George was also an organizer. He brought the men together so that they could watch over each other in case some predator wanted to bring one of them down.

"Niggah got to understand what he is an' where he come from," George would say. "Look right in the glass and say what you see. If you can do that ain't no man can contradict you."

In his stupor Socrates listened to the big man and his long lectures. Rain was seeping in and the chill made its way through Socrates' damp clothes. He wasn't awake or asleep, drunk or sober. He understood that much of what he had done and said was because of Giant George's lectures on the yard.

"Guilty or not we all servin' time in this life, Socco," the big man would say. "Ain't no reason for you to punish yourself 'cause you know there's plenty' a people waitin' in line to get in their licks."

WHEN HE WOKE UP the next morning Socrates felt dizzy, unable to rise to his feet. His breathing was labored. His chest hurt but there was no way he would make it back to the street.

He wondered if maybe he should have taken Lana up on her offer. He wondered if he should have asked Luna for her hand.

"You too quiet, Socrates," George said. Socrates wasn't sure if this was a memory. "Laugh a li'l bit, man, make some noise. You all serious an' shit but you know that don't make nuthin' any different."

He slept again and when he woke up he exerted all of his strength to rise. He made it out to the alley and from there to the street. It was daytime but the sun was setting. He was walking, though the feeling in his legs told him that he wouldn't make it far.

At Central and 103rd Street he fell to the sidewalk and rolled into the street. An old woman leaned over him and peered into his face.

"Do I know you, Mister?" she asked.

He said something but neither he nor the woman understood a word.

4.

For a long time Socrates felt as if he was in motion. Like a trunk, he felt, being moved from train to train following some traveler. He woke up at intervals that revealed strange scenes: the top of a van, maybe an ambulance, and a man taking his pulse; a dark room with cool air and colored lights pulsing in the shadows; someone moaning and people talking happily as if no one had called out in pain; someone holding his hand . . .

"You awake, Daddy?" she asked.

Socrates could only open his eyes for a second. When he did he caught a glimpse of Luna in a loose yellow dress that she wore from time to time. The strain of looking exhausted him and he nodded off for what seemed like a moment or two but when he opened his eyes again Luna was wearing a different dress, it was white with large dark blue polka dots over her belly.

"Socrates," she said.

"Hey, baby. How you doin'?"

He took a deep breath and felt sharp pain deep in his chest.

"You got pneumonia," she said as if this was somehow an answer to his question.

"I'm sick?"

"Uh-huh."

"An' this is the hospital?"

"Yeah."

"How long?"

"Three days," she said. "They fount you on the street an' brought you here. You had Cassie's card in your wallet so they called her. She and Tony got me and I been here pretty much the whole time since then."

Socrates reached out with his fingertips to touch her stretched abdomen.

There was a film over his eyes and so he kept blinking.

"You okay, honey?" she asked him.

"You look pretty, Luna."

"Are you okay?"

"I evah tell you about Giant George?"

"Nuh-uh. Who's he?"

"I was in prison with him. He was the strongest man I evah met. Nobody fucked with Giant George."

Luna smiled and Socrates passed out.

When he woke up again she was still there in her polka dots.

"What about George?" she asked.

"He used to tell me that if anything ever happened to any-body that that was a good thing unless that man was killed."

"What if somebody got his arm cut off?" Luna asked.

"Then he could learn how to live even better with just one arm."

"But suppose he didn't learn?"

"It don't mattah that he didn't. It only mattah that he could."

Socrates closed his eyes. He felt Luna kissing his cheek.

When he awoke again she was slumped sideways in the chair next to him napping. He was strong enough now to sit up. This time she awoke to find him watching over her.

"Hi, Daddy," she said.

"Can we get married?" he asked.

"You feelin' like you gonna die or sumpin'?" she asked, suspicion laced through her words.

"More like I lost a arm."

"Could we wait awhile and see?" she asked.

"You scared?"

"My mother and stepfather were married," she said, "an' she would shoot crack in his neck an' watch him fuck my older sister on the couch."

"You got a sister?"

"All I got is you."

"Socco," Billy Psalms said from someplace very far away. "Socco, wake up."

Antonio and Psalms were standing over his hospital bed. There was a wheelchair between them.

"Come on, man, get up," Billy said.

Socrates took a deep breath, noticing that the pain in his chest was gone. He got to a sitting position with his friends' help and then he made it to his feet.

"Sit down, Mr. Fortlow," the ever-courteous Antonio Peron said.

"If I cain't walk on my own, Tony, then you can lay me down in my grave."

Socrates put a hand on Billy's shoulder and followed them out of the partitioned area of a room he shared with three other men.

They walked along a hallway until they got to a huge elevator which they rode for a minute or two. Then they went down another hall to a blue-green door that was partly ajar.

Socrates wasn't surprised to see Luna in the bed with a little brown baby in her arms. Tony helped the big man into the chair at the side of her bed.

"Say hi to your daddy, Bellandra," Luna said.

"What?"

"Bellandra. I named her after your Auntie."

5.

Leanne Northford had Socrates and his new family come stay with her while Luna learned how to care for her newborn and Socrates recovered from his illness.

For three weeks the septuagenarian ex-social worker clucked and watched over the odd little family. Socrates learned how to change diapers and Luna got used to breastfeeding Bellandra. They both would get up in the middle of the night when the baby cried.

"When she gets over twelve pounds she'll be sleepin' through the night," Leanne told them. "Before that her stomach's too small an' get hungry 'bout ev'ry three four hours."

SOCRATES MOVED OUT of his garden home and rented a small house on Ogden from a friend of Deacon Saunders. They moved in and Socrates got Billy to give him driving lessons. He bought an old Pontiac that was lime green and on Sunday afternoons he and Luna would drive down to Santa Monica with Bellandra and sit on a blanket listening to the waves.

HE DIDN'T MISS MANY Thinkers meetings but he was quiet there for a few months, letting others preside over the discussions and arguments. He listened to the frustrations, fears, and fantasies of the men and women who had taken up his cause.

One day, after the meeting was over and everyone else had gone, he took Luna's hand. In the crook of her other arm Bellandra slept with her mouth open and her arms flung wide.

"Can we talk about it today?" he asked.

"We togethah right?" she answered.

"But what about if I get sick again? What if I die? How can I be sure that you taken care of?"

"Then don't die."

"You know what I mean, L."

"How come you was out on that street anyway?" she asked.

"You axed me 'bout us when Tony and Cassie got married. I didn't know what to think so I went to a bar. After that it was rainin' and I went to the place I used to live at."

"That hole in the wall?"

"Uh-huh."

"It must'a been full'a rats an' shit."

"No. There wasn't enough in there for a rat to eat. It was just the place I used to stay."

"How come you went there?"

"Closest place to prison I could think of I guess."

"Is that what you thought about when I said about gettin' married?"

"I guess."

"Then why you still want it?" Luna asked. "How come you ain't happy when I don't answer you?"

"When I was sick I had this idea in my head," he said. "It wasn't a dream or vision but I was asleep or unconscious."

"What idea, baby?"

"It was that I was bein' dragged along like a dead body off to the pyre."

"What's a pyre?"

"A big fire where they burn the dead," he said. "And then it was like I pulled away and got to my feet and said I wasn't gonna be dragged no mo'. An' after that I was free but I was stumblin', stumblin' through life like all that mattered was that I wouldn't be dragged.

"But then I fount the Big Nickel and you set your eye on me . . . I got to marry you, Luna. You the mother of my child."

"Can we wait one year?"

"Why so long?"

"I just wanna wait and see if you still want me aftah a year in the same house with a cryin' baby and the Big Nickel too. I want you to want me for a year and then ast me again."

"That's what you want?"

"Uh-huh."

"And if I wait a year from this day an' ax you again you gonna say yes?"

Luna smiled and then grinned.

"That's a goddamned miracle right there," Socrates said.

"Ain't no miracle," Luna replied, unable to keep the grin from her lips. "It's just a plan, a plan and a promise."

"No, baby. That right there will make a fool like me walk the straight and narrow."

THE TRIAL

1.

"So, Detective Brand," the state prosecutor asked, "what, in your own words, did you find when you entered the building called the Big Nickel?"

The gray haired, brown eyed, olive skinned white man in the witness chair pondered the question for a moment, pretending that he hadn't studied his answer for days.

"The two officers that had been watching the house . . ." Lucius Brand began.

"There were detectives watching the house?" Marlene Quest, the prosecuting attorney, asked.

"Objection, your honor," Mason Tinheart, Socrates' lawyer, complained. "What the police were doing outside the house is not relevant to the case at hand."

"I disagree, Mr. Tinheart," Judge Irene Tanaka said. "It will give the court some understanding of why the police felt that a crime may have been committed. Continue, Detective."

"Thank you, your honor," Brand said. "We have been watching the house called the Big Nickel for over a year."

"And why is that, Detective?" Marlene Quest prodded.

"We monitor the coming and going of many gang-related individuals at this house. We have long suspected that illegal activities have been planned and condoned by Mr. Fortlow."

"Your honor," Mason Tinheart whined.

"The jury will ignore the comment about police suspicions," Tanaka said to the twelve men and women to her left.

This jury was comprised of young and old, black and brown and white, men and women. But as Socrates looked upon them he didn't see his peers. They were from different places across a variety of borders that most of his people could never cross. It wasn't a question of hierarchy, of quality or even comparison. It was simply that they weren't colleagues at work or war. These people, Socrates thought, could judge him but they could never understand who he was.

"And so," Quest continued, "what did you find at the house?"

"Mr. Fortlow was sitting on the stairs that led to the second floor. He told us that we would find the victim in the second floor hallway."

"And did you?" the prosecutor asked.

Marlene Quest was a beautiful, Germanic woman, her short blonde hair set like seashells around her heart-shaped face. The red of her lips was a memory of some much brighter color and her figure, in the gray-green dress suit, was a promise made by fashion magazines and entertainment TV shows from San Diego to Krakow.

"Yes," Brand replied.

Most people looking at the forty-something police detective would have thought him handsome and athletic. Socrates, however, saw only a petulant boy; a frowning white version of Kelly Beardsley.

"I found Detective Beardsley bludgeoned to death in the upper hall. His jaw had been crushed and his neck broken. His service revolver was on the floor at the other end of the hallway."

"And what was your first reaction to this tableau?"

"Say what?" the cop asked.

"What was your professional assessment of the situation you came upon?"

"That a murder had been committed."

"Not self-defense as Mr. Tinheart claims?"

"Definitely not. Beardsley was a trained police officer. There's no way that Fortlow's version of the altercation could have happened. The only way that Detective Beardsley could have been killed like that was if is he was taken unawares."

"Objection, your honor," Mason Tinheart said again. "The witness, no matter his expertise, was not in the hall where this tragedy occurred. He cannot testify to events that he did not see with his own eyes."

"Detective Brand is a trained policeman, your honor," the beautiful prosecutor claimed. "Who better to decipher the events as they occurred?"

Irene Tanaka was in her late fifties. Her black hair was going gray but her eyes seemed to Socrates like those of a much older, either wise or deeply disillusioned, woman.

"I must agree with the defense," she said. "The jury is directed not to take Detective Brand's rendition of the events necessarily as fact. His reading of the physical evidence is only one possibility."

"What did Mr. Fortlow do after you found the body of Detective Kelly Beardsley?" Marlene Quest asked.

"He held out his hands."

"For what reason?"

"To be cuffed. We made him put his hands behind his back though."

"So he admitted his guilt?" the prosecutor deduced.

"Objection."

"Sustained."

"No more questions."

"So, Mr. Brand," Mason Tinheart said, "tell us why you entered the Big Nickel."

"An anonymous tip," the policeman said in a terse manner.

"Somebody called you?"

"911."

"What were the exact words in the message?" the lawyer asked, smiling as he did so.

"I don't know."

"You've never heard the message?"

"No. It was deleted from the system."

"Deleted? I thought there was always a permanent record of all emergency calls. So that later, when and if there is a trial, the call can be brought in as evidence, maybe even testimony."

"The system went down that day," Brand said, looking down at his hands. "All calls for a forty-seven minute period were lost."

"How convenient for the prosecution."

"Objection, your honor," Marlene Quest intoned.

"Watch the sarcasm, Mr. Tinheart," Tanaka reminded the barrister.

"You are aware that Mr. Fortlow says that he is the one who placed the 911 call are you not, Detective?" Tinheart continued.

"He says so but it's not true. The operator who took the call remembers that it was a woman's voice."

"If only we had the recording to corroborate that memory," Tinheart opined.

"Badgering the witness, your honor."

"Mr. Tinheart."

"Did anyone have a gun in hand when you and the two officers entered Mr. Fortlow's place of work?" Tinheart asked.

"Yes."

"One gun?"

"We all had our weapons out."

"And, after finding the body did you holster your pistols?"

"No."

"So Mr. Fortlow might have felt threatened by armed gunmen roaming around him."

"We are the police not thugs," Brand said.

"Bearing arms though. Maybe Mr. Fortlow held out his hands because he was afraid of being shot."

Brand had no retort.

"Tell me, Detective, did you find a woman in the house?"

"No."

"Was there a window in the hall that would have allowed someone from the outside to witness the alleged crime?"

"No."

"Has anyone else come forth as a witness admitting that they made the emergency call?"

"I'm not aware of anyone who has done so."

"Did you or the officers you had watching my client see a woman run from the house?"

Turning abruptly from the policeman Tinheart faced the jury. "We do have, as exhibit 12-B, phone records from the Big Nickel proving that a 911 call was made from the office phone at the time this supposed woman was alerting the police.

"No more questions."

SOCRATES WATCHED HIS LAWYER come back to sit by his side. The white man had been a constant support since even before the charges were brought. He didn't like Mason Tinheart but he had no criticism of him either.

Socrates noticed Lucius Brand glaring as he walked between the prosecution and the defense. Following the detective with his eyes he found himself looking at the gallery. His friends were assembled there. Darryl, Chaim, Billy Psalms, and Cassie Wheaton. There were others too. Every day at least a dozen folks from the Big Nickel came to support him. He didn't mind their presence any more than he cared about Mason Tinheart. The only people in the room that mattered to him were Luna, his one day wife-to-be, and Bellandra, their baby.

It was late in the afternoon and so the judge ended the proceedings for the day. Socrates was taken to a van and driven to a small jail in Redondo Beach. He had no windows but when he was escorted from the van to the prison each afternoon or early evening he caught the scent of the ocean from between ten seconds and half a minute, depending on how long it took for internal security to notice the guards and open the electronic lock.

Socrates had a cell to himself. This was a luxury. Billy Psalms had even managed to get him a small entertainment unit that had a TV, radio, DVD player, and even an MP3 unit. Socrates didn't understand the MP3 player nor did he listen to the radio or watch TV or movies. He only used the clock to test himself on how aware of time he was.

Keeping the face of the unit against the wall he'd turn it around from time to time to see if he knew the hour. He was right most of the time. Every convict kept a clock running in their mind. Time was the only thing a prisoner had; and time was always running out.

Socrates was reading a biography that Chaim Zetel had brought him. It was a thick tome about Albert Einstein.

"You'll like the book," Chaim had said. "It's about a man whose life was just as important as what he did. And what he did was very big."

Socrates did like the book. It was friendly and inviting. It was told in a loving manner, the way a relative who knows your flaws, but cares for you anyway, would talk.

When the lock to his door slid open Socrates looked up. This motion seemed to bring him from one world into another. Just the movement of his head felt like a long journey that was immediate and at the same time far behind him.

2.

"Maxie," Socrates said.

Standing in the doorway stood the first undercover cop that had infiltrated the Big Nickel's Thursday Night Meeting. He was acorn-brown with eyes that never seemed to meet the person he was talking to. His clothes were green and dark blue but otherwise unremarkable.

Socrates could see that Martin Truman, aka Maxie Fadiman, had always been a spy, a mole in his own life as well as in the lives of his victims.

"Hey, Socco," the ex-cop said. He moved to the chair across from the cot where the ex-con, soon to be con-again, sat.

"What's up?"

"I went to your lawyer and said that I was proof that the police were hounding you. He took me to the judge," Maxie said. "The prosecutor was there and they told me that I couldn't testify. Tanaka claimed it would be prejudicial."

"She's somethin' else," Socrates said without anger. "It's like she wants to help me but then she gets all worried that she's gonna break the law and so she ends up gettin' on me harder than if she was my enemy."

"What happened in there, Socrates?"

"The courtroom?"

"No, at the Nickel. I knew Kelly. We worked a couple'a jobs together."

Fortlow's attention withdrew from the judge that he had studied so closely in the last weeks. Now he was completely intrigued by his visitor.

"What you doin' down here, man?" he asked the one-time
snitch.

"Tryin' to help."

"But who are you?"

"What do you mean?"

"Are you Maxie the spy, Martin the cop, or the guy that came
to us and said he was sorry?"

"The last one."

Socrates' whole life, it seemed then, had been getting him
ready for *this time* when he was on trial for murder. And it wasn't
just the courtroom where he was being tested. It was in his windowless cell and with strangers like Maxie who came in and out
asking questions. Brigitta Brownlevy, Mason Tinheart's girlfriend, offered him sex in his cell. Luna brought Bellandra every
day that they would let her visit. The prosecutor, through Tinheart, made him offers of reduced sentences. Reporters asked
for interviews. There was even a biographer named Nell Hardwick, who wanted to tell ". . . a true story about a real man, not
some trumped up celebrity with nothing to them."

He told Brigitta no, realizing that he might well regret it one
day. Luna was his strength. She sat with him for as long as possible talking about Big Nickel business and his opinions about the
judge and jury members.

"There's a old black woman on the upper left look like I just
insulted her," he said. "And then there's this white girl who keep
shakin' her head."

"I know that one," Luna said. "I cain't tell if she for ya or
against ya."

"Ain't that life in a dark alley," Socrates said and they laced fingers.

Socrates had rejected the prosecutor's offers because no matter what they found him guilty for he would spend the rest of his life in prison since he'd already gone down for murder once.

He'd refused any interviews with reporters. Socrates had been reading newspapers for years and he had not been impressed with their ability to understand men like him. Whether they were on his side or not he was sure that they'd get it wrong.

But he agreed to meet with Nell Hardwick, the biographer.

When she came into the visitor's room and sat across the table from him he raised his manacled hands, asking her without words to stay silent. The graying white woman was tall and thin. She wore a boy's dress shirt and a red skirt. She had a notepad, papers, and a tape recorder all visible in a clear plastic purse.

"Don't take no notes and don't record me," Socrates said. "I just wanna say some things to you and then you can go. If what I say gives you somethin' then you can write your book, or not.

"I want you to know that I don't mind bein' in here, in jail. That's where I been most'a my adult life. A long time ago I murdered two people and just recently I killed a man in my place. I'm on trial because I killed him and they don't like me and they don't believe it was self-defense. In some other neighborhood they might'a believed what I said but down where I live if you kill one'a them then you got to go down. That's why I got my Big Nickel and my friends—because down where we live the law is like a mugger and a thief, down where we live at you got to concentrate real hard to know just how to walk out the door with pride and common sense too.

"I killed a man who was stealin' from me and who wanted to kill me and now I'm on trial. That's all there is to it, Miss Hardwick. Who I am, what I am, don't mean a thing. It just come down to me and him and then me and them. So go on and write your book or don't, it's all the same to me."

"I WANT TO HELP YOU, Socrates," Maxie said.

"Help me how?"

"First tell me what happened in that house?"

"How me tellin' you that gonna help me?"

"I need to know," the ex-cop, ex-snitch, ex-patriot said.

Socrates could see the pain in Maxie and he wondered if it was real or conjured in order to fool him.

"I killed him, Maxie," Socrates said after some time. "I saw him breaking into my personal file cabinet, I called to him, he pulled his pistol and before he could shoot I hit him and he died."

It was the truth in the world of bodies in motion but it was also a lie. Maxie sniffed the air almost aware of the subtlety of the well constructed fabrication but then he pulled back.

"I can get you outta here, Socco," he said.

"How you gonna do that?"

"I got all the keys. I can walk in here at midnight and walk you out the back door. I could do that tonight and by the time they know you gone you'll be in Toronto at a house up there that's ready for you and Luna and the baby too."

Socrates stared at the evasive face of the man before him, remembering that when Martin was Maxie at the Big Nickel he looked you right in the eye because he was playing a role that he could hide behind. But the real man, the one sitting before him, was ashamed of who he was and shifty and vague in his appearance.

Socrates was wondering not about the possibility of freedom but at the offer. He'd spent more than a quarter-century in prison and no one offered to break him out like a chick from its shell; no one held out a hand and said, "Come on let's go."

The gift was in the offer—like money in the bank or somebody loving you from far away. It was like the smell of your brood on the wind from the west or a nod from another black man in the street.

Socrates liked his cell with its featureless lime-colored walls and a book about the rebel physicist. He liked the courtroom and the ambivalent judge and the men and women sitting judgment on him; blind as Justice. He liked the prosecutor's figure and his own attorney's girlfriend. He had no need for freedom. The Japanese judge and the jury and even the cop who testified against him weren't free; at least he wouldn't trade places with any of them.

"If I was free I could fly to that mountain ovah there," Billy Psalms had once said on a clear Los Angeles day. "I could rise up in the air an' go there like a bird. But the ground got its chains on me. It say, 'you stayin' right here,' an' here I be."

No, Socrates didn't need freedom. He liked his cell, missed his prison life. And even when he exulted in the liberty of walking down the streets without a guard, or sleeping behind a locked door when he held the key, he was still thinking about not being locked up.

No, Socrates thought again, I don't need freedom but my child needs me; her lock and chain, her mean daddy who won't let her cross the street by herself.

"Socrates," Maxie said. "You wanna get outta here or not?"

"You like it up in Toronto, Maxie?"

"Better than this here jail."

"Your baby like it?"

"She's a baby, she don't even know where she is."

"I really appreciate the offer, Max. I know how hard this must be for you. It's a big step to do what's right when the big boss is wrong. 'Cause you know loyalty is a chain too. So's your job and your house an' even yo' dick."

Maxie laughed. "I miss the Thursday nights, Socco."

"They don't have nuthin' like that up in Canada?"

"They don't have nobody like you anywhere, Brother," Maxie said, forcing himself to look Socrates in the eye for a brief moment.

For five minutes or more the men sat looking at each other's hands. After that Maxie stood up and turned away. It was awhile before Socrates felt alone again, as if the informer had left his shadow to make sure the test was over.

3.

Weeks went by. The trial dragged on and Socrates spent his time studying the faces of the judge and jury. He was also intrigued by the young woman who took notes of the proceedings. The court reporter was white and pretty but she held herself like an ugly teenager shy of her appearance. Every once in a while she'd catch him staring at her and then she'd brush an imagined lock of her black hair away from her face. Socrates would smile when she did this and sometimes she smiled back.

The guards in the jailhouse liked him. Two of them had even shaken his hand.

The forensic doctor found it hard to believe that a sixty-year-old man could hit someone that hard with his fist alone. The police, however, found no weapon that could have been used.

Under oath Captain Telford Winegarten, the man in charge of the Anti-gang Tactical Division, admitted that Kelly Beardsley worked for him.

"But he was under strict orders to simply observe," the captain said. "It was what we call non-invasive reconnaissance. He would not have broken any lock in that house. He was just there to listen and report on gang activity."

"Did he discover any gang activity?" Mason Tinheart asked.

Winegarten did not reply.

"I have already subpoenaed your records," Tinheart reminded him.

"No."

"And how long had he been there?"

"Nearly six months."

"If he didn't find out anything then why keep him there?"

"The police have to have patience, counselor," Winegarten said. "We don't have the luxury of retaliation."

Tinheart smiled and walked away.

"THIS IS A BIG MOMENT, Mr. Fortlow," Mason Tinheart said in Socrates' cell after the trial had gone on for six weeks. "We have to decide whether or not to put you on the stand."

Socrates didn't say anything to this because he didn't know what was right.

"On the one hand you are the only witness to the killing," Tinheart continued. "You were there. You hit him."

"Twice," Socrates said.

"What?"

"I hit him twice."

"But it was a one-two punch right? You didn't wait and hit him again later?"

"No. It was one right after the other, hard and fast."

"So the problem is," Tinheart said, "do we put you in the witness chair and let the jury see the man you are?"

"They already seen me," Socrates said. "And you know I'm ugly as a mothahfuckah to most of them. Everybody got a different life but I doubt if any of them have seen a life like mine."

"But do we dare pull back the curtain?" Tinheart asked. Before Socrates could answer he added, "Brigittta says that you should do it but I think she's infatuated with you."

"Maybe somebody on the jury will like me."

"Brigitta came to see you didn't she?" Mason asked.

Socrates nodded.

"What did she say?"

"That I shouldn't give up. That I should keep up hope," Socrates said, thinking about sex as hope. "But I told her that I just take life as it comes. I don't hope its comin' 'cause it's comin' still and all."

Socrates could see that the lawyer had other questions, that he was afraid of something between Brigitta and other men. But the lawyer didn't voice his fears.

"All we need is one juror to keep you from jail," Tinheart said. "I think you should go on the stand."

Maybe, Socrates thought, Tinheart wanted to destroy him because he believed that his woman had betrayed him. Maybe Socrates on the stand would give the lawyer his own private justice.

"Lemme think about it, Mason. I'll talk to you in a few days."

"We have to decide quickly."

"I need to think about it."

"We have to plan our approach."

"Should I get me a new lawyer? Maybe Cassie?"

"No. I understand," Mason said. "I'll come by day after tomorrow."

"Two days after," Socrates said.

CASSIE WHEATON, after hearing the full explanation of Socrates' fears, agreed to sit with Tinheart at the defense table. She said that she didn't know if his testimony would help or hurt his case.

"Tinheart is right about one thing," she'd said. "You have to expect that the jury will be mostly against you even if your case is strong."

"I'M A BAD PERSON TO ASK, Socco," Billy Psalms had said. "You know me, my hands just itchin' for some dice to throw. An' you cain't make a bet wit' yo' mouf shet."

IT JUST SO HAPPENED that during the time that Socrates was deciding about his answer to Tinheart Chaim Zetel came to visit. The tinkerer liked to visit and play a game of chess on a stone board that he'd found rooting through the trash in Beverly Hills.

But that day Socrates didn't want to play.

"I got a problem, Chaim."

The old man smiled at the irony of the statement.

Socrates laughed.

"Tinheart wanna put me on the witness stand an' I don't know if I trust him."

"Because of the woman?"

"How you know that?"

"Strong women like strong men. They like to push up against them."

"What do you think I should do?" Socrates asked.

"The one thing, the only thing they cannot ask of us is silence, my friend," the old man told the killer. "We all die. We are all dragged away. But we do not have to go quietly. We owe it to our children and our friends and even to our enemies to speak out."

"Why the enemy?"

"He needs to hear the truth too."

"But what if I'm not sure about what is true?"

"Even if you are not the truth is still there."

THAT NIGHT SOCRATES HAD A DREAM about himself when he was six years old. He had stolen a ballpoint pen from a 5 and 10 on Garner Street. He took the pen to his Aunt Bellandra and said it was for her birthday. She took the present from him and smiled at it. The smile lasted for more than a minute and then she handed it back to the child.

"It's very lovely, Socrates," she said. "Now I want you to go back to the people you stole it from and give it back. That will be the best gift you evah give me."

4.

"In your own words, Mr. Fortlow," Cassie Wheaton said, "tell us what happened the day Kelly Beardsley died."

At the last moment Tinheart decided to let Cassie represent the defense in examining Socrates. He provided a list of questions but she discarded them.

"I was in the kitchen lookin' for a sandwich but we had given them all away," Socrates remembered. "And it was like I saw somethin', a shadow or somethin' like that in the corner of my eye. At first I didn't think anything of it but there wasn't supposed to be anybody in the house and it started botherin' me. So I went upstairs and I saw that the door to my office was closed. Now I knew I had left it open and so I went in . . .

"Kelly was there lookin' in the top drawer of my file cabinet. I knew that he had to have broken the lock because my file cabinet locks automatically and only me and Billy Psalms have the keys. And the drawer got a counterweight on it so I couldn't have left it open.

"I asked Kelly what he was doin' but he just walked past me out into the hallway. I went out aftah him and called his name but he just kep' on goin'. I raised my voice and he turned and at the same time was pullin' a pistol from his pants. I moved up on him real quick an' hit him two times. He went down and I checked him out but he was dead. I called 911 but the cops got there before the ambulance."

"You asked for medical care?"

"Yes I did."

"Not just for the police?"

"No, ma'am. I knew the police had to come but, but I didn't want anybody to say that I didn't try to help Kelly aftah hurtin' him like that."

"What happened after that?" Cassie Wheaton asked.

"Cops come in with their guns out. They put me in chains and took me off to jail."

"Did you intend to kill Mr. Beardsley?"

"No, ma'am."

"Why didn't you try to grab his gun hand and disarm him?"

"Might as well try an' grab a viper by his fangs," Socrates said flatly.

"Were you aware that Mr. Beardsley was a police spy?"

"Objection," Marlene Quest ejaculated. "Prejudicial language."

"Mr. Beardsley was a police agent who pretended to be a member of the Big Nickel group," Wheaton said. "He secretly gathered information on the people in that institution and reported his findings to Mr. Winegarten. In everyday parlance he was a spy."

"I'm going to have to agree with the defense on this point, Ms. Quest," Judge Tanaka said, almost apologetically. "Objection overruled."

"I repeat the question, Mr. Fortlow," Cassie Wheaton said. "Did you know that Kelly Beardsley was a spy?"

"When I saw that he broke into my file I knew that he was after something that he thought was a secret. I didn't know if he was a cop or not but I didn't think he was just a thief neither."

"So you didn't know."

"Not before I saw him in my file."

Socrates saw that Cassie was unhappy with his answer but he had already decided that he was going to tell the truth with every word he uttered in that witness chair.

"SO YOU KNEW he was gathering information on you?" Marlene Quest asked at the beginning of her cross-examination. "And that's why you killed him?"

"He died because he pulled out a pistol and I hit him."

"Hard enough to break his jaw and his neck," Quest said as if she were reminding him of something he forgot.

"I was movin' fast, counselor. A man was moving a gun muzzle in my direction. How hard I hit him had to do with how fast I was movin'."

"But what about the pistol?" the prosecutor said with the leer of satisfaction in her tone.

This question came as no surprise. The handgun that had Kelly Beardsley's prints on it was at the other end of the hall when the police got there. It was one of the central points of the prosecution that the gun was either a plant or a red herring placed by Socrates to hide his crime.

Cassie and Mason had told him to say that he had no idea how the gun got there.

Might as well not open up a can of worms, Tinheart had said.

"What about it?" Socrates asked.

"How did it get over fifteen feet away from the corpse?"

"I kicked it there."

"Kicked it?"

"Argumentative," Cassie Wheaton and Mason Tinheart announced as one.

"When Kelly hit the floor the pistol fell at his side. I didn't know if he was dead or even unconscious. I sure didn't want him to grab the gun an' start shootin' so I kicked the pistol."

"You didn't take it from his pocket and move it away from the body?"

"No."

"You didn't sneak up on Officer Beardsley and strike him down out of jealousy?"

"Jealousy?" Socrates asked. He was surprised for the first time during the trial. "Jealous of what?"

"I have it on authority that Mr. Beardsley and the mother of your child, Miss Luna Barnet, had dated more than once. I have detailed affidavits from the restaurant and bar staffs."

The laughter that came from Socrates was honest and pure. He sat back in the witness chair, comfortable in that seat.

"Lady, you don't know my Luna if you think she gonna be messin' 'round on me in a place where you could get a affidavit. She just about the onlyest person I know done had it harder than I did. She know how to keep her secrets quiet. You go to restaurant to eat, a bar to drink. But if you wanna fool around it's the back alley all the way."

For a moment the prosecutor lost her bearings. The last thing she expected from a murderer was friendly laughter. She shuffled her *affidavits* and then looked up.

"Ms. Wheaton tells us that Kelly Beardsley was a spy. Why would anybody spy on you, Mr. Fortlow?"

"Same reason I'm on trial, Ms. Quest."

"I don't understand."

"There's bad blood down around where I come from, ma'am—a lotta bad blood. It's like Detective Brand and Captain Winegarten say, there's gangs and drugs and murders and prostitution on every block. And if somebody wanna do somethin' about it he got to shove his hands in all the way to his elbows. You cain't stop a gang member from killin' unless you have him in. You cain't help a drug addict or a prostitute unless you sit down with 'em. At least that.

"And if you a man like me, a man that already went to prison over a crime that was terrible, then the cops and the judges and the juries and the prosecutors got to get together and see if that man is frontin' or what.

"I don't like spies. I don't like it when the police come into my house every other day because I got a record and they got a job. But I accept those things. That's the life I live. If I was to go out and murder people because'a things like that L.A. wouldn't have no population problem. I'd be killin' twenty-four seven."

Marlene Quest had a faint smile on her face. Socrates could tell that she thought he was doing her work for her.

"One last question, Mr. Fortlow," she said. "We know you killed Mr. Beardsley, a policeman in the execution of his duty, what we want to know, the reason you're here, is to know if you murdered him."

Socrates had refused to practice his answer to this inevitable question. The truth would be his only protection and the truth could not be rehearsed.

"I don't think so, Ms. Quest. I have thought about it ever since that day and—"

"Yes or no, Mr. Fortlow," the prosecutor said.

"I'm answerin' your question, counselor."

"Yes or no."

Socrates turned to the judge but didn't speak. Their eyes met.

"This is his day in court, Ms. Quest," Tanaka said. "We'll allow him the leeway to explain himself."

"Thank you, your honor," Socrates said. "It's not complex but there's points about it. I knew Kelly was grabbin' for a gun before I saw it, I saw it before I hit him but I was already movin' fast. Now if he didn't have a gun I might'a hit just as hard anyway. I was goin' on my instinct but instinct coulda been wrong. It wasn't but it coulda been. I saw the gun before I hit him and so when I think it all through I don't think I murdered him but that I only killed him outta the instinct of self-defense."

5.

After the last arguments were given it was the end of the day and so the jury was sequestered for the night.

Socrates went to his cell and was visited by Cassie and Mason.

"Number seven and number eleven are on your side, Socco," Tinheart said. "Older black woman and black man. They had sympathy for you when you testified."

"Seven come eleven as Billy would say," Socrates said, trying to keep up his lawyers' spirits.

"They'll probably take a month to decide," Cassie added. "Our only problem is if someone else on the jury wants to wear them down."

Tinheart nodded sadly.

"Why'ont you two go home and get a good night's sleep," Socrates suggested.

"I brought some sleeping pills if you need them, Socco," Mason offered.

"I like it in jail, Mason. I sleep like a baby behind locked doors."

"I AIN'T HAD NUTHIN' TO DO with that man," Luna said in the visitors' room a while later. It was the first time he'd had visiting hours since Quest had suggested her infidelity.

"I know that, Baby."

"I had lunch wit' him two times and drinks once but I nevah even kissed his cheek. He said that he wanted to get together and talk. I didn't know that he was some kinda spy."

"I know that, Luna."

"But she made it sound like she had pictures of me up in the bed wit' him. He was nice but you my man."

"And you my woman right, Luna?"

"Yes."

"Ain't no white woman in a burgundy suit gonna change that."

Upon hearing these words Luna started to cry. Tears flowed from both her eyes and she buried her face in his big, manacled hands. She was a child for a moment. Socrates wondered what the tears between his fingers had to do with freedom. He had the urge to be at the Thursday night Thinkers' Meeting to ask just that question.

THE NEXT DAY THE JURY FILED IN. Judge Tanaka sent them off to meet and twelve minutes later they sent word that they had come to a verdict.

A middle-aged white woman named Calla Adams rose and was asked for the verdict.

"Not guilty," Calla said, but the words weren't said with finality alone, it almost sounded to Socrates like she was going to add, "of course."

Cassie kissed Socrates cheek while Mason Tinheart slapped his arm and shook his hand. His friends, at least eighteen strong, rose to their feet and cheered. Judge Tanaka didn't ask for order. She announced that justice had been done and ordered that the prisoner be freed.

THAT NIGHT LUNA MADE Socrates hamburgers and a salad.

"I had Billy show me how to cook you sumpin', Daddy. I wanna be a good wife to you and I know that a good wife got to cook sometimes."

"Wife?"

"Yes. Wife. We gonna get married at the Big Nickel just like Cassie an' them. I'm gonna change my name and learn to cook and go to school and have at least two more'a your chirren."

"All I gotta do is go on on trial for murder an' you do all'a that?"

"All you got to do is believe me an' I don't have to prove myself," she said. "That's why I come knockin' at your do' in the first place."

"Then why you say we have to wait a year?"

"Forgive me?"

6.

Six weeks later life had returned to normal at the Big Nickel and at Socrates and Luna's house. The wedding was being planned and the Thursday night Thinkers' Meeting had settled down from the upset of almost losing their founder.

ON HIS FIRST MONDAY out of prison Socrates drove from the new house up to Lorenzo Drive in Cheviot Hills and picked up Darryl. Together they went down to fish off a pier about thirty-five miles south of Santa Monica. They went so far away because Socrates had become a celebrity after his acquittal in the highly publicized trial.

The little pier they went to was rarely used.

"So what you gonna do now?" the boy asked him after an hour or so.

"You wanna take a walk?" the philosopher replied.

BAREFOOT THEY WALKED DOWN by the ocean along the sparsely populated beach. The waves were loud and the sun beat down on them.

Darryl had come down to visit Socrates once a week while he was in jail but they never discussed the trial. They talked about Darryl's school and life at the Zetel's. They talked about Luna and baby Bellandra or sometimes about fishing.

"I'm gonna keep on doin' what I been doin'," Socrates said after they'd walked a quarter mile.

"But they wanna kill you or throw you back in prison," Darryl said.

Socrates noticed that Darryl's voice had gotten more certain in his days as a West L.A. college student.

"Yeah," the boy's mentor said, "they sure do."

"You'n me an' Luna could move up to Oakland or maybe even Portland," he said. "I could finish school up there."

"What you know about them places?"

"That they're safe. I don't want you to get killed."

Socrates stooped and touched the young man's arm. They lowered down to sit in the cool sand, laying their rods and buckets by their right sides.

"I need the Big Nickel more than I need to know I'm gonna be free," Socrates said. "It's not that they need me. It's not that they couldn't make it without me. It's Billy's chili and the look on people's faces when they tryin' to say sumpin' an' they don't know what it is.

"I don't wanna go back to prison. I don't want no lethal injection. But you know we all gotta go sometimes, D-boy."

"But you could start a new place."

"Then the cops be aftah me there too."

"Maybe they'd let you teach someplace."

"And they tie my hands and gag my mouth. Ain't no school wanna hear what I got to say."

"Luna said that you got a extra room in your house," Darryl said then.

"Uh-huh."

"So can I come stay wit' you while I'm still in school?"

"Sure you can. Yes, sir. That would be the icing on the cake, Little Brother."

"I could get a job an' pay rent. Luna said it was okay."

"I already said yeah. You don't have to convince me."

"Okay," Darryl said as he stood and picked up his rod.

"Okay," Socrates echoed, standing as his friend did. "I guess we bettah be gettin' back to the war."

Walter Mosley is the author of the acclaimed Easy Rawlins series of mysteries, including national bestsellers *Cinnamon Kiss*, and *Bad Boy Brawly Brown*; the Fearless Jones series, including *Fearless Jones, Fear Itself*, and *Fear of the Dark*; the novels *Blue Light* and *RL's Dream*; and two collections of stories featuring Socrates Fortlow, *Always Outnumbered, Always Outgunned*, for which he received the Anisfield-Wolf Award, and *Walkin' the Dog*. He was born in Los Angeles and lives in New York.